# OUT OF PLACE

For Sue
This book belongs to
MjTree...
"seek joy"

# Out of Place

## MILREE LATIMER

**LUMINARE PRESS**
WWW.LUMINAREPRESS.COM

Out of Place
Copyright © 2021 by Milree Latimer

All rights reserved. This book or any portion thereof may not be reproduced or used in any manner whatsoever without the express written permission of the publisher, except for the use of brief quotations in a book review.

Printed in the United States of America

Cover design by Melissa K. Thomas

Luminare Press
442 Charnelton St.
Eugene, OR 97401
www.luminarepress.com

LCCN: 2020921863
ISBN: 978-1-64388-508-7

*For my Mom…nurse, farmer, and mother.*
*For inspiration.*
*1896–1977*

ALSO BY MILREE LATIMER
*Those We Left Behind*

*one small thing
I've learned these years,*

*how to be alone,
and at the edge of aloneness
how to be found by the world.*

—David Whyte, *River Flow:
New & Selected Poems 1984–2007*

# Part One

*1911 ♦ Arriving*

# Chapter One

*Then she turns to go, folds up
all that light in her arms like a blanket
and takes it with her.*

—Dorianne Laux, "Girl in the Doorway"

### 1911 ◆ Dublin ◆ Martha

My mother died when I was thirteen years old.

When I was twelve, the sickness overtook her.

At night she'd cough so hard I thought her chest would fly open. I thought demons might take to the air.

She died on a Sunday night. I sat with her, listening to her breath wheeze in and out. I waited, hoping for the sound of one more breath, another, another. Early that morning she had not been able to lift her head from her pillow, the only one I could find not spattered with blood. But she smiled at me like someone who'd already left her body. I grasped her hand, sat on the bed, and rocked back and forth.

"Ma, you have to help me. I don't know what to do."

"Sing to me," she said, in a whisper, a murmur of her old self. "Sing our song."

I knelt on the floor, my hand clutching her fingers. I sang our song.

*I know where I'm goin'
And I know who's goin' with me.*

*I know who I love*
*And the dear knows who I'll marry…*

Ma drifted into a peaceful sleep, or maybe she was already leaving me. Off in the distance, I heard the bells of Christ Church Cathedral. The doctor had said I needed to find a priest for Ma, and as I listened to the far-off bells I knew I needed to go.

"Ma. I'm going now, going for a priest," I whispered into her ear. I set off running, out the door, down the stairs and beyond the old building where we lived. Down to Henrietta Street.

"No more cryin'," I said while I ran. "No more cryin.'"

We hadn't been church-going people, Ma and I, but I hoped someone, a man of God, could have the power to save her. So, I ran. I ran toward the bells.

◆

Ma and I were a pair. We were inseparable.

We'd lived with a family whose home was near the heart of Dublin, even though they were wealthy enough to move into the countryside. Ma had started as a domestic with the Quinns when I was a wee babe, working as a baker and a maid. I grew into girlhood knowing the smells and sounds of a kitchen.

I knew how to bake bread by the time I was five years old. I helped Cook make stews and potpies and gathered vegetables from the garden by the back door. I thought I was pretty tough, but truthfully, Ma was the tough one. She never talked about her past, not even to me. As I grew older, I could tell my ma was a fine lady—well-spoken, not like the maid Audrey who kept the dishes clean, dusted the floors, and used words like "bollocks" and "fecker" a lot. Ma told me, "Never, ever will you use those words, Martha Cait." I would never. I wanted to be a fine lady, like Ma.

One time Ma decided to teach me to read and write. What a time we had those evenings in our small room over the kitchen. Mrs. Quinn, a kind lady, gave me books that her daughters had used when they were my age.

"You're a smart girl," Ma said many times. And I thought she was a very good teacher.

But the good days ended.

It was a sad day when we had to leave the Quinns' house. Ma had become very ill. The "galloping consumption," they called it. Mrs. Quinn was sorry to see us go, but Mr. Quinn said they couldn't have Ma coughing and feverish while working in the kitchen. "We could all get sick," he'd said, with a tone of voice that meant it was not up for discussion. For a short while, that was the saddest day of my childhood.

After leaving the Quinns, we moved into two rooms in an old, dilapidated building on Henrietta Street in Dublin. We were better off than some. We shared it with an old friend of Ma's who'd offered us a home off the streets.

◆

SHANA WAS AN OUTCAST FROM HER FAMILY BECAUSE SHE had gotten pregnant and went to live in the tenements. Ma and Shana became friends years ago when they both were young girls.

Ma had some money, some coins and banknotes she'd earned from the Quinns, so she took care of feeding us all. The two rooms were small, but we were lucky. Our neighbors' house down the street was home to ten people—two rooms, ten people.

Ma insisted I go to the school down the street and even paid a small sum for me to attend. I was a good student. I loved to learn. Ma and Shana helped me with my sums every night. They'd clap their hands when I got every answer right. My real pleasure was reading my stories to them from my school reader. Sometimes I'd make up fanciful tales and spin them out for their pleasure.

As Ma got sicker and sicker, I stopped going to school because I needed to stay with her. Truth be told, I was afraid to leave her. Early that fateful Sunday morning, I got up to go to Ma, who was coughing with a fierce, gasping sound. Shana was at the door with her knapsack slung across her shoulder. Her fear of the consumption drove her out the door.

Without giving me a chance to say, "Please stay," she was gone.

◆

After Shana left, I ran for a priest. At the cathedral where the bells still pealed, a Father stood greeting parishioners as they left.

I uttered only two words. "My ma…"

"Yes child, your ma? What is it you want to say?" He shook the last parishioner's hand and turned to the open doors. "Yes?"

I took a breath. "My ma, she's really sick, I think she's dying."

"Then shouldn't you be going to find a doctor?" For a moment I felt small, while the Father grew taller. I rose to my four feet, eleven inches.

"Father, the doctor told me to get a priest." Silent sobs became nettles in my throat. I dug my fingers into my palms, determined not to cry.

He stood. I waited.

"All right, show me where you live."

◆

MA DIED BEFORE I HAD A CHANCE TO SAY GOOD-BYE. I wanted to tell her what a good ma she'd been—I wanted to sing her one more song—tell her I'd always be all right because I carried her spirit in my skin, but I felt the priest's anxiety, his desire to leave because he, too, worried about the consumption. I sat beside her, my hand over hers, while he gave his blessing, "Through this holy anointing, may the Lord in His love and mercy help you with the grace of the Holy Spirit. May the Lord who frees you from sin save you and raise you up."

The Father blessed her and left.

When he'd gone, I talked to Ma for only a moment because I knew she'd be on her way. Ma never dillydallied.

"Ma? What do you want me to do?" I swallowed, shook my head, and breathed a long sigh between my lips, tight from holding back. Tears needed to come another time, not now. I felt numb, a fatigue that tempted me to lie down beside her, to let the breath leave my body. To go with her.

A gentle knock at the door roused me. "Martha, Martha, dear. It's Shana."

When I opened the door, my body folded into hers. I let the ragged sobs wrench every breath from me until there were no tears left to cry.

◆

IT WAS SHANA WHO ARRANGED MA'S BURIAL AND WHO took me to Mrs. McCarthy's Home for Destitute Children. Here I found a home for the next two years.

Because I was the oldest there, Mrs. McCarthy put me to work right away, work that would give me confidence and skills I'd use for the rest of my life.

Eventually, I became her helpmate. "She's the best of all of us," Mrs. McCarthy would say. In her care, I became mother, sister, and friend to children who I felt needed love and care.

For me, Mrs. McCarthy's Home was a sanctuary. She was a woman with an unflagging spirit who taught me ever-increasing tenacity. I decided I'd never leave her. But, two years to the day after I arrived, Mrs. McCarthy died. The home was to close, even though I cajoled and beseeched those who'd given donations, those who'd believed in her.

"You are much too young to run this home, to take care of these children," they told me. Once again, as I felt home collapsing beneath my feet, another angel entered my life. Her name was Miss Ashcroft. She was from an association that transported orphan children and homeless girls like me across the ocean to Canada—she was in charge of organizing all of us to sail from Liverpool, England, to Quebec, Canada. And in her wisdom, so I believed, she asked for my help.

◆

As I was readying to sail across the Atlantic, I assumed I was going to be with the children from the Home who'd become my friends and my charges. I thought I'd be traveling, like them, to a farm somewhere in Canada, maybe even with them to a new home like Mrs. McCarthy's. But Ma changed everything. Miss Ashcroft had a letter from my ma that Mrs. McCarthy had kept. From that letter, I discovered I had family in Canada. There, written in Ma's faded script, I learned she had a sister who lived in Canada, in a town called Kingston, Ontario.

Ma had made no mention of family. But, truth told, she had a sister who lived in a place called Kingston. My world, my safe place, was uprooted again like the dog-violet we'd transplanted in Mrs. McCarthy's garden.

I read the letter Miss Ashcroft gave me, my fingers pressed into the paper like pincers.

*To Martha McGrath's Guardians*

*When I am gone, please be sure that my girl, Martha, goes to my sister's home in Canada.*

*My sister's name is Emily Johnson and she lives in Kingston, Ontario, on King Street. Her husband is a professor at the university there. I know this because he is the one who has kept in touch with me over the years. His name is Owen Johnson and he has a daughter, Anna. My sister and I have had some differences, but I am sure she will not turn away my girl. Emily, Owen, and Anna are Martha's family and I know they will care for her. Mr. Johnson and Anna took in my sister Emily, I hope she will see her way clear to accept her only niece.*

*I ask this with the hope you will be kind and look after my girl.*

*Sarah McGrath*

I tried to understand why Ma wanted to send me so far away from Ireland to a country where I'd live among strangers. My family members were the children I'd learned to care for in Mrs. McCarthy's home. I feared what life might be like among strangers who had wanted nothing to do with my mother.

# Chapter Two

*We shall be a family...all of us.*
—Anna Johnson

### June 1913 ◆ Louise Basin, Quebec City ◆ Martha

THREE LONG, LOUD BLASTS FROM THE SHIP'S HORN announced that the SS *Laurentic* was reversing its engines and docking in Quebec City's harbor. I'd arrived in a new world, an Irish girl barely past her fifteenth birthday. With each honk and blare, I jolted and hopped backward, putting my hands over my ears to cut out the raucous sounds.

I figured if Ma were beside me, she'd be laughing, that rambunctious chortle that used to come from somewhere deep in her chest. To me, it was a sound that meant all was well, but that was before the loathsome cough silenced her laughter. In her last days, she'd told me, "After I'm gone, all you need to do, sweet girl, is turn around, look with a spry eye, and feel the breeze." To my too-sensible mind, it seemed far-fetched. Ma was the whimsical one. But every so often, whenever I felt a soft breeze rustle my hair, I'd look around, just in case.

Miss Ashcroft stood beside me on the deck where all of us had assembled—other young people, little children I'd come to know and care for at Mrs. McCarthy's home in Dublin. I watched other passengers push and shove to get to the railing. They waved and shouted at friends and family waiting for them on the pier below. I couldn't understand how a person up on deck could ever recognize anyone down there. I did know one thing, though: There was nobody in the crowd waiting for me. I still had miles to go, and I'd be on my own. Yet I still had the little ones to care for. I could worry about my future, and whoever this family might be, later.

◆

The day we left Mrs. McCarthy's Home, where I'd been living for two years, I felt desolate. But I felt sorrier for the little ones, the children who were being taken away from the only home some of them had ever known.

Miss Ashcroft had said to me again and again that I was one of the lucky ones. Because of Ma's letter, I was going to a family. I was no longer a Home Child without relatives. Yet I still felt like an orphan, just as I had when Ma died. Even though I'd discovered I had a family out there, somewhere in Canada, my stomach had problems settling into that idea.

"A family in Canada wants you—your mother's sister, your aunt," Miss Ashcroft had told me quietly, away from the others. "The other children don't have relatives, so they'll be going to farms and strangers. You are the lucky one."

As tears began to drop onto my cheeks, she put her hand on my shoulder and said, "It's a far, distant place, Canada is. But, child, there are good people waiting for you." Calm as Miss Ashcroft had seemed to be, her eyes filled as she tried to reassure me. It was her job to ferry us safely to Canada, and I felt she cared about us.

Strangely, this lady, with her hair all tied up in a knot on the top of her head and a long coat that billowed when she walked, felt like a sister to me. We'd come to know each other as we crossed the Atlantic and as we shared the care of the youngsters.

Miss Ashcroft had sat with me during the voyage, told me how brave I was. "You are a remarkable young woman, Martha. I've not often been able to depend on one of my 'chicks' to help me. We had such a large group on this voyage. I'm not sure how I'd have managed without you here."

I beamed and got back to tending the children and helping her.

"Children, stay beside me. Hold one another's hand. Martha, watch the children as we walk." Miss Ashcroft stepped out ahead of me.

I'd taught them how to hold hands on board the ship and stay in a line with one another. I held Josie's small fingers. She had never given me her full palm. Like a child ready to run.

"Miss?" Josie clung to my dress. She was six years old and only knew safety when I was there. The rest, all fifteen children and I, looked upon one another as a family, and today it was important they felt protected, for the world ahead of them would be bewildering.

As we moved closer to the gangway, people started to push against us. I needed to hold tightly to the hands of the girls who were hanging on to one another, each trying to stay close.

Each had a note pinned to the lapel of her jacket, a note that gave her name and the city where she was headed. It was the notes that brought me close to tears because none were heading for the same collection point. As the children stood in their line, I helped Miss Ashcroft check off the different cities printed on the notes. Each of them was going far afield from one another—Toronto, Hamilton, Winnipeg,

Edmonton—and all I could think was how difficult it would be for them, and for me, when the time came to leave one another.

Miss Ashcroft moved in and out of the crowd like a woman on a mission. As I dodged and weaved after her through the throngs of people, my hand clutching the smallest girl's fingers, I wondered how daring I felt about being swept along into the unknown.

◆

WHEN WE FINALLY LEFT THE SHIP AND STEPPED ONTO Canadian soil, we threaded our way through the crowds to the immigration hall. Walls that seemed to stretch to the sky lay just ahead. Noise and crowds surrounded us. I was small and insignificant. The renewed hope and energy that I'd experienced when we first left the ship had drained away.

We made our way along a wooden platform by the building. We were met by two Home Children officials, who gathered up the girls and in whispered conversation with Miss Ashcroft began to lead them away. Josie, who'd been grasping my skirt, cried. What could I possibly say to comfort her? Miss Ashcroft moved to the side and beckoned me.

"Martha, you'll need to say good-bye. Give her a hug and then take her over to the others. It's the best way, I know."

At that moment, I looked back at the ship and felt a sense of loss. Josie had summoned the little girl in me who had traveled from flat to smaller flat with her ma, always on the move until moving ended with Ma's death. I'd have to send this small child out into her new world, a place that at this moment felt heartless and cruel.

I crouched down, took her in my arms, and whispered, "You are braver than you've ever thought you could be, and something good is waiting for you. Just imagine what that might be."

She looked into my face as though she knew what I had said might be true, but probably not. Tears dripped from her chin while I peeled her fingers from my hand. A woman who'd been speaking to Miss Ashcroft walked to Josie and me.

"I'll take care of Josie," she said as she bent down to pick the girl up. I could hear my little friend's cries fading into the crowd as I turned away.

I thought I would never feel so heartbroken again.

Miss Ashcroft came to my side, took my hand, and gently brushed a flyaway hair from my forehead. "We need to go to customs now, Martha, and get you on your way."

It seemed that separation and good-byes were what she did best.

◆

AS WE MADE OUR WAY THROUGH CUSTOMS, MEN BEHIND high counters peered at us and at our papers for what seemed minutes on end. Miss Ashcroft, in her efficient, capable manner, made it clear that I was to enter this country and I was to stay! I smiled for the first time as I watched tall men slouch when she said to one of them in her distinctive and clear tone, "Young man, my friend here and I have been traveling for a very long time."

Customs now cleared, we walked along the concrete aisles of the immigration hall. Tall, square, wooden pillars reached up to a flat, white ceiling that seemed to go on forever. As we walked, I gazed out at the cavernous room filled with row upon row of wooden benches. People sat and stood, waiting for their trains. Families sat on the benches and the floor. Some ate food they'd brought with them, cheese and salami from Italy that hadn't yet been confiscated by the customs officers. Others slept. There were those who sat, hardly moving, and stared at the hordes of people as though wondering what had happened and how they'd arrived at this place in their lives. Announcements about arriving and departing trains echoed every few minutes. Babies wailed. People called out for their children in languages I'd never heard.

Nine days in a cramped ship's cabin with three other people had left me hungry for air and space. The expansive immigration hall was like the New World. All around were people like me—dads, moms and babies, girls and boys running and chasing one another. Where would home be for them? How much farther did we need to travel before we were no longer out of place?

Fascinated by all the different sounds and languages (some French, some English, and some that I couldn't make out), I followed along after Miss Ashcroft and dragged my feet across the floorboards. I slowed to a snail's pace and listened, completely tuned in to the music of this new world.

"Come along, Martha. Don't lag," Miss Ashcroft said. She moved in front of me, stepped nimbly around duffel bags, and avoided feet and legs stretched out into the passageways between the benches. "Come along, come along," she called to me over her shoulder.

As I scurried to catch up to her, I spotted a row of bags lined against a wall under the windows, where they'd been deposited after the crew from the ship had unloaded all our possessions. Without breaking step, Miss Ashcroft picked up her suitcase and pointed over at my cloth bag, which looked forlorn and faded among the trunks and cases that surrounded it.

"Your bag has a check ticket on it, Martha, ready to go on the train. Now we just have to get you there." As I followed along behind her, my imagination took flight. The bleak cavern of the hall faded within my mind, replaced by a sense and vision of myself—a welcomed long-lost girl, whose loving aunt and uncle rejoiced in her return. I was the prodigal daughter home to stay. Maybe my aunt would be beautiful like Ma was. Maybe she'd open her arms to me, and we'd be right-away friends. Maybe she'd be a fairy godmother who'd come to rescue me.

"Martha, stay with me!"

My dream state was interrupted by Miss Ashcroft's summons as I made my way through the crowds toward the door and out onto the train platform. I would travel the rest of the journey on my own. Miss Ashcroft walked along the platform with an energetic resolve, weaving her way among the crowds of people who stood by the tracks, some of whom had to move aside and let her through. She was a woman on the lookout. As I was right there with her, I wondered who she'd lost.

"Miss Ashcroft…are you all right?" I asked, grabbing her hand. "What's wrong?"

A red flush crept up above the collar of her coat. She had glanced back at the door to the immigration hall. "Martha, you need to stay right here. I need to go back in there."

She pointed to the immigration hall. "That whistle we just heard. It's your train coming into the station. A woman is supposed to be meeting us to travel the rest of the journey with you to Kingston."

As she started to walk away, she called over her shoulder, "Do not move from that spot!"

"Where are…?" I started to ask, but she'd disappeared inside the hall. All the old sensations murmured in my head as I watched her leave. Those familiar feelings of being shunted from flat to flat with Ma and finally to the orphanage. I felt like a package left on the wrong porch.

I was afraid to move, so I stood my ground by the door to the hall. I heard Ma's voice in my head: "Be brave, girl." I jammed my hand into my coat pocket and wrapped it around her letter. It felt wrinkled and crushed, but it was still there. The moments that I waited for Miss Ashcroft to reappear slowed to a crawl.

After what seemed like a long time (or as Ma used to say, "Every minute I have to wait for you to listen feels like an elastic minute!"), Miss Ashcroft reappeared. "Martha! Look who I found!" she called out as she strode through the crowd. Seeing her wave at me with a broad grin took some of my anxiety away. By her side, a tall, young woman in a black stylish hat kept pace with her. "It's your cousin, Anna!" Miss Ashcroft called across the heads of the travelers moving in and around her. I saw a graceful woman standing before me.

I straightened my back and smiled my most welcoming smile. Aware of my flyaway hair, frizzed beyond help, I tried to pat down the curls and pulled my knitted shawl close around my shoulders. I hoped maybe the wrinkles in my blouse might not be so obvious.

The young woman, who looked not much older than me, welcomed me with clear eyes and a smile that drew me into her world. "Hello," I said, as I reached for my cousin's gloved hand. Her grip was firm and confident.

"Hello, Martha. I am so glad I've found you in this crowd. Welcome to Canada." She paused for a moment, smiled, and shook my hand. "Welcome home."

It all made sense to me now—Miss Ashcroft's distraction and her agitation. I wasn't going to Kingston on the train by myself. Someone, who was my cousin, had been asked to be here to meet me. Miss Ashcroft had arranged it all. She wasn't responsible for me any longer because I wasn't one of the Home Children with whom I'd traveled. But she was single-minded about seeing me safely on my way. The fears I'd had of making this journey by myself began to ebb and were replaced by awe. I let my hand linger in hers for a few seconds, long enough for me to know I was no longer alone.

"I'm Anna. Anna Johnson," she said, looking over my shoulder, extending her other hand to Miss Ashcroft. "Thank you for taking such good care of Martha. What a long journey you've both had. I hope you'll have a chance to rest before returning. It was so good of you to travel with Martha."

Up to that point I'd said nothing, neither a good-bye nor a thank you, to Miss Ashcroft. I turned to her and reached for her hand. "Thank you, Miss Ashcroft. I am going to miss you."

Her eyes flickered sadness for a moment, and I wondered how many children and young women like me she'd bid good-bye to over the years.

As she picked up her bag, she turned to Anna. "Miss Johnson," she said. "I believe you are welcoming a lovely young woman into your family." An envelope, which I was certain held my life story within it, was passed into Anna's hands. Miss Ashcroft rested her hand on my shoulder, and when she spoke again her eyes were brilliant with unshed tears. "Martha, you are one of our fortunates. Goodbye, my dear girl. Show your gratitude to the Johnsons who are taking you into their home. And, Miss Johnson, take care of our girl."

Anna stood back for a moment while Miss Ashcroft picked up her leather bag. With a gentle nod toward me, Miss Ashcroft turned and walked back toward the immigration building and disappeared inside.

◆

ANNA AND I GATHERED OURSELVES IN SILENCE. I PICKED up my bag and stood as tall as I could while I walked beside her, my stomach fluttering with a mixture of delight and unease. We moved down the platform just as the train to Kingston pulled into the station. A huge, black locomotive followed by a length of passenger cars paralleled our stroll. Neither of us spoke. I was grateful to Anna for her silence; it told me that she, too, knew about good-byes.

Astonished by it all—the huge, black engine, the crowds—and overwhelmed by how events in my life had speeded up, I stopped in midstep, dropped my suitcase, inhaled, and whispered on my exhale, "I can't believe I'm here!"

Anna, who'd looked worried for a moment, smiled and said, "You can't believe you're getting on a train, you mean?"

"No! I can't believe I'm here in another country. I feel like I've been lifted and taken out of my life. Do I really have a family? Are you part of my family?" I jammed my hand into my pocket, the one that held Ma's letter, by now so crushed and wrinkled it was almost in tatters. As I pulled it out and uncrumpled the tattered page, I said, "Ma was right! Wasn't she? I have a family. I have a place." My feet froze in midstep. "I do, don't I?" Anna wrapped her arm around my shoulder and spoke the words that would become our shared story: "Yes, Martha, you and I are family."

◆

A LINE OF CHILDREN STOOD BY THE TRAIN, EACH HOLDing a boxlike suitcase with the name of a city written across the side. Hamilton, Halifax, Toronto. Some were the children I'd left behind only a while ago. I scanned the faces to see if Josie, who'd been so reluctant to let go of me, was among them. She wasn't. Already she'd been separated from her friends and sent on her way to another place, another city, another life. Anna must have noticed the shadow that clouded my eyes. She gently squeezed my shoulder again. "They will find a place. I'm sure of it."

◆

ANNA AND I CLIMBED ABOARD THE TRAIN BOUND FOR Kingston, a seven-hour ride that would give us time together. A ride through trees and fields, and beside a river that comforted my occasional stomach jitters.

After we'd left the docks and the train station, Anna reached into her bag.

"I thought you might arrive here a bit hungry, so I brought us cheese and pickle sandwiches. And I brought you a train schedule with a map so you might have an idea where we are and where we're going. We'll be stopping and changing trains in Montreal, a city in Quebec, and from there," she pointed to the places on the map, "we'll travel on to Kingston."

We sat in silence for a while, munching on our first meal together. I had many questions but decided to leave the quiet between us uncluttered. Instead, I thought about those children who'd been standing in a line back on the station platform. I wished a quiet hope for them that they might find someone like Anna at the end of their journey.

The clacking of the wheels along the track gave sound to my growing sense of belonging. Anna relaxed into her seat and turned to me.

"Tell me about your trip across the ocean, Martha. Was it exciting?"

I grinned, and the storyteller in me launched into tales of being mother to the children being sent to Canada, Josie in particular. I told about how I made sure no one fell overboard because no one was allowed to go out on deck without me in tow. I re-created some of the fantasies I'd made up for the little ones, when we'd lie in our bunks, foot to head.

"That's how you slept?" Anna snickered. I laughed to hear her snicker through her nose. "They were so lucky to have you there with them, especially when life has been so difficult for them."

Her regard for me lingered like a warm cup of tea, and I smiled at my reflection in the window. We let the quiet circulate between us for a while. A pleasure that felt new moved across my skin. I felt safe here with Anna.

When she spoke again, Anna's voice had a new, more serious tone.

"I want you to know, Martha, that we are very glad you are coming to live with us." She settled herself into her seat, folded her hands, intertwined her fingers. "I am delighted that you and I will come to know each other. I have no brothers or sisters, and that's how I've grown up." Anna gazed out the window, which for a moment reflected her sadness.

"I'm twenty years old. It's time I set out to do what I've always wanted. I've decided to go into nursing school at the local hospital." She spoke with renewed fervor and smiled. "I hope you will agree and look forward to enrolling in the high school. Kingston Collegiate and Vocational Institute, it's called. Actually, it's where the first prime minister of Canada went, in 1830."

Her words tumbled out as though she wanted me to take in the possibility of being a student again, without a moment to say no.

I'd learned to read people when they appeared uncertain. The doctors who had infrequently visited my mother, the minister from the local church, and the child workers who eventually took me in at the orphanage, they all had ways of circumventing the truth.

"I'd be excited about going to school, Anna, especially if you are there to listen to my lessons. Will you be?"

Questions began to tumble. "Have you lived in your home all your life? What must that feel like to always live in the same place, to always be part of a family? What's it like? What's my Aunt Emily like? Does she ever talk about my ma?" I stopped for a moment. Anna's eyes had lost some brightness. "Oh, I'm sorry. I'm going on and on. You probably need to ask about me."

When she turned back to me, Anna's smile had faded, her eyes clouded. "It's your Aunt Emily, my stepmother. She can be difficult."

My hope for a new mother like Ma fractured into shards. Why hadn't Aunt Emily contacted Mrs. McCarthy? Why had it been Mr. Johnson? Why was Anna meeting me? Where was my aunt? My fingers had begun to tingle, and a tiny rivulet of sweat had formed in the middle of my back.

"Oh, Martha. I'm welcoming the chance to have a sister. We can be like sisters, you and I, and my father has always wanted another daughter."

I took a deep breath and turned toward her, my gaze locked. "But your stepmother, my ma's sister, doesn't want me. Is that true?" Her silence answered my question.

The train began to slow as we entered what appeared to be a large city. Anna looked across me and out the window. "We're already in Montreal."

I watched the scene that played out on the busy station platform as we pulled in. I looked down. The waxed paper from the sandwich still sat in my lap. Crumbs had accumulated on my woolen skirt. My chest felt hollow.

Anna reached for my hand and intertwined her fingers through mine. "Martha McGrath, listen to me. My father and I are delighted to be your family—and we are your family. I feel as though we've waited a very long time for you to arrive. Ever since we knew how sick your mama was. Now you are here. Whatever is sticking in my stepmother's craw…well…"

I couldn't help from huffing a snort at Anna's description of my Aunt Emily's craw being stuck. I'd learned a new expression.

"Yes, Martha, whatever is stuck in her craw isn't what's important. You, my dear cousin. You are the important one. And we will be a family, all of us."

My doubts that had cascaded a few moments ago began to fade and a seed of something new to me began to grow. Hope. I buried my face in the softness of Anna's coat. Her hand cradled my cheek.

I wasn't sure why, but I believed her.

# Chapter Three

*I know where I'm goin'*
*And I know who's goin' with me.*

—Irish folk song

### June 1913 ◆ Kingston, Ontario ◆ Martha

"MARTHA?"

Sun warmed my cheeks. A gentle hand shook my shoulder and a soft voice called to me, one that sounded so much like Ma's, I didn't want to wake up. My dreams had taken me back to our one-room flat in Dublin. I saw Ma standing over me, the way she used to when it was time to start the day, time to put on my school pinafore, time to have my porridge oats. As I grasped at my fantasy I watched her gradually fade into the background, her shining black hair the last image to disappear.

"Martha. We're here. We're home." The train had stopped. People stood in the aisle and reached up for baggage and packages piled on the upper luggage racks.

I stretched, folded my arms across my chest, and inhaled a long, slow breath. When I exhaled, I had a strange feeling as though I'd taken on the body of another person. No longer Martha McGrath the Irish orphan, but Martha McGrath the Canadian, cousin, niece. I wondered at this new life that beckoned, as though my life, like the train, had switched onto a new track.

◆

As we'd journeyed from Quebec, Anna had begun to tell me about her home, where I'd be living from now on. The thought that I'd have my own room sent me reeling. Nothing that I'd experienced in my life compared to her description of home.

"Your room is up on the third floor," she'd told me. "There's a window bench where you can sit and look out over your Aunt Emily's garden. The room that will be yours used to be a place in the attic where my stepmother, your aunt, kept some of her own things she'd brought from Ireland."

I turned to her when I heard "Ireland." Something I remembered that Ma had said only a few years ago. I wished now that I'd listened and paid attention. Something about a shawl that belonged to her mother, my grandmother.

"Did she have any of my mother's things, do you know?" For some reason, I'd feared Anna's reply. Why did I feel such discomfort, why the cold emptiness in my chest?

"I'm not sure. We can ask when we get there." Anna shifted in her seat. I sat back and stared out the window at the trees slipping by. Maybe I didn't want to know what might be among my aunt's possessions when she left Ireland. I smiled over at Anna.

"You know, I've never had my own room, with my own chest of drawers, and my own blankets. Ma and I shared a bed in the flat where we lived with Shana, Ma's friend. Our clothes were all in the same cupboard. Even the toilet was down the hall, and that one we shared with our neighbors. Sometimes that was disgusting." Anna laughed at my description, and I realized she'd probably always had her own toilet.

Anna talked a bit more, and I began to push away my concern about Aunt Emily and her puzzling antagonism toward me, her only sister's daughter. I'd always been able to convince people I was a good person, and I believed Aunt Emily might have a change of heart when she knew me better. Persuading someone to like me was my protection, a way to conquer the aloneness that could swamp my spirit. But Aunt Emily loomed, a dark specter who threatened my new life in Canada. I needed people who wanted to fold me into the family. Already I could see that Anna might be one of those people. But I had my work ahead of me.

As we sat in silence, I stared out the window and watched the trees, hundreds of them, some of which I'd eventually come to love for the beauty they'd bring into my life and the sense of protection I felt among them. Nothing and no one had given me any reason to depend upon anybody.

"Martha?"

I roused myself from the view out my window and realized Anna had been talking. I'd heard nothing.

"I am sorry, Anna. I've been mesmerized by the acres of trees, sometimes so thick together I can't see into the woods, and then, suddenly…" I stopped and shook my head back and forth. "There'll be field after field, empty of trees, and land as far as I can see. It's extraordinary."

"Canada's a huge country, Martha. I think on our trip from Louise Basin in Quebec to Kingston, Ontario, we probably could have crossed the whole of Ireland and maybe back again." She'd laughed, "But then, I've never been to Ireland. I only know pictures and the maps my dad has in his office."

For a while we sat, both of us hushed in the newness of our bond. I didn't want to annoy her by asking too many questions, but I needed to know.

"Anna, why do you think it is that your stepmother… Aunt Emily…doesn't want me in her home?"

I asked the question and watched the reflection of her face in the window. She closed her eyes for an instant, then put her hand on my shoulder. "What do you know about us, your new family?" she asked. "Did your mother ever talk about us, about hoping to see us someday? About wanting to see her sister again?"

Her question puzzled me and gave me pause to think all was not well. That, possibly, I had reason to worry about Aunt Emily.

Before I could ask again, Anna shushed me. "Don't worry about your aunt, Martha. What's most important is you are here with us."

Still, her question about Ma troubled me. Didn't my cousin know how hard life had been for us, particularly for Ma whose days were filled with illness? For the last two years of her life, she'd gradually been dying. She'd tried to keep up with her teaching, but the consumption made her so weak, some days she couldn't get out of bed. And then the doctors told her she couldn't go into the schools. Why would she be thinking about her sister in Canada? Ma was sick and worried most of the time. I'd known for a while that my mother had a sister about whom she never talked; my Uncle Owen had sent mail and sometimes money to Ma when she was so sick. I was sure that his wife, my Aunt Emily, didn't know how he'd tried to look after us.

Something had happened to separate Ma from her sister, something serious enough to cause silence between them. Something still smoldering.

But I wanted to make a good impression on everyone. I knew from all Anna had told me that even she, Anna, didn't understand why her stepmother, my aunt, disliked me, possibly hated me.

◆

When we arrived at the train station in Kingston, Ontario, my apprehensions held me in a private, dark world, while everyone around me bustled and hastened to leave the train.

I'd been in a fog for a while when I heard Anna's voice, businesslike and practical. "Martha. We need to hurry. Let's get your bag down."

I managed to put the worry away as Anna took charge. She reached up and pulled down my bag. When she dropped it onto the seat, she bent down and looked out the window. People stood waiting to board. Others were looking up at the train. Some were waving. I thought I saw one very tall man standing at the back of the crowd who caught sight of Anna. I was right because she waved her arms back and forth like someone signaling. As she moved away from the seat, she bent to pick up my dilapidated bag. "No, no. Anna, please let me carry my own bag. You shouldn't have to do that." I tried to reach for it, but by the time I'd caught up to her, she was already at the entrance and had one foot on a step.

"Here, ma'am. Let me take that for you." A conductor at the bottom of the steps reached up, grasped my bag, and placed it on the platform. Almost immediately, that same very tall man I'd seen outside the train appeared and picked up my bag, which by now seemed to be moving from person to person, as though it had taken on a life of its own.

"Anna," he called as we descended the steps. "I'm so glad to see you home safe and sound." He reached toward her, his arm outstretched, his hand extended to grasp hers. His smile broadened as she stepped down toward him. I'd stopped behind Anna to watch them. I saw two people happily receiving each other, two people delighted to see the other again. I realized the tall man with the gray hair, peppery beard, and smart wool suit fashioned in the current style had to be Uncle Owen Johnson, Anna's father. In my lifetime I'd not often seen a father and a daughter greet each other so lovingly. I'd not known any sort of father.

"And…Martha. Welcome. Welcome to Canada!" He stood by Anna, who'd stepped onto the platform, and he looked up at me with such anticipation, I almost felt home.

◆

"Uncle Owen," he said. "Call me Uncle Owen." He lifted my bag and set it on the back seat of his Model T Ford. Experiences were tumbling one over another: my uncle, whose large hand encompassed mine in welcome; Anna, who'd linked her arm through mine when we walked to the car. I sat in the rear of a motor car like royalty who'd come to visit.

"We'll drive to the house, meet Mother, show you your room, and let you rest," Anna had said.

I smiled from the back seat of the car. I watched, fascinated, as Uncle Owen reached in, moved some levers, turned a key, walked to the front of the car and, seeming without effort, cranked a lever half a turn. What a moment that was. I knew I wanted to learn how to drive this car. Anna turned back to me the moment the engine took hold and, like a sister might, whispered, "Dad loves his Model T."

I'd been looking after myself, Ma, and children at the orphanage for so long, I hadn't known what it was like to be the one cared for or feel such a sense of belonging. Some old voice dropped into the midst: "*Careful, Martha, this could all end, and soon.*" It was like walking a tightrope.

◆

Uncle Owen and Anna stood in what they called the "front hall entrance foyer," a room just a shade smaller than the flat Ma and I lived in for five years. A small, stained-glass window shone multicolored designs created by the late afternoon sun onto the black-and-white tiled floor.

As I stood there on the threshold, I looked down at my black boots buttoned up over my ankles. I wrapped Ma's red wool shawl closer around my shoulders, and in an instant I felt a wave of aloneness like a shoe that had lost its mate. The intimacy I'd experienced only a few moments ago, gone.

"Martha? Come in, please." Anna reached for my hand. I realized I'd been standing still, not moving at all. "You're home."

She sounded so like my ma in that instant, I thought I'd fall weeping. The trip, the sail, the train, the hugeness of everything, descended. I felt more like an orphan girl than at any time since leaving the docks in Liverpool. '*I know where I'm goin' and I know who's goin' with me.*' Ma's lilt. My face crumpled. In that moment, Anna rushed to me and folded me into her arms. I sobbed as though I might never stop.

Uncle Owen backed away from the front entrance, farther into the hallway, my bag still in his grasp.

A voice pitched with impatience descended from the landing at the top of the stairs.

"What's wrong with the girl?"

Aunt Emily's welcome home.

# Chapter Four

*"I realise now that I wanted to disappear. To get so lost that nobody ever found me."*
—Jessica Warman, *Between*

### June 1913 ♦ 53 King Street ♦ Anna

MARTHA'S BODY FELT LIGHTWEIGHT IN MY ARMS, LIKE a small child's. Not the young woman who'd been curious about the trees and the room she'd have all on her own. The sobs shook her shoulders with such force I feared she might crumple into splintered bones there in the front entrance. I'd wondered when she might succumb to all she'd experienced in the past ten days, or throughout the fifteen years of her life.

Nothing prepared me for the depth of grief that rose from her shaking body. The straight-backed, clear-eyed girl I'd met on that platform waiting for the train had disappeared.

My father, who'd moved farther into the dim light of the hallway, looked stricken. He placed Martha's cloth bag onto the black-and-white tile floor, a gentle motion. He looked to me. I cradled Martha in my arms there in the doorway.

"Dad?" I beckoned. When I was small and he had to be both father and mother as comforter, he'd gather me into his arms and whisper into the top of my head, "All is well, Anna, all is well." And today he came to Martha as he'd come to me. He wiped her cheek with his pocket handkerchief and told her, "All is well, Martha, all is well."

I gradually moved Martha away from the doorway, my arm across her shoulder, while Dad bent to pick up her bag. When I looked up the stairs, I watched my stepmother, who stood with her arms folded like a barricade. She made no move to come down to her niece.

"Mother?" I called up to her. "Will you come and help us, please?"

What cruel notion, I wondered, caused her to pay no attention to Martha's despair? Was her anger so relentless she couldn't find a place in herself to show a measure of compassion for her sister's child?

My throat filled with a desire to shout at her, as so often I'd wanted to throughout the years since she'd arrived as my governess, who soon became my father's wife. Yet my bewilderment at her behavior was like a narcotic that buffered my reactions to her cruelty. Her unfathomable bearing at that moment was secondary, even a waste of my time. Martha needed every consolation we could muster for her right now, right here. As I moved down the hall toward the kitchen, my arm around her waist, she lifted her head from my shoulder and with barely a whisper, said, "Anna, I am so sorry. Forgive me."

"Here, Anna." My father walked toward me as we approached the kitchen. "Let me help." He offered his arm to Martha, like a man inviting a lady for a stroll. I saw endurance begin to flow back into her body as she moved away from me and crooked her arm into his. Years of practiced perseverance rose up. Tears dripping from her chin, she straightened her shoulders and walked into the kitchen, arm in arm with my father.

"Martha, have a seat here at the table, and let me make a cup of tea. You do drink tea, don't you, Irish as you are?" He helped her lower into the one chair at the table—his chair. I wondered if I'd ever loved him more than I did at that moment. He didn't fuss, and he didn't deny her sadness. He gave it place, time, and reverence.

When I moved over to the electric range to take the teakettle and fill it at the sink, Dad beckoned and pulled out a chair close by Martha. "I'm making the tea, Annie. You sit here and talk with your cousin."

Martha's sobs had subsided and only a few soft hiccups remained. I reached over and drew back the strands of dark hair that had fallen over her eyes. "Do you know how brave you are? You've just traveled thousands of miles to be here. You've left home and country. I'm not surprised at all that you are overwhelmed." We sat, the two of us. The only sound in the room was the beginning whistle of the kettle on the stove. Martha nodded, inhaled one long, slow breath, intertwined her fingers, and rested her hands on the table.

"We'll help in every way we can to make a home for you here, won't we, Dad?" I looked over at him. He stood, pouring water over the tea leaves in the strainer of the teapot as though he'd done this every day of his life.

I heard my stepmother descending to the front hall, where she stopped and opened the French doors into the parlor.

"Mother, we're having tea in the kitchen," I called to her. Nothing. No response.

"I'd like to go and speak with Aunt Emily, if I could," Martha said.

I turned and glanced over at my father. He stood at the counter, teapot in hand, his back to us, and shook his head no. When he turned to us, I couldn't read his expression. My only indicator of any disquiet he might have been feeling was a sadness that shadowed his eyes.

"I think you and Anna should have your tea and a good talk. I'll take your bag up to your room." He paused, set our cups and the pot on the table, and walked to the hall door where he turned back. "Try not to worry about Mrs. Johnson, she'll come around. She's just a bit fretful. That's all."

What an interesting word I thought. Fretful. It felt protective. Who was he protecting, Martha or her?

◆

MARTHA'S ROOM WAS ON THE THIRD FLOOR OF OUR house. It had been a place where steamer trunks, filled with baby clothes and photos weathered and yellow, lay closed and silent. As a little girl, I'd often retreated to this attic room to re-create what was left of my mother before she died. A wedding dress, blue silk with a diamond clasp attached, a faded photo of Mama and Dad on their wedding day. A rocking chair with peeling paint sat in a corner. I'd found these treasures one day when I opened the door to the attic and discovered steep stairs leading to what I'd decided was a magic place. Even as a twenty-year-old woman, I still thought of this room as magical. I'd persuaded my stepmother and my dad that Martha should have this room. I said it would be a place of her own where she could look out over the gardens and see the lake from her window over the roof. Soon after I pleaded the case for Martha, my stepmother hired two men, whom I found one morning hauling the steamer trunks and the old rocking chair down the flights of stairs. I was returning from my shift at the hospital.

"What are you doing?" I'd asked the men who were standing at the bottom of the stairs, each holding an edge of a steamer trunk.

"We're haulin' these away to the junkyard, ma'am."

"Put it down, please."

A voice echoed down the hallway. My stepmother.

"What is the problem here?'

"Emily, these men say they're taking away our steamer trunks and the rocking chair."

"Of course they are. That's what we decided. If we want to put the girl in that room, we have to clear the room of unnecessary clutter."

"No, Emily, we had not…decided. You decided. And," I pointed at the rocking chair and the trunks, "these are not clutter." By now, I'd found myself standing, blocking the door.

"Must everything be so difficult?" She breathed an impatient sigh.

"If you keep changing the rules, yes."

I realized she'd taken what to her was a natural step toward ridding the house of my mother's memory. Martha, her sister's child, was arriving and needed a room, the attic was to be that room, and thus required disposal of everything in it.

"Emily, the trunks go back upstairs to the attic room as we decided. They will be covered with blankets and used as small tables. The rocking chair? I'll paint it and sew a cushion and I'll make curtains for the window. Done. Understand? Now gentlemen, if you will. Please trek everything back up the three flights of stairs and put it all back into the attic room."

Emily's face became crimson, and her eyes bored into me.

"Do what you want. It matters nothing to me." She spun, turned, and with one last retort, "You've always been difficult," left.

◆

I watched Martha when she walked into her room. My dad was behind her. Emily had chosen to stay in the kitchen. Sulking, I expect.

Dad and I had worked on the room soon after the nasty scene.

We'd painted the walls a clear sky-blue, and I'd fashioned crisp, white curtains that hung over the windows. A small bed fit against the wall under the sloping ceiling. The rug I'd found rolled up in the cellar, one I'd had as a young girl in my bedroom, fit exactly from wall to wall.

Flowers from our garden graced the white bedside table I'd scrounged from the used furniture room at the hospital. The steamer trunks I'd salvaged, piled one on top of the other, would hold Martha's books and treasures, the few she'd brought with her. And a narrow wooden wardrobe that Dad had in his office at the university stood sentinel-like at the bottom of the bed.

Martha was silent. She looked across the room to the window, and with two strides walked over, turned, threw her arms into the air, and whirled, laughing.

"Bloody great!

A once-despairing Martha had transformed again before our eyes.

"I'll leave the two of you to it." Dad laughed and turned to the door. "Martha, if there is anything you need, anything, just tell Anna. We want you to be happy."

I'd never heard my father be so solicitous. I knew he

could be a kind man, but he bridled emotions carefully. Love, for him, was a field surrounded by hedges. His cat, Oliver, and I were safe within that field. I wasn't even sure about Emily, his wife. But now he'd invited Martha into his world. I was puzzled, and pleased.

After Dad left, Martha dropped down onto her bed.

"Is there anything you need now?" I asked.

"Anna, would you understand if I said I need to be alone for a while?"

"Of course I would. Do that." No more words were necessary. As I slipped out the door, I turned and looked back at Martha, who'd pulled her shawl, her mother's shawl, around her shoulders. She lay back against the cushions and pillows I'd scattered across the top of her bed. I thought surely she'd be asleep by the time I reached the ground floor.

As I came down the stairs, I stopped at the second-floor landing, where I could hear the murmur of voices drifting from the parlor.

I didn't want to eavesdrop, and I didn't know if I'd be welcome in there. Emily's crisp tones had risen. As I came near the door into the parlor, Dad emerged, his face clouded into a deep frown.

"Dad?" He was moving so quickly down the hallway toward the kitchen I had to speed up.

"Dad? What's happened?"

"Anna, come into the kitchen and close the door…please."

# Chapter Five

*So...this is how invisible feels.*
—Martha McGrath

### June 1913 ◆ 53 King Street ◆ Martha

FLOATING. I FELT AS THOUGH I MIGHT STILL BE FLOATING on the ship, mid-ocean. The sense of being transported, the breeze wafting across my face, enveloped me. Was I being lifted and taken? Was this how it felt to die? My next breath determined that I was not being raised up to some better place. The next breath woke me with a start.

The sheer curtains that covered the dormer window blew across the head of my bed. The branches from the willow tree were so close that in my dreamy state I'd thought someone might have tried to pick me up and carry me off. The sun just to the east had not yet broken through the branches. I'd slept through the night and awakened only when the wind brushed against the curtains.

A tentative knock at my door reminded me that I was not alone, and possibly might never be again. Family. I was with family. How does that feel? Family?

The next knock was not so hesitant, and it was followed by a loud whisper. "Martha, are you awake? I have tea."

Anna was at my door. She'd climbed the three floors up to bring me tea. How was it my ma had never talked about this family? Anna and Uncle Owen, kinder than any

I'd known. Why hadn't Ma told me? Did she even know them? The door opened only a sliver, then wider. Anna backed into the room with a tray that held a delicate china cup and saucer, with a napkin folded over a small teapot. Never in my life had I been served tea in bed. She smiled down at me, looking like some kind of angel, dressed in her crisp, white uniform, her starched apronlike bib billowing over her chest.

Her hair was pinned up under a white cap bordered by a black velvet ribbon. To me, the orphan child, she was a vision.

"I thought I'd bring you tea before I leave for the hospital."

I sat up, pulled my legs up to my chin, and wrapped my arms around my knees, still covered with Ma's shawl.

"You are all so kind to me." I still had a feeling that I'd been misplaced, that I'd landed somewhere magical, and soon the spell would be shattered.

The rag rug on the floor reminded me of all the bits and pieces of me, sewn together hither and thither, mismatched colors and raggedy edges.

Anna set the tray down on the steamer trunks that were now a table. Her crisp uniform rustled as she walked to the window and pulled it shut. When she turned to me her smile had disappeared. Instead, her eyes seemed cloudy, her mouth set in a sad downturn.

"Anna? What's wrong?"

Without protest or comment she dropped down beside me, the folds of starched cotton wrapped around her legs, somewhere amid all that material was Anna. It seemed natural to sit shoulder to shoulder, rather like sisters might.

"Is it Aunt Emily?" I asked.

"Yes. I don't know what's going on. She won't talk about it with me or with Dad." Anna stayed still and said no more.

"What can I do, Anna? Should I leave?" I wondered if it might be less terrifying just to go. "I'll be all right, whatever I need to do," I said.

"Oh, Martha, no. Don't even consider such a possibility." Anna dropped back onto the bed beside me and grasped my hand. "We'll all figure this out. Whatever it might be that's troubling Emily, you will not, and I repeat…will not…leave. This is your home. You are my cousin, and you belong here. Dad's only niece."

I couldn't help myself. I began to smile, which soon became a throaty giggle. Anna's fearless backbone reminded me of Miss Ashcroft and all the stories she'd told me about how women deserve the vote. "We are people too," she'd declared to me as we'd sailed that journey across the Atlantic.

Here was Anna, my cousin, beside me on the bed, her starched apron bunched under her chin, declaring my rights. I had been blessed with my ma teaching me about my worth. Sick as she'd been during the last years of her life, Ma taught me about strength. She'd get herself out of the bed some mornings when I knew every part of her ached, just to be sure I had some Irish oatmeal bread to take to school for lunch. To the end, she was my ma.

"Oh! I have to go." Anna leaped from the bed and straightened her uniform. She looked at the watch pinned to her apron, then sprinted to the door of my room and flung it open. Like a cloud chasing across a blue sky, she was gone.

I lay back in the quiet of the early morning house and watched the sun create patterns across the vaulted ceiling. I needed a plan. Just as I had when I arrived at the orphan home in Dublin, I needed to concentrate on how to be accepted by Aunt Emily and become someone who belonged to the Johnson household.

◆

"Where is the girl, Owen? I haven't heard anything at all. It's almost eight in the morning. What if she's skulking around looking to steal the silver?"

I stood at the closed door into the dining room. I'd tiptoed down the stairs as quietly as I could, fearful that Aunt Emily and Uncle Owen might be sleeping.

I waited a moment, hand on the doorknob.

"Emily, Martha is your sister's child. She is no thieving street urchin. So, please, for all of us, stop this nonsense." Uncle Owen sounded irritated.

I backed away from the door, turned toward the stairs, and began to climb as stealthily as I could. As I reached the first landing, the door to the dining room opened and Uncle Owen strode into the hallway. As I took the next step, a creaking floorboard caused him to turn toward the stairs.

"Good morning, Uncle Owen," I called out. My voice was a rasp.

"Stay right there. I'll come up."

"No, no. I'll come down. Might I get you something to eat? I make a lovely Irish breakfast." I talked myself down each step. He reached for my hand as I neared him.

"My goodness, no, Martha. That will come soon enough, I'm sure. Come in here and join your Aunt Emily and me. Do you like to read the newspaper?"

The woman at the far end of the table was a cold presence. She sat, her arms and hands positioned on either side of her breakfast plate, her fingers flat on the white tablecloth.

I tried to find something of Ma in her. Her mouth folded into a frown as though she'd bit into something sour.

"Good morning, Aunt Emily." I stopped by her chair. She made no move to stand or reach out. She looked over to a place midway down the table and pointed.

"There," she said. "You can sit there. Owen? Are you coming in, or are you leaving for the office?"

*So, this is how invisible feels*, I thought.

"No, no, Emily. I thought I'd stay for a while and make sure that Martha has a good breakfast." He stood by the door, his hand still grasping the latch, possibly ready to change his mind and leave.

"Well, child, are you going to continue to stand?"

This was a kind of rudeness I'd experienced before—being a child of a single mother and living in poverty invited cruel comments and coldness.

I pulled the chair away from the table and sat down on the edge of the pillowed seat, my hands folded almost automatically. *Is this how a young woman might behave in a posh dining room?* I wondered. *Might this be how to please her?* A knife, a fork, and a spoon lay properly beside a blue china plate. A glass of orange juice was carefully placed at the edge of the fork. I waited for someone's next move. It came soon enough.

"You can address me as Mrs. Johnson," she said. "Or Aunt Emily, if you must."

Uncle Owen had walked around to the other side of the table. He stood ramrod straight, his fingers spread across the top of the chair, his knuckles a white hue as he grasped the carved wood.

"Martha, I want to be sure you have a good breakfast before I leave for the university. Let me get you some warm biscuits and homemade jam." He turned to Aunt Emily for the first time. "I suspect you made these biscuits, did you not, Mrs. Johnson?" She nodded briefly. *What an unusual household,* I thought. Uncle Owen's manner with Aunt Emily was distantly polite. As difficult as life had been, Ma sick, us living with her friend Shana all in one room, we'd tried to be gentle-like people. I taught the young children at the orphanage how to be kind with each other. This coolness toward one another in a family puzzled me.

I smiled my best good girl smile for Aunt Emily.

"I'm sure your biscuits and jam are delicious. But, please, may I go to the kitchen and make up my own plate? I'm not here to be a bother. I want to earn my keep."

"Suit yourself," she said and went back to her tea.

With that, I slipped from the chair and stood behind it, not sure what to say. I looked to Uncle Owen, who pointed to the door.

"I'll come with you," he said.

I'd been in the dining room for only a few moments; I'd been in this house overnight. In those moments, in those hours, only Anna's presence and Uncle Owen's earlier assurance gave me heart or kept me from running.

Out in the kitchen, I realized I was shaking. Uncle Owen took a chair, pulled it out, and beckoned to me. While I gathered myself, he busied himself pouring tea for the two of us.

"Martha?" His black-rimmed eyeglasses perched on the tip of his nose.

My tremors slowed and I picked up my cup, still not trusting myself to speak.

"Martha, I think I know how hard this must be for you, but you are no longer alone as you might have felt at other times. If there is any part of you thinking of leaving, please listen to what I'm saying."

I'd not been able to look into Uncle Owen's face, until now. His eyes urged me to believe him. "Uncle Owen, I will stay as long as I have Anna and you. I will stay because Ma wanted me to come here."

He nodded. "Work calls me, Martha. I must go."

His words ringing in my ears, I took my cup with a biscuit on a plate and walked back down the hall to the dining room. Emily hadn't moved from her place at the table, except to open her morning paper. I sat on the chair beside her and began to slice my biscuit.

Without looking up, she handed me the jam.

When I bit into the biscuit, I raised my eyes to see her staring across the table at me.

"I'm not sure how this all came about. None of this, you living here, was anything I agreed to." She stood up, plate in hand, and walked to the door.

"Do not expect me to coddle you, as Mr. Johnson and Anna seem to be doing. You are my sister's child, I won't turn you away, but I don't have to pretend I'm pleased."

She was gone.

I left my half-eaten biscuit on the plate, waited till I heard the kitchen door shut, and left to climb the stairs to the attic.

◆

ANNA TOOK VACATION DAYS IN JULY, AND SHE AND I would walk to the lake early in the morning. We took sandwiches and lemonade, read our novels to each other, and sometimes lay on a blanket and talked. Some days, Uncle Owen took me to his office at the university where I'd sit under a tree and disappear into a novel. Those were the times I lost myself to *Jane Eyre* or imagined a friend like Dorothy's scarecrow.

But I missed the cool breezes off the River Liffey in Dublin and the sounds of the bustle in the markets. There were times when I'd walk to the lake by myself, sit at the shore, and listen for the Irish sounds of the water lapping up on the stones.

One afternoon, I took myself to the public market downtown. I'd told Uncle Owen I wanted to go, and so I did with his blessing and money in my pocketbook. The calls of vendors, the scent of flowers, the colors of vegetables in their crates, all transported me to Dublin and Ma. I remembered our shopping days when we'd find the reddest apples and the sweetest butter, then head back to the house where Cook and I would bake pies and tarts, ready for the Quinns' dinner.

That day at the Kingston Market, I decided to surprise everyone and bake pies and tarts for supper.

No one was in the house, and with a sense of cheer I'd set about baking, until...

"What on earth is going on?"

Emily, home from her quilting group, had come into the house through the kitchen door.

"This will not do. Clean up this mess right now."

I stood frozen, a rolling pin covered in flour in my hands, pie dough half rolled on the counter.

"But, Aunt Emily. I want to bake for everyone, I want to be useful. Ma…and I…used to …"

"Let's not talk about what used to be, child. This is my kitchen. Now clear away the mess."

The words bounced inside my head as she tromped and rustled down the hall.

That day I packed my bag and shoved it under my bed. How much angrier could I become before leaving?

◆

TUESDAY, SEPTEMBER 2, 1913

"Martha. Are you ready?" Anna called up the stairs to me.

I sat on the edge of my bed, one shoe in my hand, the other still unlaced. I was a swirling mixture of anxiety and anticipation. It was the first day of high school. Over the summer I'd decided to stay here for a while and then agreed to go to high school.

Since the scene in the kitchen, I'd decided I'd be so perfect that Aunt Emily would have to want me to stay. I'd help with housekeeping, although she always left the kitchen or the room I was dusting. She spoke little to me directly.

Anna and Uncle Owen were my saving grace. When I thought about the other children I'd lived with at Mrs. McCarthy's Home in Dublin, I had to believe that my life might be better than theirs. But some days, I wasn't sure. Anna had to work at the hospital, sometimes very long hours. Uncle Owen, the mathematics professor, spent days at Queen's University. He was part of a small faculty and was devoted to his work and his students.

On this day, the day after what I came to know as Labor Day, I'd begun the next new path of my life. Anna had insisted, Uncle Owen had made sure it happened, and Aunt Emily, in her usual manner, stood back without comment.

Ma was my teacher at home until I went to the school down the road. She'd taught me to read, and she'd insisted I go to the school nearby. Those days near the end, I stopped going to school and sat by her bed reading to her. Ma, with all the problems she'd experienced in her short life, was a determined woman. Determined to make something out of her misfortune, her mistakes, and her alienation from her family. There were times when I wanted to ask Aunt Emily if she knew how brave my ma had been, but the moments when there were just the two of us were brief and dispassionate. I'd made few gains winning her over throughout the summer. I wondered if the longer I stayed, the more she resented me.

"Martha. You're going to be late! Not a good way to start." I'd been sitting immobile on the edge of my bed and hadn't heard Anna running up the stairs to my room.

"Come on! Dad is waiting to drive us."

"I'm not sure this is a good idea." I hadn't finished my thought before Anna grabbed my shoe, my hand, and my book bag, all in one motion.

"This is not a discussion, Martha." She pulled me across the carpet, as I hopped and stepped and tried to keep up. "We've gone over all the reasons." Still, she pulled.

"Anna!" I spoke with such ferocity, she stopped.

She turned to me and dropped my hand and my shoe, but still held my book bag. "Martha, are you frightened? The girl who crossed the ocean, who came to live in a whole new country? My idol?"

Stunned at her declaration, I dropped to the floor and sat without ceremony on the top step.

"Me? Your idol? Anna, how can that be, when you are mine?" And, as though synchronized, we began to laugh—me with one shoe still flapping open and another shoe partway down the stairs where it had dropped, and Anna with her starched uniform bubbling up under her chin, hanging on to my book bag and the railing. The moment ended in laughter.

"Girls, we really must go." Uncle Owen stood at the bottom of the stairs. He looked every bit the serious professor, but I could tell he wanted to join in our ruckus.

◆

ANNA SAT ACROSS THE TABLE AT DINNER THAT EVENING, quiet and subdued. Uncle Owen was preoccupied, so I thought. The air felt blurred. We ate in silence. My uncle sat, still sipping his before-dinner whiskey, and looking beyond us all. Aunt Emily concentrated on peeling the skin from her boiled chicken. Anna looked tired from her day but made a point to smile over at me every so often. She'd been the one who insisted we light candles for the dinner table, a custom Aunt Emily had declared as "silly." I'd come to understand that some silent specter separated Uncle Owen and Anna from Aunt Emily.

I ventured to break the silence.

"One of my teachers at the collegiate is straight from Ireland. He even knew where Ma and I lived on Henrietta Street in Dublin." Before I could carry on my story, Aunt Emily hissed, her lips tight, her jaw clenched.

"There'll be no more talk of Dublin in this house."

The air that had felt blurred now crackled.

"Emily, I think if Martha wants to tell about…" Uncle Owen had emerged from his preoccupation. He looked wretched as though he wanted nothing more than to be silent, eat his dinner, and retire to his study.

"I agree with Dad." Anna roused and looked around as though waking from a dream. "Martha, tell us."

I felt a kind of unspoken quiet war. Aunt Emily, Anna, Uncle Owen, each drawing up a position about me, about my place in the family. I sat for a moment and let my roiling stomach settle. Just as I had done for my fifteen years, I'd try to fix what seemed to be broken.

I'd start now. I'd make myself part of this family. I'd start with what Ma had taught me: 'Talk intelligently, my girl, let people know you have a brain.'

"Did anyone see the newspaper this afternoon?" I asked. "Mr. Ryan has been asking us to follow the articles about what's happening in Europe. He thinks young people need to pay attention to world affairs."

Aunt Emily harrumphed. Uncle Owen nodded while he buttered his bread. Anna said, "I agree."

"Maybe we need to talk about what's happening, you know, be ready for a possible war. That's what Mr. Ryan says…he…" Before I'd finished my attempt at diverting, Aunt Emily cut in.

"Oh, for heaven's sake, child, stop talking nonsense. I want to eat my dinner in peace and quiet."

I squeezed my shoulder blades back. My throat felt tight. My spirit that had rallied again and again over the weeks was weakening and in its place a simmering rage.

I could hear Ma in my head as the words began to tumble. "Martha, Martha, words matter, a small spark can light a forest. So be slow to anger." *Oh, Ma, I've tried. I've tried.*

Nothing I could do swayed her. How pleasant I was only irritated her. I believed that Anna and Uncle Owen's growing fondness for me offended her, possibly infuriated her. I felt like I was holding my breath just to please her. I could not do this anymore.

I dropped my fork on the plate, stood, and pushed back the chair. My napkin fell onto the floor. Aunt Emily stiffened.

"Aunt Emily, I don't know what I've done to make you dislike me so. Ma loved with her whole heart. How could the two of you be so different?"

I was swallowing tears as I got up to leave. Sure that my packed bag up in my attic room would soon be needed.

"Stop right there!" She had risen from her chair, hands balled into fists slamming down onto the table with such force the plates rattled. "Never, ever speak of your mother in this house…"

"Emily, this is so unnecessary." Uncle Owen's voice cut through Aunt Emily's tirade.

But she only looked at him with a hateful stare.

"I will say what needs to be said."

At that moment I saw another Uncle Owen. "Emily, sit down…please." His voice was tight with a raw bitterness. Everything, every hidden resentment, every disappointment was becoming unraveled.

I'd never heard Uncle Owen speak that way, but most shocking was Anna.

"Martha, sit down." Anna spoke with such authority, I walked back to my chair and I sat down.

Anna turned in her chair full body to face her stepmother.

"I am no longer going to allow myself, my father, or your niece—the only blood family you have in this room—to be plagued by your ill humor."

I watched Emily, who was visibly shaking. Anna stood and walked toward her.

"No, Emily. We will all stay here in this room until you start to tell us why you are so irritable. You need to tell us what is stuck in that craw of yours."

Aunt Emily's face became a crimson mask. Her eyes flared. "How dare you. How dare you speak to me in that tone. I will not have you question me."

A quiet, stinging voice spoke from the end of the table. Uncle Owen. "Emily, I'm not saying it again. Sit down." Shock registered around the room. If he'd slapped her, I doubt she could have been as stunned. "You, you of all people, Owen. I came all the way from Ireland to you, and to you."

She turned and thrust a pointed finger at Anna. "And you," her hand waved with such force in my direction I felt the air rush past my face. "You swagger in here like some grand lady—putting on airs, just like your mother. She's the very one who took us all down. Your treasured Ma."

Anna stared wide-eyed at her stepmother; Uncle Owen shook his head from side to side, his hands curled around the napkin in his lap.

My heart pounded. My breath stuck in my throat.

"Aunt Emily? How could you talk about my ma? How could you say hateful things about her?"

"Your precious mother. My sister destroyed our lives. Don't talk to me about how wonderful she was. She was a tramp. Your father…was no fisherman lost at sea."

The air in the room collected into stony silence.

Emily reached into her apron pocket, pulled out a small tattered book, and thrust it at me.

"Here. Read about your sainted mother."

It was Ma's diary.

# Part Two

1891 ◆ Leaving

# Chapter Six

### 1891 ♦ Near Dublin, Ireland ♦ Emily McGrath

AFTER DOCTOR BURKE LEFT THE HOUSE THAT NIGHT, I stood at the top of the stairs and listened to Da's sobs—a sorrowful sound that caused my heart to pulse against my chest. When I called down to him, my voice scraped against my throat like sandpaper.

"Da? Da? What's happening?" The sobs diminished as he walked to the bottom of the stairs where he stood head bowed, shoulders slumped.

"Emmie. Come down, come to your ma. She's gone. She's…"

I grasped my long flannel nightie in one hand and the wooden stair rail with the other. I had barely placed one foot on the step when I heard Sarah call from her room, "Emily? What's wrong? I hear Papa?"

"Shush now, Sarah. Stay in your room. I'll be back up in a moment." Words locked in my throat. Ma was gone. Our ma was gone. My legs were jelly.

As my body collapsed onto the third step from the bottom, I felt the soul I had shared with my mother leaving me. I was alone. But I couldn't stay sitting there. Da needed me and soon I'd need to comfort my little sister. I stood up, clutched the railing and, one step at a time, moved into a changed world.

As I reached the hallway, I saw Da in the front parlor, the room where Grandpa had lain in his coffin just last year.

My bare feet touched the cold floor. I rolled my hands into fists and tucked them into the long sleeves of my nightshirt. My body felt rigid.

I saw Da slumped in his leather chair by the peat fire, his forehead buried in his hands.

"Da? Tell me?" Earlier when I'd heard the horse and wagon rattling up to our house, I'd looked from my bedroom window and watched my father rush the doctor inside. Any hope I'd held vanished when I saw Da's anguished face.

"Oh, Da. It's Ma, isn't it?"

"Ah, Emmie, your beautiful mother is gone. How can I live in this world without her?"

Bent down on my knees, I took his outstretched hands and pressed my forehead against his. "Da, oh Da…" My words were keening laments. "I promised Ma. I told her I'd always be strong for you and for Sarah." I sat back onto the floor, placed my hands on his knees, and sat in prayerful sadness. "Ma was our rock. I depended on her for all of my twenty-one years. Now, she's gone."

Da nodded—his head still bowed, his long hair falling around his face. I heard Ma's voice real in my mind. "John, please get your hair cut 'fore I die."

"Ah, Emmie." He lifted his head and looked at me, his eyes brimming. "She was so sick, Emmie, she was so sick."

When he took my hand again, he pressed it to his cheek, and he spoke as though Ma were standing there. "I thought she'd just hurt her hand when she hit it against the wood stove, but we didn't pay attention, Emmie, we didn't pay attention. She knew whatever that bump on her hand was, she knew it wasn't going away. We should have known." His words rode on gulping sobs.

"She had the cancer. She had the cancer."

I stood up and moved away from him, toward his whiskey cupboard. It felt wrong, watching agony overcome him without trying to do something.

We'd not been close, Da and I, and I didn't know how to take on his pain. Mine was too great, so I brought a friend to him. I poured a stiff shot of Irish whiskey and handed it to him with trembling hand.

"Damn you, God, if you care at all, why did you have to take her?" he shouted. I froze, fearful that he'd strike out at me.

It was that moment when he said the unforgivable.

"Where's little Sarah, Emmie? Where's your sister? We need her here. She's your Ma all over again. We need her here." Ma and I had had each other for nine years before Sarah came along. Sarah the beauty, Sarah the love of everyone's life.

I swallowed the bile that rose in my throat and poured a whiskey for myself. Even in Ma's death, Sarah was given first place.

Sarah, born nine years after me, was just twelve years old on the night Ma died. I wondered if it might have been Sarah's fault coming along when she did, Ma being in her forties and having a difficult pregnancy bearing and birthing her.

It wasn't right or Christian to hold such evil thoughts about my sister, but still, I had a place in me that simmered like a pot of water about to boil over.

I sat on the floor by Da's chair and hid the wetness that clouded my eyes.

Ma would expect me to be strong, and Da had nothing left to give us after he lost his Annie. His life rested in her memory. Now he'd live in the spaces she had left.

◆

MY SISTER, SARAH, WAS A SPIRITED GIRL. FROM THE TIME she was born she let the world know of her arrival. I watched her grow into a dark-eyed, dark-haired beauty. At twelve years she turned heads when she skipped and danced down the small street in our village.

Now, with Ma gone, I knew I needed to care for both Sarah and Da. In the days after Ma's death I woke with a dull ache behind my eyes, one that cut into my breath—could I possibly take her place? Could I care for them, and for me, the way she did?

Each day, after the three of us did the early morning chores, Sarah left for school in the village. Later, I walked down the road to my country school where, among the little ones I taught, I felt a brief respite from sadness. Da? He headed out to the barn with his whiskey bottle in his back pocket.

Da was a good tenant farmer who worked diligently for the lord of the manor; however, he actively agitated for himself and those men who rented and tilled the land. He became a landowner when the Land War receded, one who plowed and harvested his own fields and took care of his own animals. This house, this soil, belonged to him—something that brought him a sense of pride. But after Ma died, Da lost that spirit. He was no longer the man who once stood up to the absentee landlords. He was broken.

When Da needed company after he wandered in from the barn, I sat in Ma's rocker and talked with him. I told him about the day and the children's antics at school. Often, if he was feeling talkative, he told Sarah and me stories about Ma and how much she loved us all. But, on the nights he staggered over to his chair beside Ma's rocker, I felt lost without Ma there to tell me what to do. Those were the nights when Sarah, wrapped in her flannel nightgown, would sit at his feet and sing to him songs he'd taught her. My favorite was "Rose of Tralee." Her voice was a lilt that lifted us from the sadness we all felt.

*The pale moon was rising above*
*the green mountain,*
*The sun was declining beneath the blue sea;*
*When I strayed with my love to the*
*pure crystal fountain,*
*That stands in the beautiful Vale of Tralee.*
*She was lovely and fair as the rose of the summer,*
*Yet 'twas not her beauty alone that won me;*
*Oh no, 'twas the truth in her eyes ever dawning,*
*That made me love Mary, the Rose of Tralee.*

Other nights he joined her when she sang, just as he used to with Ma. But there were more and more times when he rose from his chair and made his way up the stairs.

One night during a blizzard, Da lifted himself from his chair and reached for his woolen jacket from the hook by the door.

"I'm going out to the barn and see to the sheep."

"Da, let me come with you."

"No, no, Emmie, it's bad enough out there for a strong man like me, let alone a waif like you." He laughed a bit. He always liked to tease me about my five feet almost one inch of shortness. My "little" sister, Sarah, could already look me straight in the eye. "I'll be fine," he said.

Often Da would stay out in the barn with the sheep, sometimes just passing out on the cot he kept out there. We didn't go looking until the morning when he didn't come back to see Sarah off to school.

"Where's Da?" Sarah asked. She'd been standing at the door as the sun rose, waiting for him to call out for her. A sense of doom shivered through my body.

"You go out, Sarah, see if he's already there. I'll pull on my coat and boots and be with you in a minute." I grabbed my woolen scarf and my winter jacket, pulling on my boots as I walked out the door. Snow still whirled everywhere, blocking our view of the barn. I panicked when I saw Sarah go down into a snowbank at the sheep pen. She stood rigid as I ran to her, snow over her boots.

"Da. It's Da," she screamed. There at her feet lay Da, curled into a frozen sleep.

I ran to her side to reach for her, to try to drag her from the horror of Da's wide-eyed face, stiff with snow and ice. She refused to move.

"He must have fallen," I yelled at Sarah.

She fell too, onto her knees, almost buried in a drift, cradling Da's head and shoulders in her arms.

"I fell over him, Emmie. I fell over him," she sobbed.

"Oh, Sarah." I sank, gathered her into my arms, and clutched her as though I feared she too might leave me. The three of us—the lifeless frozen body of Da, Sarah's wailing small being, and me transformed to stone—moved into our newly changed worlds.

Her wails became a high-pitched scream. She scratched and grabbed at my coat like a terrified animal. I wanted to throw her off me. I wanted to toss her small body into the snowy grave.

My soul joined Ma and Da. I was empty. Nothing was left.

Sarah pummeled my chest until she collapsed into the snow.

◆

A MONTH FOLLOWING DA'S WAKE, THE SOLICITOR MR. Barry told us Da had left us the farm and each of us a private income.

After Mr. Barry left that night, I sat at supper staring at potatoes and turnips growing cold. The glowing peat whispered in the fireplace. Sarah stared at the flames. We held the grief of a new world in our hands.

"Sarah?" I leaned toward her. "I'm thinking we need to sell the farm. I've an idea of where we might go."

With no warning, she smacked her hand onto the table with a force that rattled the dishes.

"Emmie! You can't do that! This is home. This is where we belong!"

"But, Sarah, we can't look after the place. I need to teach. You need to go to school. We can't look after the animals, and the neighbors won't help us forever."

A knot tied in my stomach at the sight of Sarah who now stood, her shoulders tight, her arms folded across her body, fingers digging at the sleeves of her sweater.

"Emmie, I'm not sure if I could forgive you. Da and Ma would have never, ever sold the farm." She threw her arms into the air and swung her head from side to side, the combs that held her wild black curls hurling to the floor. "I'll stay home from school. I know how to look after the sheep. We can get help from the neighbors. We'll be fine…Emmie, please, please, don't sell our farm."

I bowed my head and closed my eyes to blot out Sarah's desolation.

When I looked up at her, I shook my head. "No, Sarah, it's not possible. We have to be realistic. We need to move." Before she could punctuate the air with more pleas, I put my hand up, palm out. "Stop, no more. We must move. When you are rational, we'll talk about what's possible."

"No. I say no. You may think you're moving, but I will never, ever leave this farm." The outer door cracked against its frame as she slammed it shut. She was gone.

I found her later in the corner of the barn, sobbing. When she looked up to me, I knew she wanted my comfort. I realized I had nothing to give her. I walked out of the barn and left her to her weeping. I was determined we'd not be poor or have to move to Dublin's tenements. So afraid was I of such a possibility, I enacted the plan that would eventually tear us apart.

I began a letter to Lady McCormack the next day.

*Dear Lady McCormack,*

*I am writing to you today to ask if there might be a position within your household. I am a teacher at the local school, however, Sarah and I will be moving soon from the farm. We will need to find other accommodation, as my teaching role and our work on the farm are part of an agreement. We run the farm, and I teach the farmers' children.*

*I understand you may be in need of a governess for your young boy, Roan. Might it be possible for me to assume that role?*

*Please do not think me presumptuous in my request.*

*Humbly yours, Emily McGrath*

◆

"Miss McGrath? Emily McGrath?"

I turned from the blackboard where I was printing the sums for the children who were due to arrive at 8:30, when I'd go out to ring the school bell. I thought, before I looked around, that the woman speaking to me might be the mother of one of the boys. But when I turned, I knew she was no mother of a farm boy.

A young woman in a black maid's dress stood at the door. I dropped my piece of chalk into the box on my desk and walked toward her, my hand outstretched. Whatever might a lady's maid from the manor want here in my schoolroom?

Sarah and I grew up knowing all the staff at the McCormack house, known always to us as the "Big House." Christmas parties, birthday celebrations, we'd always been invited. Lord and Lady McCormack were classic gentility in the old British sense. Even after the agitation of the Land War, they'd remained kind and good people to those who now owned parts of their land. Might this be an answer to my letter?

"Miss Rourke, please come in, what a pleasure to see you. How is the Lady? There's nothing wrong, is there?"

"No, not at all. There's no problem. I'm here only to deliver a note from Lady McCormack. I believe it is in response to your letter from last week."

A note from Lady McCormack? Curiosity pushed apprehension aside. The maid stood at the door.

"Come in, Miss Rourke, do come in."

"No, Miss McGrath, I'll not trouble you further. I'm just here to deliver your letter and return to the house."

"Well, I thank you, and please convey my good wishes to Lady McCormack."

With a nod, she turned and walked out the door and down the grassy path to the big house over the hill.

When I opened the letter, the fears I'd begun to heap upon myself about losing our home and possibly becoming poverty-stricken were quashed. Sarah and I were soon to be "well-set," as Ma would say.

I was to be the new governess at McCormack House, and Sarah had been invited to come along as part of the household staff.

Lady McCormack's offer gave my sister and me a future.

# Chapter Seven

### 1898 ◆ Near Dublin ◆ Sarah McGrath

THE ROOM BECOMES OBJECTS, A STOVE HOT WITH FIRE, a boiling pot of water, a chair where Emmie sits rigid, ready to bolt.

All I know is pain. The contraction eases and I drift out and beyond, away from the room, far from Jeanie the midwife, down into a valley of memories.

*The cottage by the Big House is small—a kitchen, two chairs by the fireplace and a room with one bed for Emmie. My twelve-year-old self climbs the ladder to the loft, where a straw mattress covers a single bed. I'm afraid. Nothing is familiar. The edges of my fingers blur into the wooden slats of the ladder. I lose myself in the dim light between memory and pain.*

The pain holds me like a leather vise. The fire in the stove flares up, sending heat into the flat where Emmie and I live. Nothing around me is familiar, nothing gives comfort. Someone wipes my brow.

"Emmie? Help me, please?"

I can't do this. My body lets go. Is this how it feels to die? The vise releases and images drift back into view. Memory shifts. A door opens onto a young girl sitting by the fire weeping. I hear her. I see her.

She's me.

"*This is not home*" I cry. "*I want to go home. I want to go back to the farm.*"

The pain releases and I sink into darkness.

*For the first two years after we moved to the cottage by the Big House, I missed the farm, the house where was I born, the chairs where Da sat me on his knee. I missed the loft where Emmie and I slept. I missed my own pillow. I missed Da and Ma. Those first years after they were gone, I cried each night into a pillow that didn't hold the familiar hollow of my head. A pillow in a room in a cottage that was not yet home.*

◆

THE PAIN CRASHES IN AND PUSHES BACK ON MY DREAMS. I want to hold the images of me, of Emmie, of the farm, but the spasm refuses to let me be.

I hear another howl.

"Sarah, Sarah." Someone calls me and I reach for her hand. I wonder, has Ma come to rescue me?

"Sarah, I'm here. It's Emmie."

Another moment or another hour, I'm not sure. Voices hover like shadows, anxious with fear.

"Emily, ma'am. Will you please let me run for a doctor? I'm not sure…" Jeanie clutches my hand.

"No! No doctor. We must do this ourselves. No one must know."

Her voice becomes muffled. The flannel on my back feels as warm as the ground under the gorse bushes.

*Roan and I had created moments to be together. At night we crept out beyond the back door across the fields to the river.*

*We discovered a lovely place under the yellow gorse bushes one summer when he was home from school. During those days, when he rode the estate, checking on the production from the landed tenants, ensuring the farmers had fine-working equipment and the animals were healthy, he* often took me with him, because I had a farmer's daughter's knowledge of farming. He treated me like a partner, asking me what I thought about the state of the fields, the look of the animals, the condition of the pig sheds. Last summer, his final year at school, we'd become comfortable with each other—he at ease with our conversations about the estate he would inherit one day, me slipping into an embroidered view of my importance and of this handsome man who noticed me.

The shady spot under the gorse bushes was the place we'd stop, tether our horses, and sit talking about what we'd just seen on the farms.

He used beautiful words that he spoke with a lovely lilt.

"Sarah, you will be a brilliant wife someday, a woman of sensitivity and fine mind." I blushed that afternoon because I knew I wanted to be his brilliant wife and I'd set out to make it happen. I felt the possibilities rising.

I walked along the laneway one day early that summer, feeling the familiar anticipation of spending time with Roan who was newly home from boarding school, this time to stay.

He appeared from behind the trees like an apparition.

"Sarah." I was stunned when I saw him that day. He'd grown taller than I remembered, his eyes danced with familiar teasing, but instead of sweeping me up and twirling me around as he'd often done when I was younger, he stopped.

"By Jesus, you've grown into a woman, and a beautiful one at that. Sarah, would you care to walk with me while I go over to the McRoy's farm? You can see how well they are caring for your family's old home."

"Oh Roan, how I'd like to, but I have work to attend to before supper." My hands were trembling, my legs like jelly.

"Ah, yes, your duties. Then I wonder might you consider an evening stroll by the river? The gorse bushes are particularly lovely at this time of year in the moonlight."

◆

ROAN DRIFTS AND MOVES ABOVE ME. HE'S MURMURING and groaning. He reaches down and lifts my hips, moving them in an unfamiliar yet wondrous cadence.

◆

I FEEL AS THOUGH MY BODY IS BEING TORN OPEN. SOMEone is shouting, "Push, Sarah, push." Emmie is weeping. A baby is crying out.

◆

IN 1891, EMMIE AND I LEFT THE FARM TO TRAVEL TO THE Big House, there to live in a small, brick cottage just beyond the garden.

Lord and Lady McCormack, Master Brandon, Miss Rebecca, and Master Roan welcomed Emily, their new governess, and me, her thirteen-year-old sister, into their family.

Five years from that day I lay in my bed in our cottage. Emmie hadn't come out of her room yet, and I knew she needed to dress and have breakfast with the children. I needed to go set the logs for a fire in Lady McCormack's bedroom.

Lord McCormack had left for Dublin early in the morning and wouldn't be back until Friday. I found him to be a kind man and a good Catholic. It was unusual in these parts of Ireland, a Catholic man owning a large estate; most landowners in the west were absentee English lords, but Emmie and I welcomed the McCormacks' kindnesses and their religion. We were allowed to attend Mass with the family each Sunday, and I welcomed those times for it meant I might have an opportunity to be near Roan McCormack, Lord and Lady McCormack's eldest son.

◆

When Emmie and I arrived at the estate I was thirteen and Roan was fifteen, a young man who greeted us with unexpected warmth. He'd talk with Emmie in an adult way that endeared him to her. He shared his experiences with her when he came home from boarding school. For me, he was a wondrous reminder of Da—tall, with handsome, black eyes that suggested excitement and a smile that settled somewhere in my soul. Truth be told, I was smitten. He became like a god to me, and I knew something stirred in him too.

But I was too young to understand what could happen. As years unfolded, Roan treated me as though I might be someone precious to him. He'd go off to school and I'd wait, counting the days till his return.

*Maybe this is how it feels to be loved,* I'd wonder.

We'd find times at the end of a day to go off together—he riding his favorite horse, me sitting sidesaddle in front of him. I discovered later that Emmie often watched us go.

I had never felt such gentleness from any person. Over time, summers played out and we'd find moments, the two of us, under the huge oak tree by the stream, to talk about how our lives might be.

But one afternoon as the sun dropped past the hill, all was quiet. We lay beside one another, staring up through the leaves. Roan turned to me, his elbow resting by my shoulder, his head propped on his hand.

"Sarah" he whispered. Something in his voice stirred inside my body, like a feather drawn across my chest.

"Roan, I feel very strange."

"Don't worry, dear Sarah. I do too. I want to touch you."

Without understanding what he meant, I turned to him.

"I want you to touch me, Roan."

That evening everything changed.

I could feel his hands, soft, up into the folds of my skirts. I tore my knickers from under my skirt and let him discover my womanhood. I'd not known such fever nor such craving.

I was eighteen. We'd known each other for those years, maybe loved each other. I wasn't sure. But whatever I was feeling for him, I wanted it to go on forever.

Other nights we'd steal out to the oak tree, and on those nights I'd tiptoe back into our cottage, where I'd lay under the quilt and remember the warmth of Roan's hands, his gentleness. He'd talk to me as he caressed me, about how we'd be partners someday. Some nights I couldn't hear his voice—only skin and feelings penetrated me, as though I were suspended beyond in some other place. Many nights I'd stuff my fist into my mouth to keep from calling out.

There were mornings Emmie glanced at me, without comment.

One morning, as we walked to the house from our cottage, she stopped me and grabbed my arm with a fierceness that left a bruise. "Be careful, Sarah. You are growing into a woman and men have designs. Sometimes unsound ones."

I didn't know how unsound.

◆

It was Emmie who first noticed my thickening waistline. "Sarah, have you been eating too many of Mrs. Ryan's gooseberry tarts?" When she asked the question, I looked away.

Emmie says I destroyed her life.

When I discovered I was pregnant, I did only what I knew to do. I told Emmie.

"What do I do? You need to help me, Emmie."

"You foolish, foolish girl," she'd said when I told her what I suspected. "I watched you leave at nights, and I knew you were taken in by him. He got what he wanted." She spat the words at me.

I'd heard about young girls who were whisked away because they'd disgraced the family. But surely that couldn't happen to me, because a lord's son was the father of my baby, and he was a good man. He'd do the right thing.

"It'll all be fine, Emmie. I know it will. Roan and I will be married. We'll just have to be sure we do it before I show any more."

I couldn't believe her anger as she grabbed my arm and pushed me onto a chair.

"Don't you see? Don't you realize? You're nothing more than a whore to him. You mean nothing. You are a lower-class convenience."

The familiar sting of Emmie's words penetrated like the thorns they were meant to be.

◆

When we left the Big House, we said nothing about the baby.

"But Emily, why would you leave us? The children love you. Sarah gets on so well with everyone. You can only gain stature in your life by staying on here." Lady McCormack was stunned the day Emily and I announced we were leaving and moving to Dublin.

"No, Lady McCormack. We must go. You have been gracious to both Sarah and me all these years. However, it is important that we travel to Dublin. My mother's sister is very ill, and I need to go care for her. Sarah needs to go to school there. She'll learn to become a teacher. Like me."

I was astounded at how easily the lies slipped from Emily's lips. Even as angry as she was, Emily could not bring herself to give the reason for leaving. Her humiliation would not allow her to speak the truth.

To accuse Master Roan of impregnating me, her sister, was unimaginable.

We left with few good-byes. Rebecca and Brandon stood beside their mother and father at the front door of the Big House as Emily and I climbed into the carriage that was to take us to the train and on to Dublin. Roan stood apart, his hands folded like any gentleman might, his eyes avoiding mine.

I knew then. I was nothing to him.

Life turned and turned like the wheels on the carriage, taking us away from the good life, to a city and an existence far from the countryside fields, the gardens, and everything we loved.

◆

FROM THE MOMENT MY WEE MARTHA SUCKLED, HER head tucked into my arm, I knew a love I never had experienced. Nothing prepared me for this little girl.

No one would take her from me.

◆

EVERYTHING WAS CROWDED. OUR ROOM IN THE FLAT ON Henrietta Street was small and carried the smell of the city.

The streets were filled with people, trams, and horses. Most days I felt I couldn't breathe.

Emmie, too, was crowding me out. She left in the morning to go to a school somewhere down the way, where she had accepted a position to teach primary-age children. Most days she was gone from early in the morning till late afternoon, but then when she arrived back at our flat she spoke little, only paying attention to baby Martha in her cradle.

We'd continued the lie. I might have been taken to some home for wayward girls, Martha grabbed from my arms, if there were no husband.

Our story seemed to satisfy the landlord when we found a room in a building that once had been grand and now was crumbling. A room with two beds, an old range for cooking, and a basin for our daily personal cleaning. Two chairs sat by a window. A dilapidated fireplace kept us warm. We did our best to cheer the place. A red, yellow, and green hooked rug lay on the wooden floor. My flowered quilt that Mrs. McCormick had given us when we left the cottage covered the bed. However, we felt more like paupers than we ever had in our lives, and I knew Emmie blamed me.

Until one day, a month after Martha was born, I met Emmie at the door, Martha's little body tucked into my arms.

Emmie brushed past me, her face a mask, her eyes dark points of light. She had been cold and distant since we'd arrived in Dublin.

I grabbed at her arm as she tried to pass me.

"Emmie, how long are you going to be angry with me? How long are you going to punish us?" I held Martha closer and wrapped a wool blanket around her head as though to protect her from Emily's resentment.

The heels of her high-top shoes punctuated her antagonism toward me.

"Emily! Stop!"

A sickening gall rose into my throat.

Emily's outrage had consumed us since we moved to Dublin. Martha was the only reason, Emily said, that she was staying at all.

She turned toward me and swept her arms as though pushing me away.

"Sarah, your loathsome desires have destroyed us. We live in a disgusting flat because no respectable landlord will have us—you, an unwed mother, and her bastard child."

Her words flew across the room like poison arrows.

"I work every day in a school where the children have no respect for me or for learning. Our savings account is dwindling. We live wrapped in a lie. I stay for Martha's sake, but soon, Sarah, soon I'm going, and you'll have to decide what you need to do."

"Emmie? What do you mean? Where will you go? Where will we go?"

I held Martha with such a force she began to whimper.

That was the evening I discovered that Emily, my sister who had sworn to Ma and Da that she would care for me and protect me, that was the evening I realized how angry she was and how much she hated me.

◆

LATER THAT EVENING, AFTER I ROCKED WEE MARTHA to sleep and sang her Da's song, I crept out to the room where Emmie and I sat each night, she sewing or reading the work she'd given her students that day while I prepared the lessons I would teach to children at the school just down the street. I'd take Martha there in her wicker basket. Good baby that she was, she'd sleep as I worked with the young children.

Emily had spoken to the headmistress about me carrying out teacher-training at the school where she worked. How could she offer such kindness to me and still be so resentful? How could I redeem myself?

Emmie sat, her head down, the needle between her fingers moving swiftly as she finished a smocked dress for Martha. She neither looked up nor acknowledged me. My stomach churned with the fear of everything happening too fast. When I reached over to place my hand on Emmie's arm, she froze, needle in midstroke.

"Emmie, please. Talk to me."

Her silence replied.

"I am sorry, Emmie. You're right. I'm to blame for everything that's happened, but please, you and I, we can sort out what to do."

Dress, thread, and needle left Emmie's hands and flew past my head. She lifted herself from her chair and stared down at me, her face flushed, her mouth tight.

"Sort out? What to do? You have disgraced yourself and shattered my life. No, there will be no sorting out."

She stood, picked up her sewing, and dropped it in my lap.

"You'll have to finish this," she said, and left.

◆

THE NEXT MORNING, I SAT AT THE TABLE WITH MARTHA curled in my arms. Emmie sat apart from us in the middle of the room, a battered suitcase at her feet.

Her hair was pulled back into a severe twist. The frilled collar of her best white blouse grazed her chin, and her brown wool skirt fell around her. One black boot dangled in her hand.

"Sarah." Her voice this morning was steadier, firmer, and chilling. "I've answered an ad in the Irish Times. A widower is looking for a governess for his daughter, and I applied and was accepted."

"Where?"

Martha lay dozing—her eyes flew open when I jerked forward.

"Canada. A town called Kingston."

"But, Emmie. Canada is thousands of miles from here. I'll never see you again."

"You'll be fine. You have Martha, and I'll leave you money to live on, and you'll keep up your teaching, or find domestic work."

Her plan to leave was clear. I was stunned when I realized how complete were the details of what she intended to do. Not only was she leaving Dublin, Martha, and me, she was leaving Ireland.

Today she'd leave by train for Liverpool, and in two days she'd sail to Canada. I'd always known that Emily McGrath was sufficient unto herself, something she'd taught me, but I had never imagined she might turn away from her family.

This woman sounded like a stranger to me, someone I'd never known.

"Sarah, remember. When people ask, Martha's father was a fisherman lost at sea."

"Emmie…" I wanted to tell her again and again how sorry I was.

"No, Sarah, there is nothing else to say."

As she stood, her face crumpled and her eyes dimmed, and, for a moment, I thought she wouldn't leave. But she straightened her shoulders, then reached down and picked up her luggage, which held all she owned.

When I stood, my legs were weak, my heart a stone. I gathered Martha into my arms and held her as though life could flow between us. Her head rested on my shoulder as she turned—a small smile for her Auntie Emily whom she'd never see again.

"I have to go, Sarah. There is a hackney carriage waiting to take me to Kingsbridge Station."

"When will you sail?" My voice quavered.

"In two days." Her back to me, her hand on the doorknob. "I've left my address in Canada on the mantelpiece."

"Emmie?" This is not real, I thought. "Can I write to you?"

Her hand still on the doorknob, she turned back to me. "I will write to you, Sarah."

We stood, two women, locked in the shackles of pride and disappointment. Only the weight of Martha against my body confirmed that I was living this moment.

I reached one arm toward her, my sister.

The door closed.

She was gone.

# Chapter Eight

### October 1913 ♦ 53 King Street
### Kingston, Ontario ♦ Martha

ANNA AND I SAT ON THE BACK-PORCH SWING.

The chill October air moved through me like the bleakness I felt as I held a letter my mother had written and never mailed. It was her plea for forgiveness, and she'd tucked it away in her diary.

*Emily, I am so sorry, I've ruined everything. Please, someday, might you find a place in you that forgives me?*

I'd wept nights on end since reading Ma's diary and her last letter to her sister. Ma had died feeling anguish, guilt, and the pain of wrongdoing.

I was left with her heartache and the knowledge all I'd been told was a lie.

In the midst of my thoughts, I heard Anna plead with me, "Martha, you're going to need time. Please don't decide to go because of everything that's happened in the last month. Don't talk about leaving. Don't do what my stepmother did. Don't be a coward like her."

My shoulders fell forward and my chest filled with a feeling that I might never breathe again.

"Anna, everything's a lie. Everyone has lied to me, everyone."

"Martha, I haven't lied nor has my dad. Don't punish us."

"But my life is a lie! My father? Not some fisherman lost at sea! My father, some rich lord's son who cared nothing for Ma and didn't even want to know I existed."

I dug my fists into my eyes, trying to rip away all the false images.

"We'll figure it out. We will. I promise. Maybe you and I will just escape together." Anna leaned into me and wrapped her arm around my shoulder. "Maybe the world will offer each of us a way out."

For me, I needed to take my life into my own hands. That night, with Anna's help, I began a letter to the Canadian government.

### TO THE OFFICE OF FARM SERVICES

*Dear Sirs:*

*My name is Martha McGrath. I came here from Ireland in 1913 to live in the household of my aunt and uncle. Emily and Owen Johnson.*

*I am writing to you today wishing to offer my services on one of the farms where there may be children I traveled with when I sailed on the SS Laurentic. These were orphan children being sent to Canada for a better life.*

*I came to know these children both in Mrs. McCarthy's Home in Dublin and on board the ship. Miss Ashcroft, who was our guardian from the Society, could tell you I am a reliable and trustworthy person.*

*Please sirs, I feel I might be helpful. I am a good worker.*

*Please advise how I might gain employment on a farm in Frontenac County.*

*My address here is 53 King Street, Kingston, Ontario, in care of Dr. Owen Johnson.*

*Yours truly,*
*Martha McGrath*

# Part Three

## The War ♦ 1914–1918

# Chapter Nine

> **THE GLOBE, TORONTO, FRIDAY, AUGUST 7, 1914**
>
> *Canada Prepares For War*
>
> ACTUAL MOBILIZATION IS NOT BEING RUSHED
> Enlistment is to Proceed, Then Selection

### August 7, 1914
### Kingston, Ontario ◆ Professor Owen Johnson

NEWSPAPERS COVERED THE TOP OF MY USUALLY CLEAR desk. My orderly world had tumbled into uncertainty. The headlines called out war. I held my forehead in my hands as I leaned over the desk, my elbows resting on the newspaper, my eyes following the words, which one by one created a chill across my skin.

> Ottawa, Aug. 6—A communication handed out by the Prime Minister at the conclusion of tonight's Council meeting states that a message has been received from the Imperial Government stating that Canada's offer of an expeditionary force for service abroad, if required, had been accepted. It was further announced that this force will be organized at once by voluntary enlistment.
>
> The important new feature of this announce-

ment is that the Imperial Government has now intimated that the Canadian army division will be expected to leave Canada for service abroad, either in the United Kingdom or Belgium as soon as the word comes that they are required.

All the worry about Emily, her rancorous nature, her harshness toward Martha, seemed secondary. Caught in the knowledge that the war was about to come home to roost among my family, I moved the newspapers aside and reached for a pen. I sat for a moment or two. Anna's late-night revelation sat like a stone in my chest—when I looked out to the lawns and buildings beyond my window, I could picture only Anna's face, her eyes shining with a dark determination.

Last night she'd come into my study after everyone else had gone to bed. I was preparing to have a cigar and linger by the waning fire. As she crept into the room, the glow from my lamp caught the porcelain of her skin, the shining length of her hair swept back and up under her nurse's cap. Her starched apron rustled like the calming sound of a breeze through a maple tree. My girl, my Anna.

"Papa." She hadn't called me "Papa" for fifteen years, not since Emily arrived and told her "Papa" was too babyish for a big girl. "I saw young boys heading for the train station today."

"It'll be a while, I think, before any Canadians are called up." My weak attempt at allaying her fears and mine.

"I ran after them, Papa. They're going to somewhere in Quebec. They've started to mobilize."

I couldn't find words to tell her not to worry. Something horrendous was on the horizon. Even though people were cheering and marching in the streets, I felt a sick dread.

Anna sat opposite me in my winged chair where she used to sit on my knee as a young girl, those nights when we told stories to each other. Those nights when we escaped from Emily's worrying.

Anna was agitated. When she leaned forward to take my hand, her mouth tightened.

"Dad, I'm going to France. I'm going to volunteer with the Canadian nurses. They are going to need me."

I almost said, "No! I won't allow it."

But instead I grasped her hand, as though she'd disappear if I let go.

Now I sat wondering how I might dissuade her, keep her safe from harm, and with my gaze fixed upon the image of Anna there in the winged chair, I began to write my plea to her.

*Dear Anna, my girl,*

*I'm here in my office, newspapers spread before me, all announcing everything you, Martha, and I have talked about and feared over the month.*

*So much has happened throughout the past year, I hardly know where to begin, thus I'll begin with how fearful I am of losing you, and Martha. She, like you, seems caught up in a growing tumult to join the war effort.*

*Be assured that Emily holds the same fears, but her abhorrence of revealing any sort of kinship keeps her silent. I can't attend to her right now.*

*When you told me last night of your hope to contribute to the war effort, I felt deep pride thinking only that you were imagining yourself helping out more at the hospital, working with the Red Cross. But your revelation terrifies me. Please, might we talk more about all this?*

*Your loving father*

I folded the letter and decided to give it to her later, but my heart ached. I felt a love for Anna that filled my throat, along with fear for her, and for all of us.

As I walked outside down the steps from my office building, I stopped and watched a company of young Queen's students drilling. I knew there already were young men who'd been training during the years preceding the war, but I was startled to see them there on campus, a labyrinth of wool khaki, rifles over their shoulders.

Eyes clear, heads held high, feet landing on the pavement with a slam of leather soles, they seemed elated. I mustered weak envy for their youthful daring, mingled with a chilling portent for Anna. Brave, guileless Anna.

◆

HOME, KING STREET, WELCOMED ME.

"You're home! I'm so glad!" Anna flung the door open, lifting an arm to beckon me inside. "I talked with a head nurse at the hospital today."

Before I could give Anna the letter, she called us all to come for tea—even Emily.

"Come in here, come sit, please. I need you to listen."

I decided at that moment I'd tear up the letter I'd written. Anna was not going to be persuaded to stay out of this war.

When we were all gathered, I turned to her.

"Anna? You wanted to tell us something?"

The silence in the room felt coiled, ready for someone to strike words into the air. I began to wish I'd decided to stay longer at the university that afternoon. Before I could stir myself to answer, Martha broke the silence.

"Anna?"

"Yes," I said. "Let's listen to Anna."

She leaned into the space that Martha, Emily, and I created for her. She was the cornerstone of her story—we were her columns. Ordinary life stopped in that moment. Anna's eyes were bluer than I'd remembered. They were her mother's eyes.

"You know this war is going to need nurses, Dad."

She'd said all this the night before, but now she was telling the whole family. There would be no pause, no turning back. Her surety shone in the color on her cheeks. I folded my arms across my chest.

"At the hospital today, Matron was telling us how she wanted to go as soon as she is called."

"But do you think they'll be calling up nurses?" Martha asked. "Women?"

"Yes. And I mean to go."

There it was. For Anna, the conversation was over.

I sat in my chair and absorbed all my daughter's distinctions: her lips set tight like the period finishing a sentence. She was that same young girl who'd been determined to go into nursing school.

She reached her hand over to me. I unfolded my arms, with no need to protect myself from the truth, and leaned to her.

"Dad. I have to do this. Do you understand?"

"I do, Anna, knowing you all these twenty-two years, I understand."

I wanted to say *No. I'm your father. I won't let this happen.* Yet all I could do was sit and feel the agony of losing my daughter to war and its ghastly possibilities.

She stood from her chair and threw her arms around my neck. She was almost giddy.

"I'll go today and tell Matron. I expect as soon as those young men go to fight, they'll need nurses to tend the wounded."

I grasped her outstretched hand. "Anna—"

"I'll go get the tea," Emily said. She left the room and closed the door with a click, her own acknowledgment of Anna's desire. I wondered if she remembered that four-year-old Anna who'd greeted her all those years ago here in this room. I wondered if her heart ached like mine.

"Come here, Anna. You too, Martha."

I enfolded the girls in my arms, Anna's head tucked under my chin, Martha's face buried into my woolen vest.

I wondered how many other families—mothers, fathers, daughters, sons, nephews, nieces—how many others were holding on to one another, not wanting to let go.

# Chapter Ten

**Unit: C.A.M.C. ATTESTATION PAPER**

CANADIAN OVERSEAS EXPEDITIONARY FORCE

What is your name? Anna Jeanne Johnson

In what town, township, country were you born? Kingston, Ontario, Canada

What is the name of your next-of-kin? Professor Owen Johnson

What is the address of your next-of-kin? Kingston, Ontario, Canada

What is the date of your birth? January 1, 1893

What is your trade or calling? Professional nurse

### May 1915 ♦ Ottawa, Ontario ♦ Anna

*Dear Martha:*

*Everything is a whirl. Since I arrived here and got off the train in Ottawa, I feel as though I'm a character in a storybook. Remember when you and I used to talk about how we felt out of place sometimes, as though home was not where we thought it might be?*

*I wonder, was this your experience when you set off from Ireland? Was there a feeling of home when you arrived? I'm feeling odd. As I set off for Europe, I*

have a sense I'm moving toward somewhere, a place where I belong. How could that be? Who knows what lies beyond? Just as you didn't know, Martha.

Have I ever told you how brave you are?

Thank you for watching over Dad. He was so stalwart when I left on the train the other day, but I'd never seen him tear up before, not since Mama died.

What can I tell you about how I feel? Here I am in my navy blue uniform and my navy cape. Martha! It's lined with scarlet—can you believe how elegant I look? I wonder, though, if I might be playing at being a military nurse. Did you know? We all have the rank of lieutenant!

I don't know what lies ahead, and if you asked me whether I'm frightened, I'd have to say yes. I have no idea what awaits us. Or what awaits these young men who are traveling to Halifax with us. Who will return?

I must sign off for now. I'm not sure how soon I'll be able to get another letter to you. We will arrive in Halifax tomorrow and board our ship after a brief training.

Take care of yourself, dear Martha. Hold firm when Emily tries to weaken your resolve. You are your mother's daughter.

Ever your loving friend and cousin,
Anna

◆

## 53 King Street ◆ Martha

I SAT IN THE SWING UNDER THE LILAC BUSHES AND INHALED. Anna's letter lay in my lap. Her handwriting was perfect.

All at once, I felt both the closeness of her presence and the sharp pang of her absence. Anna might already be sailing across the Atlantic.

Uncle Owen had been keeping up with the war news, and all of it was frightening. We'd heard about horrific strange clouds of yellow-green smoke, a kind of chlorine gas. What if Anna breathed that stuff? How unfair it was that I sat here inhaling the sweetness of lilacs while Anna could be choking on poison gas.

"Martha," Aunt Emily called from the back porch. She'd been out of sorts all day. When I arrived home that morning from my volunteer night shift at the hospital, I had found her on the chesterfield by the fire in the kitchen, a damp cloth across her eyes. I felt queasy with the thought of her ill temper.

"Martha! Did you hear me? I need you out here."

Life in the Johnson household was determined often by Emily's moods. Uncle Owen dealt with the ebb and flow of her spirits by disappearing into his office at home, or more frequently, he'd walk over to the university. On one or two occasions, he had even slept there. This was a house grieving Anna's departure, but more than that, it was a house filled with unresolved hostilities. Before Anna had left for England, we'd talked about how I needed to handle Emily. It was a hard road, but I'd decided to hold my memories of Ma and not allow Emily's bitterness to poison them. Ma's voice whispered, "You take the noble path, Martha."

I hadn't found the inner grit to approach Emily and challenge her story about my ma; how Emily had left her, and me. I was sick with what she'd done to us and her lies about who my father was. Some days I couldn't be in the same room with Emily. I was growing impatient. I needed to hold fast.

When Anna left, I wanted to be brave, to show everyone how Anna's decision to become a Canadian Nursing Sister made me proud of her. It was my one way of being with Uncle Owen in his sadness.

I took one last breath of the lilacs' scent and lifted myself from the swing.

"Martha!"

"Coming, Aunt Emily. I'm coming." I folded Anna's letter and placed it in the pocket of my volunteer nurse's apron. Emily stood on the back steps, one hand across her forehead. She held a paper. Horrified, I realized it was a reply to the letter I'd written to the Ontario Farm Service. It must have arrived in the mail, and Aunt Emily had found it.

She waved it toward me as I climbed the steps.

"What is this?" Her eyes were red and bloodshot. "Why are you writing to these people?"

When I tried to brush past her, she grasped my arm. "Martha. Answer me. Please." Weakness overtook me for an instant like a dispassionate collection of hopelessness. I felt as though she'd drawn the wind from my breath.

"Where did you find that letter? I'd like to have it back."

"Why, Martha, why are you asking about going to live on a farm? What's going on? Owen doesn't need any more upsets."

"I asked you where you found that letter, Emily." I remained standing while she pulled out a chair and sat.

She placed a hand to her forehead. Her elbow rested on the table, and with her other hand she grabbed the tablecloth and gathered it toward her. I thought that this might be her way of crying out her old frustrations, her disappointments, and maybe her sense of guilt. But she just couldn't form the words. A vase of sunflowers tottered.

Before I could get to them they fell onto the table where water rivulets dripped across the cloth.

"Damn!"

I'd never heard Emily swear. Silence was her form of anger.

I watched, captivated, frozen as she grasped the tablecloth. Vase and flowers tipped and crashed onto the linoleum floor, a cacophony of broken glass. Emily sat mesmerized by the water pooling on the floor, the pieces of glass scattered around her feet.

Had she entered some strange state?

"Emily? Are you all right?" I started over to pick up shards of glass.

"No! Leave it! I want to know now what this is about. What's this Ontario Farm Service thing—I don't understand?" She grasped the paper as though to crush it. She began to spit out the words I'd written:

"*Please advise how I might gain employment on a farm here in Frontenac County.* What is that about? A farm? And where did you learn to use such haughty language—*please advise?*"

I felt nauseous to the point that I thought I might vomit. When I grasped the edge of the sink, my knuckles turned white.

"Emily, I'm going to clean up this mess. You go over there to the chair by the fire, sit, and rest yourself. I'll talk to you when you calm down."

As though she hadn't heard me, Emily folded her arms across her chest.

"I thought you were fine," her words tight with impatience. "What is this about finding lost children? Who are these waifs? What in heaven's name is this about?"

"I am intent on going to a farm where young children might be working. Children who have come from Ireland. Children I might have known."

She snapped the paper at me. "What Irish fairy land are you living in? There are no farms where children are sent. There are no farms where you could work. You are living in some kind of dream world! You need to grow up, Martha."

"They're not waifs, Emily. Each was a child without a home, but they were not waifs." I bent down to clean the mess, my back to her, shutting out her distaste for me. "And I don't live in a fairy land. I need to do something. I need to be part of something, like Anna is. I know there are children out there. I've seen them. I've lived with them. Children who've been abandoned, one way or another."

As I began to sweep the pieces of glass into the dustbin, a muscle in my neck stiffened and sent pain into my shoulder. I swept and swept the pieces into the dustpan until nothing of the vase of flowers lay on the floor except bent stems and scattered fragments of yellow petals. I dropped to my knees and picked up small leaves from under the table.

My life here without Anna, and with Uncle Owen's self-inflicted absences, was like living in the heavy air just before a thunderstorm. I had to get away from Emily's explosions, her silences, her anger. By the time I stood up, petals in hand, stems drooping, I was ready.

"Emily. I can't stay here any longer."

◆

Speaking truth had usually been my best road. When Ma was so sick that night long ago, I knew I was right when I ran down the street looking for a priest. She knew and I knew she was dying.

I'd taken care of myself and my ma throughout my young life. I remember helping her while she baked and cooked in the kitchen in the home where she worked as a domestic. She taught me how to peel turnips for turnip pie, how to make a crust that tasted like candy, and she taught me how to look after myself. *"When I'm gone, my girl."*

Never in our years together, which weren't many, did I feel unloved. She told me every day she was alive how smart I was, how capable. Sometimes she reminded me that to look after myself, I'd need to find and trust good people. The letter I'd written to the government was my way of setting out on my own, once again.

◆

Later that night I lay in bed and listened to Uncle Owen's goodnight to Emily, his nightly pilgrimage down the stairs into his study. He hadn't come home for supper. When I left Emily fretting in the kitchen, I knew what I wanted to do.

I decided to talk to Uncle Owen. My feet barely touched the carpeted stairway as I stole down to his study. A tap at his door brought forth a gruff "Yes?"

"Uncle Owen," I whispered." May I come in?"

"Martha? Of course."

He'd pulled up two chairs facing the fireplace where the crackling spruce branches lit his face and warmed the room. I wondered why two chairs were already there, and I remembered: He and Anna often sat before the fire at night and talked about life, about her day at the hospital, about his latest mathematical conundrums, and lately about the war. He kept the chair in that space awaiting her return.

He stared into the fire as I approached and, with an outstretched hand, beckoned me to sit.

"So, you've decided," he said.

"What?"

"I talked to Emily. She told me about your letter." His eyes didn't wander from the fire. "And, you are sure?"

Whatever frustration I'd felt earlier when I left Emily in the kitchen, whatever determination had propelled me forward into a clear decision, landed there in Uncle Owen's study.

He turned to me and placed his hand on the arm of my chair. It was the moment I waited for, not knowing what to expect. What he said saddened me.

"It's going to be lonely and sad without you here, Martha, and you have to promise to come back when you can. With Anna gone, you've become my bright light. Maybe wherever you go, I'll come to visit you? But I think this is the best for you. For many reasons. I'm not blind to what's going on with Emily." I wasn't sure if I was relieved or hurt that he'd so willingly see me go. His next words gave me heart.

"You and Anna seem to be cut from the same cloth, even though you are not blood cousins. You talked this over with her before she left, did you?"

I nodded yes. "Then I'm also sure, knowing Anna, she'd have tried to discourage you or cheer you on. Which was it?" Uncle Owen, I believed, was giving me his blessing in company with Anna. "She helped me write the letter, Uncle Owen."

"Then you and I have our answer. What do you need from me?"

A sense of well-being flowed through my body. Uncle Owen, professor of mathematics, wanted to help. I wondered if this was how it felt to have a father.

No longer did I feel shameful about my leave-taking from this welcoming home. Like Anna, I was moving toward something worthy, something that said I mattered.

"All right. Tomorrow we plan. We'll respond to your letter. Tomorrow you, Martha, will join the cause, too. Well done, my girl! Well done."

The logs crackled and spit out sparks.

# Chapter Eleven

*I cannot quite remember...There were five*
*Dropt dead beside me in the trench—and three*
*Whispered their dying messages to me...*
—Wilfrid Wilson Gibson, "The Messages"

### Summer 1916 ◆ Kingston, Ontario ◆ Martha

THE DAY WAS MUGGY, AND IT WAS HOT BY THE LAKE.

I sat on a bench and watched a sailboat float across the water with a slow easy roll. My thoughts bobbed and hovered like that boat. I felt suspended in time, about to move into another passage of my life.

I'd walked over through the park to find a place to sit and read a letter I'd received from Anna. After I left Uncle Owen's office midway through the morning, I couldn't decide where to go, or what to do next. Everything I'd wondered about or hoped for was unfolding. During the past month I'd made a decision to move to a farm north of Kingston. I had to thank Owen for easing my way through a government maze of red tape.

◆

IN HIS WISDOM, HE'D CONTACTED A COLLEAGUE AT THE university.

Dr. McAllister, who often visited our house, had a sister married to a dairy farmer. Uncle Owen's plan, and soon mine, had been to go out to the farm to meet the Sloans and, in my uncle's words, "Start things rolling."

I'd be doing something good. I'd learn to farm. The arrangement felt rousing, as though I'd set in motion something that was carrying me into a new place in my life. Oh, how I wanted to tell Anna all that was happening. I wanted the nod of her head and the reassurance of her smile. *Am I doing the right thing, Anna?*

"Pardon me, did you say something?" A young man in a khaki uniform sat at the other end of the bench. I realized I'd spoken aloud.

"Oh, no, no. I'm sorry to disturb you. I've received some good news, and I guess I'm a little excited."

"Good news is rare these days, so go right ahead and be excited."

I smiled and turned to him and regretted it right away. His face was badly scarred across his cheek and into his hairline, his smile a bit crooked.

"Don't be alarmed, miss. I'm not as fierce as I look. They did a good job patching me." My first experience of what the war could do chilled me. He couldn't have been more than nineteen. I took a breath before I spoke to be sure my voice was steady.

"My cousin is over there."

"What unit is he in?"

"*She*, actually. She's a Canadian Nursing Sister."

"Your cousin is a Bluebird! Well, when you write to her, tell her she's a bloody angel. Excuse me, miss. I didn't mean disrespect."

"None taken. I'm very proud of her."

"Do you know where she is?" His right hand shook as he shifted closer.

"I couldn't tell you. I only know she's in France."

"She may be one of the nurses who saved my life."

"Do you remember the nurses?"

"Oh, miss, I do, I remember them well."

"Are you waiting for someone now?"

When he shook his head from side to side, I moved closer till we almost touched shoulders.

In that second his eyes clouded and I saw fear.

"I'm going back, miss. I'm due to go back there. I can't…I can't. They tell me I'm just scared—that I need to be brave." Tears came. He let them wash across the scars on his cheek.

Silence seemed best.

The moment was broken by someone running. "Frank! Frank! I've been everywhere looking." He swept his hand across his face.

A woman stumbled across the grass, one hand up on her straw hat, another clutching her skirt. I felt him stiffen beside me. He stood, walked to her, and reached out an arm.

"Mom. I'm fine. I just met this lovely lady."

He smiled over at me and I waved back to him. A wave good-bye. As they walked away arm in arm, I heard him say, "I wanted to sit by the lake for a while before I caught the train to Ottawa tonight. I'm feeling better, Mom. Really I am."

With a glance over his shoulder, he walked away from the lake toward the street, his arm linked to his mom's, his trembling hand stuffed into his pocket. He leaned into her and rested his head on her shoulder. For a moment. Then, I watched him lift his head, stand erect, and move away from her. His voice, loud and strong, rang across the air, like a sergeant calling men to arms.

"Time to go. Eh, Mom?"

Whatever had happened in those few moments left me saddened. Something said he wouldn't be back. Was this how my life was to be? A good-bye, a farewell, a nod, a glance, only the lake a constant?

The muggy afternoon had cooled. Drawing in a breath to cleanse my sadness, I thought about my next hope: the farm. Possibly there is where I'd find a place to settle. I leaned into a new breeze from across the lake and took in the clear, moist air. I sat back against the bench, let the coolness brush my cheek, and reached into my shirt pocket.

Anna's letter!

Crumpled as it was, I smoothed the paper across my lap and felt her presence.

JUNE 1916

Dear Martha:

*How do I even begin to describe the horror?*

*I'm so sorry to begin my letter to you this way, but to pretend otherwise is dishonest. I can't write about what I hear and see, or where I am right now, except to say somewhere in France. I try to write about the glorious moments when I write to Dad, but I know he reads between my lines. Does he ask what you and I talk about?*

*There were times when I felt strong and grateful that I'd been given this chance to be part of something worthy, however, each day brings me closer to wondering the point of it all.*

*Today the rain and wet weather persist. I can't remember feeling this damp. At nights when it cools down, I wonder if I'll ever be warm and dry again.*

*Some of the tents are old and they leak, but I'm in a hut, which is mostly dry. I light my little oil stove and pretend I'm back in the warm back kitchen on King Street.*

*We've had some good news. The powers that be are going to construct a wooden hut city to replace our tents, and there's a golf hotel nearby that is being turned into a hospital. I shouldn't get too excited, because it's possible that we could get settled and be asked to move to a new area. Some nurses are even taking leave outside France, somewhere like Lemnos in Greece.*

*I'm discovering that the military is very good about giving us leave, for which I am thankful, even short periods. A couple of weeks.*

*The nurses whom I've come to know can be transferred in the snap of a finger, but for some reason, I've been pretty stationary at this particular hospital. One of my friends, whom I met when we sailed to England, has received orders to move to a casualty clearing station. She'll be very close to the front, the nearest any nurse will get to the trenches and the artillery. It troubles me to see her go, but even more, I worry that we may never see each other again.*

*Oh, Martha, I just read through what I've written so far, and I feel as though I'm using you as my wailing wall, so I'll tell you more about our short time in England. The hospital was on an estate house far out in the countryside among beautiful gardens. If I'd had my wish I could've stayed there for the rest of the war. The awful part was and is experiencing what this war does to our young men. Many are here who suffer from something the doctors are calling shell shock. The hor-*

rible experiences these men have had in the trenches have left some mute, some trembling uncontrollably. There are those who scream out in their sleep.

Now here at this hospital where I am stationed, I listen to their stories. When the wounded come to us, I try to sit and talk with them when I have time (which is not often enough), especially the boys who have bandages over their eyes, or those who are being transferred to hospitals in England because they've lost limbs.

Sometimes after I return to my bed, exhausted as I am, I weep for them. And for myself. I wonder, will I ever return to the person I might have been?

But there are still times, Martha, when I get into my cot with a hot water bottle, tuck in for the night, and feel a sense of comfort. I want to tell you about those moments because I can often feel you—your spirit—watching over me. There are times I am lulled to sleep by the distant sound of guns, strange as that may seem.

Please let me know how you are. I know you are anxious to "do something" for the war effort. I can almost see you throwing your arms in the air and gritting your teeth with that funny grimace, and saying "there you are Anna, putting yourself in danger's way, and what am I doing?"

Be patient, dear one. There is much to do on the home front. There will be work for you.

Remember, Dad needs you close by, and Emily—in her way—will need you even more.

Must sign off now. Lights out soon.

With love,
Anna

Bluebirds. That was Frank's word. He called the nurses Bluebirds, and that moment when I sat beside him on that bench, he saw something from his world of war that held its own horror. "I can't go," he'd said. "They want to send me back. But I can't."

I read the first line of Anna's letter again: *How do I even begin to describe the horror?*

What could I possibly do here, safely on this side of the ocean, incapable of fathoming the depths of Anna's dread?

Ma had urged me to always be needed. "Never be satisfied with the way things are," she'd said, hardly able to lift her head at that time. In my life, I knew as long as I was needed, I'd be safe. I wondered about Uncle Owen telling me it's best for me to go. Did he say that for me so I might get his blessing to move on? Yet I was torn by Anna's words: *Remember, Dad needs you close by.* Still wondering, I was. Wondering where home might be.

I stood, folded Anna's letter into my shirt pocket, and began my walk back to King Street. Little did Anna know that I'd been accepted to work on a farm in the north of the county. I'd soon be heading into the next chapter of my life.

A new family and unexpected adventures awaited on a farm where a farmer and his wife would create an unplanned journey that would change the course of my life forever.

◆

I DISCOVERED THE SLOANS' KINDNESS AND WILLINGNESS to take me on as a hired hand when Uncle Owen and I made the trip out to their farm. Young women were leaving towns and cities to work on farms for the war effort. I was fortunate to have Uncle Owen to vouch for me and to be there early on as "farmerettes" became popular. The Sloans' farm reminded me of the countryside in Ireland. Barns and a milk house sat among a grove of trees that opened onto broad fields of grain. Beyond the trees and fields lay a sparkling lake.

Mr. and Mrs. Sloan had greeted me with smiles, yet I'd detected a wistful sadness in Mrs. Sloan's eyes. I wondered if they'd already been touched by the war. Many people in the community showed the same low spirit, as though they were waiting for bad news to arrive any day. My inborn need to cheer came rushing forth as I met them on the porch. I'd smiled my best smile and shook their hands with a warm grip, as Ma had taught me.

Mrs. Sloan had turned to Mr. Sloan. "If Charlie's going to be gone..." She paused. I felt it—her heartache sat between us in the palms of our hands.

"You're right, Rose." He looked over at me as he spoke. "Mrs. Sloan and I have been talking about needing help now that Charlie will be going to war.

"Does this mean I'm hired? You want me to live and work here with you?"

Mrs. Sloan put her hand on my shoulder. "My girl, we would be glad to have you with us for as long as you need to stay. Are we agreed, Earl? Owen?" Both men nodded yes.

To my surprise, Mrs. Sloan reached over and put her hand on my cheek. "I think this'll work very well for all of us."

"Thank you, Mr. Sloan, Mrs. Sloan. Thank you for your kindness. I feel as though I'm doing something that matters."

"Martha. We are happy to have you—we all need to give what we can. Mr. Sloan and I can use all the help you can give us. Life here and everywhere is changing fast. This war..." Mrs. Sloan had looked away for a moment, as though she wanted to say more, but her hand dropped to her side and she stood silent.

Uncle Owen said, "Martha, Mr. and Mrs. Sloan have a son who is preparing to go overseas." He stopped and looked over to her. "When does he leave the farm, Rose?"

"I'm afraid he's already gone to Barriefield, the Army training camp, Owen. We haven't heard anything since his last letter, which was a few weeks ago. I'm worried. Most of Charlie's friends have enlisted."

That moment, while we stood thinking about all those sons, a young boy, maybe nine years old, ran from the hen house stumbling and shouting.

"Papa Sloan, Ma Sloan! The eggs are cracking, there's chicks in the nests, come see, come see!" Melancholy lifted from all of us like the gust of a breeze.

I had met Ryan MacDougall. And life took on a new sheen.

Ryan was a young Irish immigrant sent from the same shores I'd left—he was a Home Child. One of the "lost ones." Rather like me.

The farm and the fact the Sloans needed me, wanted me there, roused in me a hope for this new chapter. Emily didn't want me around.

Why not go where I'd be needed and wanted?

That's the day I packed to go.

# Chapter Twelve

## PRELIMINARY NOTE ON THE TREATMENT OF GASSED CASES

Treatment by Regimental Medical Officers

1) All ranks should be warned of the need for seeing that the helmets of wounded men are kept properly in position until the danger from gas has passed away.

Library and Archives Canada

*Vol. 4, Agar Adamson War Letters, May 1916*

### 1916 ◆ No. 3 Canadian General Hospital ◆ Anna's Diary

*So many wounded. So few of us. I feel dizzy from experiencing so much of their pain. I feel like I've been wounded. I know I'm not supposed to write about the things I see or the screams that I hear and can't shut out when I go to my bed at night. Were it not for the young orderly working beside me, I'm not sure I could go from bed to bed.*

"Anna? Are you there?" A knock at my door. Who needs me now?

"Anna. It's Sally. Can I come in? I think I'm sick." Sally, my dearest friend since I'd arrived here at this hospital near Camiers. We were some distance from the battles, but close enough to hear and feel the bombardments. A convoy of wounded had arrived early this morning from a battle at the Somme. I'd been on duty for almost fifteen hours, tending to exhausted men lying in beds, row upon row. Limbs had been blown away by artillery fire that wasn't stopping. Blood flowed everywhere. Here in my room, my head throbbed as I remembered the smell of it. Another knock…weaker. "Anna?"

"Wait, Sally, I'm coming." I slipped from my bed and realized I was still wrapped in my uniform, my apron crumpled and bloody. When I opened the door I gasped at the sight of her. "How long have you been like this?" Chills racked her body. I grabbed a blanket from my shelf. "Here, lie down on my cot." Even as she lay down, she struggled to sit. "I shouldn't stay. I need to get home. Mama is expecting me." She was delirious.

"Stay still. I'll go for help." I flung open my door and looked back at her. She'd stopped shivering, but her pallor was dreadful, like those pale young men who'd succumbed to their wounds this morning. I knew she'd been working on the isolation unit, where there were patients with "greenish pus" caused by infected wounds. This was a dangerous sign. She could be infectious. Sally's blood might have become tainted while working with any of those soldiers. Possibly she'd contracted pneumonia.

I raced out and down the outer corridor to find a doctor, someone who might come, someone not still operating, not still amputating limbs or boring through skulls.

The young orderly who'd been working with me most of the day stumbled from one of the wards and tore off his bloody butcher apron. His face was clouded in gloom. When I saw him I called out, "James! I need you!" Breathless,

I slowed and waited. Only then did I realize he was weeping. "I can't stop now, Anna." He leaned into the wall of the corridor, his forehead against the cold roughness of the stone.

"James?"

"Anna. I can't." His body buckled. He landed and sat, back to the wall, his arms crossed around his knees. A glance up at me revealed the sadness of everything he'd experienced that afternoon and all the days before. He gazed at me with empty eyes. I sank down beside him. Gathering every part of my body, every breath I could rally, I placed my arms around his shoulders and held him close. He was nineteen years old and had been on the front lines doing ambulance duty for almost six months. There was no version of hell he hadn't experienced. When he stopped shaking, I untangled myself from his grasp and stood. There was no more time for sympathy. I dropped my hand to help him rise. "James, I need you to come help Sally. She's sick."

For the past while, each day had been crashing into the next, each crisis heaping onto the next crisis. And now my friend Sally was dying. How much deeper might this well of grief pour into my body? What could be left to feel?

But I needed to rally. Now.

I sat with her. I bathed her forehead and felt the wet cloth bring cool to her feverish brow. I made hot mustard plasters to cover her chest and try to ease her racking cough.

At some point I approached helplessness. The kind of impotence I felt for the young men who bled out, while I and doctors and other nurses accepted how powerless we were.

Young men with holes the size of fists in their chests continued to die in the early hours of the mornings. There'd been a glimmer of hope for Sam from Newfoundland that day. Sam, who'd laughed and teased me about my eastern Ontario twang, and I his Irish brogue. Sam, who'd hemorrhaged, coughed up black blood, and called out once for his love, Sarah. Sam, who'd turned his head and died. And that death rattle. How I hated that sound.

Now I was tending to my friend who was giving in, and I had nothing left for her. What possible use was I in the face of pain and despair, hers and all those young sons and brothers? I couldn't stop the guns. I couldn't bring back Sam. I couldn't help Sally. There was no reason to even try anymore. What help was I, one nurse?

I covered Sally with my quilt and placed my hand on her cheek. "I'll be back in a moment, love. You rest." As I left the room to go out into the hallway, I heard her raspy breath and what were her farewell words to me. "Thanks, Annie."

There in the hallway, I leaned against the wall and let the tears come. I cried for them all, the uselessness and for the futures taken.

One of the doctors who'd been working with me that day came along at that moment of despair.

"Anna? Is it Sally?"

"Yes. She's dying." My shoulders began to shake, my breath caught into sobs, head bowed as I, like Sally in my way, gave in. "None of it, none of it, none of it makes any sense. I don't see why we even keep trying. What help are we just to patch them and send them to die?"

He stood, quiet. When he spoke, he whispered, "It's part of this horrible war, Anna. We're here to calm them, repair if we can their broken bodies, and give some kind of peace. But it's not our job to make sense of it."

◆

Sally died the next day. Pneumonia took her. She'd come to this place where young men lived and died in holes in the ground, she'd come to bring healing and maybe hope. She'd sat with them, bathed them, fed them, listened to their stories. Now she lay in a makeshift morgue. For what?

I heard my father's voice as he said good-bye that day on the station platform. "Anna, somewhere in you is a woman who has a spine of steel. One who won't be daunted. You bring her home to me. Bring her home to Martha." Martha. Martha? How could I have forgotten her? That straight-backed, clear-eyed girl I'd met three years ago. That girl who'd left her country and what was left of the familiar in her life. Her journey was a solitary ocean voyage and she'd looked to me. I couldn't give up.

But oh, how I needed to go home.

In the midst of my despair a tracer crossed the sky, fell into sparks, and lit the muddy ground. A reminder? First there was work to do. Then I could think of home. I wrapped my cape around my shivering body and said good-bye to Sally. "Goodbye, my friend. Safe journeys."

A convoy of horse-drawn ambulances carrying wounded men rattled along the road beside the hospital. Nurses and doctors ran down the lane toward them. Sleep would have to wait.

# Chapter Thirteen

### Summer 1916 ◆ Northern Frontenac County

"Ryan McDougall, come in for supper!" Martha stood on the back step of the farmhouse, hands on her hips. Another holler, "Ryan!" and she set off running across the yard, her apron billowing, her boots sloshing in the muddy grounds. A near-collision occurred as Ryan wheeled around the corner of the milk house, sweater flying out like propulsion, hair standing in the wind.

"Coming, Martha. Coming!" Jake the border collie trotted at a dignified pace beside Ryan, ready to break into a wide-open gallop any moment. Martha slowed her pace as Ryan sought to avoid the misadventure of a crash.

"Where did you run to this afternoon?" She giggled as she grabbed the back of his sweater and hung on. He kept his legs and feet going like the wheels of a train screeching to a stop. Martha, bent at the waist, hands on her knees, dissolved into laughter. No one, no other person in her life, had the capacity to bring her to helpless hilarity.

Martha had delighted in meeting Ryan McDougall, a young, energetic Irish boy, when she'd arrived at the farm in late summer. He brought Ireland home to her. A Home Child, he was like all those children she'd sailed with on her voyage to Canada.

His story was brief, and he chose to tell it so.

"I was whisked away, ma'am," was the tale he'd told Martha. Sadness flickered briefly beneath his long, dark eyelashes, and like a child recovering from a bad dream, he'd straightened his shoulders, offered his hand, and spoke as though he'd practiced being the young gentleman. He'd worked very hard at being accepted.

"But I am ever so better for being here with Ma Sloan and Da."

Today, he was a boy reveling in the tricks he liked to play on his new friend, Martha. Tricks like hiding by the milk house and dashing out when she came looking for him. Now both stood straight, then Ryan grinned and turned toward the house. "Race ya!" he called as he rocked on his toes, ready to sprint.

"You'll never make it!" Martha yelled as she lifted her cotton skirts and bolted around him. By the time she reached the farmhouse, her breath was coming in great gulps. It had been a while since she'd raced with such verve. Somewhere back on some street in Dublin, years ago, running with Ma.

At the door to the kitchen, she stopped and waited for Ryan pulling up beside her, about to clap her on the back with congratulations. Ma Sloan was at the sink peeling potatoes, and Martha smiled when she heard her comment, "They're a pair, aren't they, Earl?" Mr. Sloan was sitting on the bench by the door as Martha opened it. She grimaced as she watched him pull on his thick-soled rubber boots. His groans told her she was a needed addition to the farm. Earl's joints were swollen and painful.

"Best they get in here so they can get out to the barn and help with the milking," he said as Martha slipped into the kitchen.

"I'm here, Da Sloan. What do you need?'

"Thank God for Owen Johnson," Ma Sloan said. "He sent

us a healthy girl to help." Just at that moment, Ryan slid into the kitchen and across the linoleum floor.

"And you have me, Ma. You have me."

"Ah. Ryan. You're an Irish blessing." She set the knife into the sink and laughed, ruffling his hair.

Martha knew Ryan was important to Mrs. Sloan. He filled some of the spaces that her son, Charlie, had left. Ma didn't talk much about worrying, but Martha had caught the pained glances between Mr. and Mrs. Sloan when word got around that the Newson boy who'd lived down the road was reported missing.

"Here. Let me peel those." Martha scurried over to the sink. Earl, cap plopped on his head, jacket over his shoulder, interrupted her lively steps.

"No, missy. There are cows to be milked and fed. And you too, young man. Work to be done, then supper." With cane in hand, Earl moved to the back door, turned, and straightened the framed picture of Charlie in uniform. He'd sent it just a month ago with his second letter of the three his parents had received.

As Ryan, Martha, and Earl left for the barn, Rose inhaled a breath that filled her lungs with clear late afternoon air. She felt in the pocket of her apron for the letter that had arrived that morning. John, who looked after the local post office in the village, had made a special stop in his new mail wagon.

"A Ford it is," he had proudly told Rose. "I thought I'd make this trip special. I know you don't get mail till tomorrow, but I figure this letter is from your son, Charlie, and you'd want it pretty soon." With that, John had turned and walked to his truck without a glance back. People in the countryside gave room for news about the war, always fearing what the next news might be.

As soon as Rose saw Earl, Martha, and Ryan round the corner of the barn, she took the letter from her pocket, moved to the rocker by the fireplace, and sat where she had soothed her boy for so many years. She took time to unfold the thin paper and felt the ever-present tears that lingered most moments. She missed him, and feared for his safety. She leaned her elbow on the cushioned arm of the rocker, her hand under her chin, and began to read.

*Dear Mom and Dad:*

*Sorry I don't get around to writing so often. They keep us busy. Three months isn't a long time to train for what's going on over there. It's raining right now, and has been for about two days, something that makes guard duty not much fun. We're taking extra duty because there's a bunch down with measles and another in the clink because they decided to take some unauthorized leave. Just wanted to have a bit of fun, they said.*

*How did you get on with the haying? Wish I could be there to help. I might be able to go home for a while if you'd come down here and tell them you need me, or you could write to the Colonel and tell him.*

*They're pretty careful about giving out furloughs, but I think they're still giving out some if there's a family need.*

*If you could, I'd really be grateful. I know this battalion is leaving Canada in a few months, maybe even in a shorter time than that, and I'd like to say good-bye to you and Dad before we go.*

*I hope the girl who's there, Martha was it? From the Johnsons'. I hope she'll be a help, Dad, and you'll need help. That's a lot of work and farming for the two of you...*

*If you or Dad could come here to Barriefield someday soon, I'd stand a better chance of getting some time for a furlough and I could help get things ready for winter. Do you think you could?*

*I hope you'll think about this.*

Your loving son, Charlie

Without a pause, Rose left the rocker, dropped Charlie's letter into the pocket of her apron, and strolled along the gravel path out to the barn. Earl was standing near Martha and Ryan, watching as they cleaned a stall. They weren't speedy; however, that would soon change with Earl's vigilant supervision. Martha cleaned and scraped with a fervor that belied her lean body—"like a rail," Earl would say. Ryan's enthusiasm sent old hay and some dirt flying in directions other than the side gutters, but Earl, patient man that he was, waited for another time to work along with him. Right now, Rose could see, he wanted Martha and Ryan to get used to working together. While the two young ones set to their afternoon work, she beckoned to Earl to step outside. When he shook his head no, she pulled Charlie's letter from her pocket and pointed to it. "You need to read this."

"I think this'll be a father's job," he'd said to Rose after he read the letter.

The next day he was on the train to Kingston, to Barriefield Camp, to talk with the colonel. Earl was a man who believed in action. Particularly when it meant seeing his son, Charlie. Who knew what could happen?

Earl arrived home on the 6:30 train coming from Kingston to Athens station. "It was a good idea, and a worthwhile trip," he told Rose, who'd waited and wondered what message he might have. "He'll be home on furlough for almost a month, time to get the haying done and in the loft, and time to harvest those fall vegetables. That colonel was real helpful. He must have come from a farm himself."

Both wondered to themselves, not daring to say it aloud, was whether Charlie might be going to France after his furlough and be gone for *"who knows how long?"*

◆

THAT NIGHT MARTHA, RYAN, EARL, AND ROSE SAT OUT in the barn on the workbench. Earl was teaching Ryan the intricacies of carving the driftwood they'd found when the two of them trekked down by the lake and out across the fields. Rose liked to sit and listen to the lowing of the cows and the occasional grunt of the pigs. In these moments, she found peace in the familiar.

Earl puffed on his pipe with long in-breaths, as though each inhale became a prayer from him, and each exhale of smoke a prayer from Rose for Charlie's safekeeping.

Martha sat beside them, her legs drawn up, her knees under her chin. She'd spent time working out in the sun, and her "Black Irish" complexion had taken on a smooth olive sheen. Her dark hair hung past her shoulders with only a couple of red ribbons anchoring the flyaway tendrils. Over this time with the Sloans on the farm, Martha the young Irish girl had flourished and blossomed into a strikingly beautiful woman. Nothing about her spoke of guile. Her beauty lay in her innocent directness. "Earl? Rose? Tell me more about Charlie. Why did he decide to enlist? He's barely nineteen. Did he decide himself? Did you both encourage him?"

Martha's need to know about Charlie filled the air. She laid her hands among the folds of her skirt and turned away as Earl spoke.

"Whoa, whoa lady. One question at a time." He tapped the bowl of his pipe onto his hand and put it on the workbench. He leaned back, taking pleasure in Martha's desire to know, and his own yearning to talk about his son. Rose said nothing at first, but waited for Earl to tell his story of Charlie.

Earl's throat tightened for an instant, with the sharp sadness of knowing how soon his boy would be in the midst of artillery, mud, and slime. He brought his son back into his own landscape of memory.

"You want to say something now, Rose?" asked Earl.

"Charlie is a fine young man, and in answer to your question, was it his idea to enlist, yes it was. I have to admit, Earl and I differed a bit on encouraging him, but in the end we agreed. We were hoping he might finish out his years at Queen's, but so many of his friends were signing up, we couldn't think of a reason to hold him back." Rose leaned back against the bench, put her hand under her chin, and turned to Martha. "Our Charlie, honest and good. We're hoping someday he'll take the farm and bring home a wife."

A faint redness crept along Martha's cheeks when Rose talked about Charlie and a wife. A faintness that could be called a blush. Earl stood up and knocked his pipe into his hand. "So, Martha, Rosie, do you think maybe it's time we go inside? These fall nights are cool out here in the barn."

Martha realized she was imagining Charlie, home for a month.

It didn't take long for imagination to become real.

# Chapter Fourteen

*"When the history of this Great War is written, a page should be reserved for these heroic young ladies who are nobly doing their bit as part of the war effort. These young ladies, considered to be heroes by many because they harvested the food that fed the soldiers."*
—Grimsby Independent, 1917

### Late autumn 1916 ♦ The Farm ♦ Martha

Why, I wondered, is autumn such a mixture of beginnings, middles, and endings?

This world has felt for two years as though it's ripping apart at the seams. Endings have hovered over us all. Anna's letters to me have spoken so often of death that I worry for her spirit. Yet, still, untoward happenings have landed in my lap like the shooting star I watched cross the sky last night.

Today held one of those unexpected moments as I headed down the path over to the hog pen to feed the pigs. Charlie, who'd just arrived home for a month, came striding from the barn toward me. The Charlie-image that I'd concocted was heading toward me—tall, strands of blondish hair falling across his forehead, blue overall strap hanging down, flannel shirt sleeves rolled up. Everything about him spoke of confidence and certainty—his stride, his smile, and his direct gaze.

His boots, untied, flapped as he stepped into my view. I'd never known till then how tongue-tied I could be. "Didn't expect to see me, eh, Martha?"

I watched a grin spread across his face and break into two matching dimples, one on each cheek. He was a charmer, to be sure.

"Martha? Charlie?" Mr. Sloan said, pointing first to me and then to Charlie. His brief introduction. I wondered if he saw the redness creeping up my neck and around my ears.

"Aw, Dad. Give 'er a moment. She looks kinda surprised. Are ya surprised to see me back home, Martha? Probably not as happy and surprised as I am to be here." I felt a pulse that might have been a heartbeat or a quick breath.

"Oh, I'm just a bit surprised. Guess I didn't know you might be home for a while," I said. I wanted to clamp my tongue shut. Everything I said sounded like nonsense.

"Well, here I am. And thank you, Martha McGrath, for being here. You taking over here, filling in my place when I leave to go fight the Hun, is a godsend." Something rustled just behind me. And Ryan appeared

"Me too, Charlie. I'm here to help. Remember what you said? Remember?" I laughed as I watched Charlie take Ryan by the waist, swing him around like a human top, and drop him on his feet directly in front of me.

"This is your biggest ally, Mart. Be good to him. He knows this place like the back of his hand, and every single animal has a name. Right, Ryan?"

If he'd whirled me 'round, I'd not felt any dizzier.

I lifted one foot and planted it firmly on the ground to make the world stop rotating. Unfortunately, that one foot landed in the middle of a cow pie. Charlie's eyes traveled from my face down to my foot where I could feel the squishy warmth of cow dung. I wanted a place deep in the bowels of the earth to swallow me up.

"Here, Mart. Grab my hand, hop into the barn, and we'll throw clean water over your boot. It won't be the first time you have to do this, eh, Ryan?"

"Ah, to be sure."

And thus, I hopped, one foot dropping cow poop as I went, Charlie at my side, his arm about my waist.

All the images I'd conjured up of how it might be when this man noticed me, that grin he'd worn when he saw me… none had included the humiliation I felt to the bottom of my cow pie foot. Mr. Sloan looked as though he had something caught in his throat; his hand covered his mouth, yet I could see his eyes glistening and a chuckle rising.

"Charlie, Martha. Got to attend to the chicken coop, you two just stay put." He was gone in an instant. Charlie told me later, his dad didn't want me to see how he'd laughed at my predicament. Kind man, Mr. Sloan.

After Charlie, Ryan, and I found our way into the barn, I sat on a bench by the door while he pulled at my baptized boot and put a milk stool under my sockless foot.

"What are you doing not wearing socks out here on the farm, girl?'

"I never wear socks in my rubber boots, my feet get too hot."

Again. My images of how we'd be, how our first conversation might sound, rapidly disintegrated. I felt mortified.

"Well, you'll soon find out, girl, that you'll need socks—and thick ones. I have plenty I'll not be taking with me to France, so you can have those."

I began to feel a small burn of irritation somewhere at the back of my neck. "I have my own socks, ya know, and I'm no eejit girl, haven't been one for donkey's years!"

Overhead, a large bird flapped its wings and soared into a dive to search for lunch on the barn floor. It was that moment when all three of us began to laugh. "Eejit girl"? Who calls herself an eejit girl, here in this country? Eejit girl was Ma's favorite Irish name for me whenever I made her laugh, or said something daft.

Ryan understood the word well. "Around here, Martha, 'eejit' is an idiot." And his snorts of laughter started again. He wrapped his arms around his body, shaking with silent laughter. He looked like someone about to fall over. Charlie, whom I discovered was a silent laugher too, was wheezing like a man who'd lost a last breath. That was the moment I knew we'd all be friends, Ryan, Charlie, and me. And that was the moment I knew I didn't want him to go to France. I didn't want him to go to war.

"Give me a minute." Charlie wheezed, inhaled, and spit a snort through his nose. That started Ryan all over again and sent him running to the house, probably to tell Earl about his joke and how we all laughed.

Charlie was the first to take a long breath. He leaned back against the barn wall, took a grayish handkerchief from his back pants pocket, and blew his nose. Next moment he turned to me. "It feels like a long time since I had a good laugh like that, Mart. It must be something about you. There's not much to joke about in this world. Maybe, could I take some of your spirit with me when I trek back to Barriefield? The lads there surely need something."

A quiet moment drifted around and through the two of us. Me, foot on the stool, my arms folded across my chest. Charlie, his back propped against the barn board wall, his hands and arms behind his head. He broke the silence just as I began to be aware of his breathing, how his chest moved as he inhaled and exhaled, how long his legs were, stretched out, his ankles crossed.

"Mom and Dad are lucky people having you here on the farm. They'll need some good laughs when I'm gone."

My boot lay on the floor, now dried from its hosing. I took a moment and leaned down and stuffed my foot into it. I needed that moment to stop myself from shouting, *Don't go!*

"Aren't you scared?"

"Don't have time to be scared."

"What do you mean, Charlie, you don't have time to be scared?'

"Mart, you gotta know and my parents have to know. I could get shot. I could be gassed. But I can't think about that. So, no, I don't have time to be scared. Poor Jim Anderson from down the road is gone. I'm really sorry for Mrs. Anderson, there on her own and losing her only boy. We've lost some good men just from this county, and everyone says they died for king and country. Maybe that's true, but I'd rather do my duty and then come home. That's being honest, Martha."

While he talked, he clasped and unclasped his hands, one over the other.

One of the cows began to low, a protest maybe. A declaration against the stupidity that Anna had described, and now here was Charlie saying something that felt true.

Dusk was beginning to settle. The laughter from a few moments ago was distant.

Laughing about cow pies seemed almost wrong, as though we were purposefully ignoring how brutal the world was.

I was eighteen years old. He was almost twenty. How many other young men and women across the world were marching into battle and secretly crying out—*Stop this war*!

"Charlie?" I drifted my hand over to him and held it open, palm beckoning. His arm came from behind his head, and his hand coasted into mine.

We sat still, hand in hand, and we listened. The gathering sounds of the cows feeding, the scurry of mice across the hayloft, Jake's quiet snores, and our own breath comingling.

"You started to say something," he said.

"Would it be all right if I wrote to you? Would you mind?"

I thought he held onto my hand for a moment longer.

"Mind?! Aw Mart, I'd be happy if you wrote to me. I'd be…" He stopped. "But aren't you already writing to your cousin Anna?"

"Charlie Sloan, I could write to you and Anna. And be glad for it."

Our hand clasp became a handshake. But the moment crumbled, broken by Rosie Sloan. Her head, followed by her body, appeared around the door.

"Martha? We've been looking for you. And you, too, Charlie. Your dad needs you out in the milk house. And Martha, there's a call on our telephone line and it's for you. It's your Uncle Owen."

Some hard object landed in my chest and I yanked my hand from Charlie's grasp.

I jumped from the bench.

"Uncle Owen? Did he say…? Is he all right? Is Emily all right? What did he say?"

She glanced down at our hands, then up again.

"No, Martha, all he said was, 'Please, may I speak to Martha.' Best you come. He did sound a bit upset. I think you need to scurry."

# Chapter Fifteen

### Late autumn 1916 ♦ Kingston, Ontario ♦ Martha

A SUMMER HAD PASSED SINCE I'D RESTED MY ELBOWS ON this windowsill. Months since I'd looked out over the garden where the willow touched down and grazed the lawn. The kitchen at 53 King Street was caught in time. Nothing had moved, nothing had changed. The plates along the rack above the door were gilded with the same designs, the oilcloth on the table lined with the usual blue and white stripes, the new electric stove with the side oven still spotless. Two people lived in this house, but it felt empty. It reverberated silence.

Owen moved from the kitchen cabinet to the stove and back to the kitchen cabinet like a cat pacing, figuring the next move, ready to pounce.

"I should remember, Martha. What do you take in your tea?"

"Just a spoon of sugar. But let me fix my own, Uncle Owen. You come sit for a while." I felt a twinge in my stomach, one that translated into an uncomfortable sense I may have crossed a boundary. What did I know about what he needed? Might he tell me to mind myself?

I waited to be chastised for being bad-mannered. For speaking out of turn. Were Emily here, she might have corrected me. Instead, Uncle Owen sighed, poured the hot water from the kettle into the flowered teapot, Emily's favorite, and walked to the table where he dropped into one of the wooden chairs. "Come sit, Martha. You are right. I need to gather myself. Too much, too much, there's too…" His words drifted into nothing. I wondered for a moment if he might be preoccupied with serious thoughts. I'd known Uncle Owen to become distracted while whoever was listening waited for his next word. Professor Owen Johnson held many ideas at one time, which made it difficult to stay with his conversations.

But whatever he was distracted by today must have been more serious than mathematical equations or structural conundrums. Serious enough for me to have left the Sloans and taken the train to Kingston. I'd promised them I'd be back in a week, possibly less.

All he'd told me on the phone line was he'd received a letter from France from one of the surgeons who worked closely with Anna. He sounded distressed on the phone, so much so that I dropped everything to go to him. I caught the train to Kingston that night.

Now I sat in the Johnsons' kitchen and wondered how I, an eighteen-year-old girl, might help Uncle Owen, professor and noted mathematician, the man who had saved my life in many ways.

"Martha." He slumped into the chair, his shoulders curved around his neck. "Martha, I need you to do something for me. I feel like everything is crashing around me and I think you can help."

I sat in the chair by him and I took his hand, a gesture so natural, even though he was an older guardian whom I called uncle. All I could see was a man who'd given me a home, a man in pain.

A letter lay on the table. He beckoned me to pick it up and hand it to him.

"I want to read this to you, and then I want to ask you some questions. It's about Anna."

"What about Anna?" The kitchen door opened. Emily appeared.

"What about Anna?" she asked once more. I saw a woman I might not have recognized had I met her on the street. Emily, who never allowed anyone to see her disheveled or untidy, stood in the doorway dressed in a rumpled dressing gown, her gray hair hanging loose, strands tangled in knots. Her dark eyes were set in shadowed circles, and her hand trembled.

Uncle Owen stood up from his chair as though catapulted. "Emily! You need to be in bed." It appeared to me that the letter he was about to share with me might not be the only crisis in Uncle Owen's life.

"Martha? Martha?" Emily called to me. My breath got caught in a long-ago scene…my ma struggling to walk from her bed calling for me: *Mart? Mart?*

"Please, Uncle Owen, could Aunt Emily sit with us?" I was worried.

I pulled a chair closer to her and reached for her hand. "No! You shouldn't touch me, I don't know what I might have, or if I might be contagious."

Uncle Owen reached for Emily's hand. With no hesitation she grasped onto his wrist.

"Em, if you were seriously contagious, I'd have whatever it is you have by now. I think you will be all right, my love. But I truly think you need to rest now. Why don't you go back upstairs and I'll bring you tea, very shortly."

I was stunned by Emily's frailty and Owen's solicitous attention. I watched as she struggled from the chair and only turned back at the door. "Martha, I'm glad you're here." Before I could answer she was gone.

"Martha." Uncle Owen beckoned me to move closer. "Emily hasn't been too well lately, but more than that, she has begun to mourn both for you and for Anna. It's one of the reasons I asked you to come. I called because…" He paused. "I called because I thought you could help."

"Uncle Owen, I'm not sure …"

"Please let me finish, Martha. I think Emily's sad, in fact, very sad. She may be feeling ashamed, and it's possible you are the one who's caused her to face up to what she did all those years ago. That's why I think you're the very one who needs to talk to her. But much more than that—it's about this." He pointed to the letter.

I wasn't sure. I didn't know what to feel. Emily and I had not started well; I'd left partially because I felt no welcome from her. What could have changed? Why was I the chosen one? I took a breath to be sure that I could find sustenance somewhere. A chill lodged in my chest. "I'll do what I can, Uncle Owen. That's not the only reason you called, I'm sure…please…what's happened to Anna?"

He nodded and picked up the letter to hand to me.

Anna's spirit was in that room, I'm sure, for him and for me.

Next morning I sat in the kitchen with Emily, her hair back up in a chignon, her dress wrinkle-free. But something had changed. When I'd walked into the room, she'd reached out her hand and beckoned to a chair beside her. The sun creating patterns across the hardwood floor added hope to a delicate moment.

"Martha. Please, I know you are here because Owen called you, not because you want to be here, but I want to say…" She stopped and took a breath, "I need to say how sorry…"

"Aunt Emily, you and I, well, we have some things to talk about—but this is not the time. What we need to do is read this letter." Before she could protest, I took the letter from my pocket. "It's from a surgeon in France." Emily grasped the arm of my chair.

"Oh, God! Has Anna died?" The thought hadn't occurred to me, until now. *Oh, no. Oh, no.* "Emily? Have you been thinking Anna's dead?" Her fingers clutched the padding on the arm of the chair.

"How long have you been thinking this?" I thought for a moment that maybe Owen knew something more and hadn't told me. I scanned the letter again quickly. It said nothing about death, but Anna was in trouble.

Emily turned to me, her face rumpled into creases, and said, "Owen hasn't said anything about her in the last while. Anna's last letter, before this one…" She pointed to the letter lying on my lap. "…Owen read to me, and I know he was leaving out parts that he didn't want me to hear. Now he's called you to come. Why won't he tell me anything? She's my daughter…stepdaughter…she means the world to me."

I remembered how attentive and concerned Uncle Owen had seemed, and how melancholy Emily had been. Had everything—the war, the horrendous reports in the newspaper, Anna's absence—had it descended on the two of them without mercy?

*Without mercy,* I thought. *Had I had left them just the way Emily had left her sister, without mercy?*

"Martha, please now, please read the letter. I need to know what's going on."

I nodded my head yes. As I straightened my shoulders and picked up the letter, I felt a cold chill where my breath needed to be. It was the same chill I'd experienced when I knew I couldn't save Ma, when I felt I'd let her down, that same chill when the Home Children left the dock at Quebec. Had I let them down too? Had I not stayed the course here with Emily and Uncle Owen the way I should have?

◆

"Martha, please. Read."

One inhale, a long exhale, and I began to read aloud. I was reading a letter from an unknown person who'd written to Uncle Owen and Aunt Emily about Anna. I felt I was eavesdropping on something private. I spoke softly, my voice tempered by my self-doubts.

"Martha, read so I can hear." Emily reminded me again in that manner of hers that sometimes felt sharp. I sat straighter, held the letter at my eye level, and began to read.

*Dear Dr. Johnson and Mrs. Johnson,*

*My name is Andrew Wilson. I am a doctor serving with the 3rd Battalion. I am here working at a hospital in England while on furlough from France. Your daughter Anna is one of the reasons I chose to take my furlough and work at this particular hospital.*

I paused at the word "hospital."

As I continued reading, I had a sense that Emily was hardly absorbing words but had begun to think the worst. I put my hand over hers.

*She and I have worked together frequently throughout the past year and I want to tell you what a magnificent nurse she is. Since she first entered*

> battle zones working alongside orderlies and doctors, she has been relentless in her care of the boys who come to us, some broken and wounded, all battle weary.

I smiled over at Emily.

"Of course, she's relentless," I said. "She'd be no other way, would she?"

"Martha, my dear, if you're going to keep interrupting yourself, I'll just have to hold my breath till you start reading again."

For a moment I felt chastised by Emily, until I noticed a small smile. Emily was teasing me. Emily, teasing. The air in the room seemed less heavy. Maybe we could be with each other and hold our fears for Anna together. Maybe Emily and I could do what I imagined families do, help one another through the hard times.

I started again, this time determined to read through to the end.

> Her nursing care is exemplary. I have stood for hours operating, and your daughter has been there at my shoulder. There have been moments when the convoys of wounded slowed and we had time, junctures when we rested. Yet Anna in those times would walk among the men, talking to them, listening to their stories, sometimes writing letters for them.
>
> There have been arduous days and nights during these last battles, some of which I can't name, only that the nature and acuity of the patient's illnesses have created mental as well as physical hardship for the nurses.

*Some hospitals are actually clearing stations where convoys coming in and evacuations going out are merciless.*

*I want to let you know that Anna, stalwart as she has been, succumbed mentally and physically to overwork and the daily grind of nursing. She has bowed down to the suffering and to the wretchedness that surrounds us. This is no weakness on her part. If I were to try to describe the abominations of this war I would be considered without patriotism. Gentle women and good young men are damaged in ways impossible to describe, possibly with no restoration in sight.*

*She has been allowed a month in a Nurses' Convalescent Home here in Kent, and I have taken a furlough to work here and watch over her as she recovers. One of the reasons I chose to be with her is that I am very fond of her, and I've asked her if she might consider marrying me.*

I stopped reading. How could I continue? My eyes had fogged with tears.

Anna, married? I glanced at Emily, sitting with her eyes closed.

"Well," she said. "Our girl has an admirer. And it sounds as though he's looking after her. Might we all feel a little less fearful for her?"

But I had moved on to another troubling thought.

Nothing had prepared me for the idea that Anna might not return—was this captain Canadian? What if he was British? Could she be gone for good?

I sat back in the chair and held the paper with a tighter intensity.

*You probably know, Dr. and Mrs. Johnson, that Anna has a clear set of truths by which she lives, and marrying me flies in the face of her duty as a nurse. Women who are married cannot remain here as nurses. However, she has promised when all this is finished, she will consider my proposal.*

*I will go back to France in another two weeks. In fact, by the time you receive this letter, I will be back there.*

*I will ensure that Anna takes the time she needs to regain strength and mental health. Her tremors (her hands were trembling when she became ill) have subsided, she no longer lapses into vacant stares, nor do her headaches return as often. Many of my colleagues discount symptoms like this, yet a new phrase is being used—"shell shock"—one that is more often used to describe the soldiers who succumb. The nurses are often just diagnosed with nerves, an opinion I consider unwarranted. Anna is not experiencing a case of nerves. Anna is exhausted.*

*There is much more I could say, yet I will sign off for now. My hope remains that we will meet when we all return. My home is in Montreal, where I practice and teach on the medical faculty of McGill.*

Ah! He's Canadian! Thank goodness! I gave a silent cheer.

*I have included a short letter from Anna that she wanted to write and send to you. She may make mention of our friendship. May I finish by saying how grateful I am to have met her. She is magnificent!*

*Yours,*
*(Captain) Andrew Wilson*

*P.S. Did Anna ever tell you that as a nurse she is Lieutenant Anna Johnson and has earned every stripe?*

I finished reading and gave the letter to Emily, who smoothed the wrinkled paper onto her lap and looked over at me, eyes brimming. "Anna, a lieutenant," she whispered. "My Anna."

The moment gave me pause. I could see something in Emily I hadn't recognized until now—she was a mother. And for a brief instant I remembered Ma's face. "Let's see what Anna tells us." I clutched the envelope as though I wanted Anna to know Emily and I were here, and we loved her. When I reached into the envelope, I found two thin pieces of paper folded carefully, one into the other. Anna's signature handwritten script with its careful curves and clearly dotted i's somehow brought her into the room. As I read, I felt her presence.

*Dear Martha, Dad and Emily:*

*I wanted to be sure that you received a letter from me, especially as Christmas approaches. This will be my second Christmas away from you, but I want you to know, I am doing fine.*

*There have been some rough times over the past while, and I really didn't want to worry you, but Dr. Wilson, dear man that he is, decided I needed to share what has happened.*

*I feel rather muddleheaded these days, and not sure what exactly occurred.*

*Dr. Wilson has been my saving grace throughout.*

I realized that Anna in a few sentences had mentioned Dr. Wilson's name twice. But my wondering was interrupted. A rhythmic knock at the back door broke into my thoughts. I slipped off the chair to walk over to the door. Emily turned toward me, "Who could that be, coming to the back door?" I motioned for her to stay seated. I opened the door, and there he stood. Charlie Sloan.

"I didn't know if you'd be coming back to the farm before I leave for France, so, I came to get you."

Not many times in my life have I been lost for words.

Thoughts of Anna's letter evaporated.

# Chapter Sixteen

*It is truly frightening to see such tall, muscular men fighting for every breath. Blue in the face they gasp and foam. Frothy white bubbling mucous pouring from their mouths and noses. We pray for their release from suffering—there is nothing else we can do.*

—Penny Starns, *Sisters of the Somme: True Stories From a First World War Field Hospital*

### December 1916 ♦ Margate Nurses' Convalescent Hospital ♦ Anna

As I sat in the lounge chair in the sunroom that day, I closed my eyes and felt the warmth of the afternoon sun and waited for Andrew to bring tea. I listened to the calming rustle of the gorse bushes outside my window and felt something like renewal. A desire to rejoin the living.

Voices drifted from the common room where nurses tended those whose spirits, like mine, had been broken. I felt I was back in the world again, where nightmares did not consume my restless sleep. I sat and wondered at the beauty of an afternoon garden. Although the Christmas season had just come and gone, the magic of blue sky and yellow gorse brought the promise of spring, someday.

I'd sat for hours during the past three weeks, staring out at the sky. Gradually, the sounds of war thundering in my ears and the flashes of blazing guns began to fade.

Lately, I thought I'd caught the scent of the ocean on the breeze. What a long time, it seemed, since I'd smelled anything but acrid smoke or bloody bodies. I'd spent time trying to fathom the horror I'd experienced. How could it be that I remembered ghastly wounds, the buzz of bone saws, the screams of young men, yet an ache to return there was settling in? Being in the midst of the bloodshed and the barrage, I could give aid and solace to broken men. Was that not why I'd come?

"Anna? Do you need to go to your room and have a nap?" Andrew's voice broke into my thoughts. "I have your tea. I can take it there."

When I opened my eyes, he smiled. "You looked so peaceful."

Andrew had been with me since I'd arrived at the hospital. He'd sat with me when I thought the tears would never stop. He'd lain beside me and held me when the nightmares consumed me. I knew he couldn't stay much longer, but we wanted these moments together and I needed this time to explain my decision to him.

"I was just thinking how remarkable this last month has been and how grateful I am to you."

I took the cup and saucer from him and placed it on the small table by the floral settee. I patted the cushion beside me. He looked askance at the overstuffed pillowed couch.

He was hesitant to sit, his khaki uniform and shiny brass buttons out of place among the blue and green flowers splashed across the loveseat.

"Come sit, Andrew. We haven't much time."

"Are you sure you're warm enough? This is a summer room and these windows…" He moved to sit, but stopped and put his hand on my shoulder. That same hand that had worked to put shattered young men together, and the same hand that at times had grasped my back as I stood by him in operating room after operating room.

"I'm fine. You need to leave soon. When is your train to London?" I felt I was urging him to go. Maybe I was.

"An hour from now." He sat and leaned forward, elbows on his knees, his chin resting on his hands.

"Anna. What can I say to change your mind?"

I sighed. I wanted to untangle my reasons for him, reasons for going back to France.

"The day I recognized the beauty of the trees beyond the windows of my hospital room, in a strange way, was the moment I knew that I'd be going back to France. I know it's difficult for you to understand." I took his hand, turning it over and tracing the lines on his palm as though I were reading it and trying to write some kind of justification. He sat, head down, and watched the movement of my fingers against his skin. I wasn't sure if I could find the words to convince him.

"I'm having difficulty, Anna. You sit here and you seem so peaceful, more than I think I've ever known you to be since I met you. Here the world holds beauty, there only bleakness and chaos. Why would you? Tell me. Why must you put yourself in harm's way again? You've proven your courage over and over again to me, to everyone who's worked with you and who knows you."

I turned to him and touched his arm, an urging to listen to my reasons. He sat back and let himself fall against the cushion. "There's little more to say, Andrew. I'm like you, a person who will travel across the channel because you believe you are bound to do something. Like you, I can't walk away from the suffering. I'm not that person."

"Oh, Anna. You're not thinking clearly. Your illness has clouded your senses."

I heard the frustration in his tone.

There we sat, our hands intertwined, our knees touching. The ruffles on the wrists of my white blouse brushed against the coarse wool of his sleeve. We were two people hanging onto a moment that we knew could be the final moments of what might have been.

"I need to try to make sense of this horrible war, Andrew. The only way I can do that is to go back to France and help in the ways I'm trained to. To marry you now, to go back to Canada, I'd never be able to rest. And truthfully, I'm not really sure that's what you want me to do."

He sat straighter in his chair when he thought I'd run out of words, and with a gentle smile that spoke of regret, he placed my hands back into my lap. I felt a sense of relief and sadness.

"All right, dear Anna. I must admit you are a confusion to me, and yet there's a part of me who is in love with your steadfastness." Silence descended. "I must go."

"Let me walk you out to the front hall. But before we leave this room and the sunshine…" I reached up and placed my hands on his cheeks. "Thank you for saving my life, Andrew. I'm grateful for your care and I will not soon forget all I've learned from you. This good-bye will stay with me for a long time."

He put his hands over mine, still on his cheeks. "Will you let me know where you are when you go back?"

"Yes. I will. And you, you go safely." I had the words *I love you* on my tongue, but decided to hold them there.

## February 1917 ♦ No. 16 Canadian General Hospital ♦ Orpington, Kent

I sat in Matron's quarters in the large hut designated for the nursing staff. I'd been waiting for almost a month since being sent from Margate to Ontario Military Hospital at Orpington. I was anxious to prove I was well and ready to go back to France. My once-crisp white apron was spotted with blood, and strands of my hair hung outside my veil. I did not look like a candidate for immediate transfer back to the front, yet I was determined.

That morning I'd been taken from the ward to assist in one of the operating rooms, where a convoy of men had been delivered, brought almost directly from the hospital ships that crossed the channel. Zigzagging its way across the channel, the ship had narrowly missed being torpedoed by a lurking German submarine. Matron was puzzled that with everything happening around us here in the relative peace of Kent in England, I was agitating to go back to France. She looked over her glasses at me, placed one hand over the other on her desk, and asked me again.

"Sister Anna, whatever is it that draws you back to harm's way?" Those had been Andrew's words, and I remained suspicious that the delay in my transfer had something to do with him. I knew I was exhausted from the hours spent throughout the day on my feet assisting one of the surgeons. A friend, another nurse, had circulated the word that I was one of the best surgical nurses here at Orpington, and that I'd been sent to train other nurses. I'd assured her none of this was true.

"In fact," I admitted, "I've been on sick leave for almost a month." I think I probably took some twisted delight in seeing her baffled expression.

"Yes, but I watched you in that operating room this morning. You were brilliant."

"Maybe I'm proof that a person has to be a little wrong in the head to be good at war," was my retort.

Now, here in Matron's quarters, I watched through her windows that looked out over the long wards with their green walls and rows of beds, each one occupied by a wounded soldier—fractured thighs and arms, gunshot wounds of heads and abdomens, and the moans. I could hear the moans through the walls of Matron's office.

I inhaled slowly and exhaled the breath that caught in my chest. The young men I saw in that ward embodied what I'd experienced at the Somme, all the ruins of the wounded.

"Sister?" I heard Matron's voice from a distance. "Anna?" I stirred myself. "Oh, Matron, I apologize, I was just looking out into the ward." Without pausing, I stood and walked to the window. I needed to see them, go to them. "I see two young men I assisted with in surgery this morning." Matron rose to her feet and walked to join me at her window. We stood side by side, like keepers of the watch over their damaged lives.

"I understand you were instrumental in saving a life today." She turned to me, putting her hand on my shoulder. "You are a good surgical nurse, but more than that, you've experienced the horror, and you listen to those boys from a place that knows. We need you here at Orpington." She pointed out to the ward. "They need you here. You've proven yourself in battle over there in France. Stay here with us now."

"Matron, I'm not the best nurse on this ward. I've watched some of the others and I am stunned some days by the skill and the care that's out there. I'm good at what I do, but one of the reasons I am is that I'm duty-bound and answerable to those men who, for all the reasons given by governments and generals they'll never meet, have placed themselves in hell."

My hand struck flat against my chest, crunching the stiffness of my apron.

"Your fervor reminds me of a young nurse during the Second Boer War. She was filled with passionate zeal much like you."

"And where is she now?" I asked.

"You're talking to her."

"Then, you understand, Matron? You understand I have to go back. To France."

"With everything you and I are. Yes, I understand," she sighed. "I'll see what I can do."

◆

MY SUSPICIONS ABOUT ANDREW WERE CONFIRMED later that month when I received my first letter from him. He'd been back in France in the midst of battles since leaving me at Margate. He knew how to contact me because he'd arranged that I be assigned to the Ontario Military Hospital in Kent at Orpington. His letter only confirmed what I wondered.

In the beginning I was angry, and I told anyone who'd listen, particularly my friend who shared quarters with me in the nurse's hut. We lay on top of our cots the night I received his letter. Still dressed in our uniforms, Maggie and I had been waiting for a convoy of ambulances transporting wounded men from a hospital ship that had arrived at England's coast from France. The convoy was to arrive near midnight, so we hadn't even bothered to take off our clothes.

I lay on my bed and read Andrew's letter aloud to Maggie. I held a torchlight in one hand, the letter in the other. Maggie dozed on and off as I read.

"Listen to this!" I threw my legs over the side of the bed and sat upright.

"What?! Don't do that, Anna! You scared the bejeebers out of me! What's he said?"

"He says...*I hope you are happy there at Orpington. I knew it would be the best place for you and for them. I hear from Matron that you are bringing your talents as a surgical nurse to the operating rooms there. It was a wise decision I know, on my part, to recommend you go there.* "Recommend. Recommend?!"

"But, Anna, you have been a great help here, the doctors say you are the best surgical nurse..."

"That's not the point, Maggie. He had no right to block my request to go back to France. I've a mind to write to him and tell him exactly what I think. Just because I turned his marriage proposal down. I won't let him stop me from going to France."

Maggie, gentle Maggie, slid off her cot and crept over to sit beside me. With hands folded, she leaned against my shoulder. "Anna, I think Dr. Wilson...Andrew probably had your best interests at heart. I've been in France, I was at the Somme, I know just how awful it is. You, my friend, have been there since it all began. Can't you give yourself some time? You're doing good work here."

"I know he wanted to protect me. I know, too, that I broke down over there. Which is the very reason I have to go back."

Maggie sighed.

"And what happens if you go back and…"

"Mags. You know we can get lost in the 'what ifs.' We, you and I, have to do what we came to do."

"I'm too tired to argue with you now, Anna, and I think I hear ambulances approaching."

The noise and rumbling of Model T Fords suspended my next retort, but not my determination.

# Chapter Seventeen

*Beneath the roar of the shells overhead the underground tunnel entrances were blown out for the infantry to surge forward. Other Canadian infantrymen in the trenches, some standing in mud up to their knees, climbed ladders to emerge into the maelstrom.*

—Tim Cook, *Vimy: The Battle and the Legend*

### Charlie

FRANCE, APRIL 1917

Dear Mart,

Just a note to let you know I'm okay.

It's been raining and sleeting here so much that I've forgotten how it feels to be dry. Next time you talk to Mom, could you ask her to send me some socks? Thick wool ones would be great.

I've been thinking about you a lot. Helps me stay warm. You are the best hot water bottle.

Everything has happened so fast, this war, the battles, watching fellows die. I'm needing home, I'm needing you. The memory of you protects me. Keeps me alive and safe. I'm sure of that. The memory of us and those two days in Kingston left me convinced I must return to you. I want us to be married.

*But in spite of it all, I'm holding up. The fellows are good men, some funny, some very lonesome, and I seem to be the one they want to talk to. I've had some experiences lately that I'll tell you about when I get home, but I can't say much now. The censors are cautious. I'll just say that some nights, sleep won't come because of the loud artillery. Then other nights we fall asleep just right here in a trench, our heads leaning against the sandbags. Yesterday I heard that a new group of nurses is being sent to the Casualty Clearing Centre (CCC) near us. Do you remember Cecil Stewart? Lived two farms over from us. He's in my platoon and was taken to the CCC the other night to get his head stitched. He ran into the wooden beam that holds up the doorway to the Lieutenant's dugout and knocked himself out. None of us know what he could have been doing to hit his head that hard. Joey Williams, one of the guys, thinks he might have done it on purpose. Not sure about that. I got a letter from Dad yesterday. He says Ryan is a big help and that you are being kind to the boy, especially when he gets homesick for Ireland. Do you miss your country, too? For sure, when I get home, Mart, you'll never be lonely again. Do you go to visit Mr. and Mrs. Johnson every so often? I know that time Mr. Johnson came out to see us, after you'd arrived, he spoke well about you, and your good nature. That's all I'll say for now, Mart, except glad you're there with Mom and Dad. I'll see you again.*

*Yours,*
*Charlie*

FRANCE, APRIL 1917

*Dear Dad and Mom,*

*Well, I wanted to write to you and let you know I'm still alive and kicking. There's a lot happening here. We've been out of the trenches, training to go over the top, and we think that might be happening soon.*

*It's cold here, but maybe not as cold as you've been telling me it is back there. I'll probably never complain about mud and dirt out in the fields again when I get home. The mud here is hellish and it just never goes away. Sometimes it's up to our knees. The sun is sure a wanderer here. Thanks for the parcels you're sending. That last one with the cake was delicious. Did Martha bake it?*

*I'll write back to you soon.*

*Your son,*
*Charlie*

### April 1917 ◆ The Farm ◆ Martha

THE WALK DOWN TO THE LAKE COULD HAVE BEEN A mistake. This early spring has been a cold one, but I needed to get off by myself, to sit, to think about Charlie and everything I wanted to say to him when I write back to him. That last night together at the Queen's Inn in Kingston before he left for Barriefield Army Camp seems so long ago, it's left me anxious for his return. Were we wrong to do what we did? Was it this war, the thought we might never see one another again? His letter has hushed some of my fears. *I want us to be married,* he wrote. I read those words over and over.

I've folded and tucked Anna's letters into pages of my journal, thickening my old composition scribbler with stories of a war still being fought in places that are only names to us here in the north of Frontenac County.

I could hear Ryan tracking his way to find me as I sat by the lake. He'd tried to move stealthily among the trees and through the grasses. With little success. His hoots of delight rang out each time he discovered animal tracks or clumps of newly blossomed trilliums. His joy in being the explorer endeared him to me and to Earl. However, Rose found his dirt-encrusted boots and his collection of worms for fishing in the lake a bit beyond her tolerance. I needed to remind her every so often how good it was to see Ryan becoming an ordinary boy.

I sat on a wooden garden chair that had weathered a few winters by the lake, turning when I heard a scratch of feet on dirt. The boy delighted in sneaking behind me.

"I heard you coming, Ryan." I grinned. "Rose could probably hear you from the house."

Every description of a raggle-taggle kid fit Ryan: His hair stood straight up and out from his head, his loose bootlaces were forever in danger of tripping him. I'd grown to love this boy. We had a bond that linked us to Ireland and the separation that we felt some days, when we were uneasy in the midst of unfamiliar worlds, or when holidays like St. Stephen's Day passed by with nary a notice.

He landed with a clunk on the rocky ground by the chair and immediately picked up a stone that he sent sailing into the lake.

"What are you doing down here, Martha? It's afternoon, don't we have chores to do?"

He sent another stone skimming across the smooth surface of the water.

"I like to come here to read Charlie's letters because it's quiet."

For a moment a shadow of sadness dimmed his eyes. It used to be Charlie, not me, whom he followed.

"Would you like to hear something that Charlie said about you in his letter?"

"He wrote about me?" His wide grin reappeared. His eyes lit up.

As I took the letter from the front pocket of my overalls, a newspaper clipping fell onto the grass. Ryan reached over and picked it up to hand to me.

"What's this? Those are pictures of soldiers. Do they know Charlie? It says 'Canadians' in big letters across the top."

Ryan and I had been working on his reading, me giving him extra lessons after he returned from school in the afternoon.

"No, Ryan." I stopped for a chilling moment. The headline under the pictures read: Officers Who Figure In Today's Casualties.

"I think these are some officers who are fighting along with Charlie." A cold breeze brushed against my body and I wrapped my arms about myself, pulling my sweater closer.

"Let's read what Charlie said about you. Come sit." I edged over to give him room.

*'I got a letter from Dad yesterday. He says Ryan is a big help and that you are being kind to the boy, especially when he gets homesick for Ireland.'*

"Martha! I'm not homesick, never was."

"I know that, Ryan. I think Charlie worries about us, that's all. But he thinks you are a big help to all of us, did you hear that part?"

He nodded reluctantly. "But what's this?" He pointed at the newspaper article.

"Uncle Owen sent this to me. He gets the Toronto newspaper and he knows where Charlie is, at least I think he knows." Places in my heart felt like pieces of ice cracking. Shards of *What if?* "Read it, Martha. Please?

I inhaled a long breath, let it go, and began to read parts of the newspaper article about the Canadians who were battling in a place in France called Vimy Ridge.

*"Canadians score again, capture miles of trenches south of Vimy Ridge by a brilliant stroke today."* Before I could continue, Ryan leaned against my shoulder and pointed to the words 'Vimy Ridge.'

"Where's that place?" he asked.

"You recognize those words?"

"Yeah, one begins with a V and the other an R. See how good I'm getting, Martha?'

"Vimy Ridge is a place in France. It might be where Charlie is."

I knew that Ryan would have questions falling upon questions as soon as I mentioned Charlie's name. "Ryan, you need to get back to help Papa Earl with the milking. You go and tell him I'll be along in just a few minutes."

"What're you gonna do now?"

"I just need a couple of minutes alone—could you do that for me?"

"Are you worried about Charlie being at that place called Vimy Ridge? Are you scared?"

The wisdom of this Irish boy could make me weep.

"I am Ryan, I am. It's such a horrible war."

"Are you scared he might die? I know about some men in Ireland that killed people with bombs." I shook my head no and held up my hand to stop him.

"Ryan, I'm scared for Charlie, but it's not helping me right now to imagine what could happen."

For a moment he dropped his head. "I'm sorry Martha. I didn't mean to upset you. You sure you don't want me to stay with you for a bit?" He stood up and let his hand rest on my shoulder.

"No, Ryan, I'm sorry, I should not have snapped at you like that, you are just being kind. Now you go find Earl and get started on the chores. Tell Rose I'll be there soon to start peeling potatoes for supper." Off he went with a gait that transformed into something between a skip and a gallop.

After the leaves settled and the sound of Ryan's dart through the woods faded, I sat down in the chair and spread Charlie's letter across my lap. I placed my hands on it, one on top of the other, closed my eyes, and spoke to him as though he could hear me.

"Charlie. I need you to come home. Remember how you said let's be married the instant you get back, and I kind of hesitated? Well, I'm sure now. I want to be here on the farm with you, I want us to have children, maybe adopt Ryan. So, I'm throwing a pebble into the lake and letting the circles widen. Those are my wishes. Come home, Charlie Sloan. Come home."

The pebble hit the water with a splash. Ripples spread near the shore and beyond, a small wave making its way inland.

◆

The next day, Rose and I drove the horse and buggy into Athens, the nearby village where we shopped for food and groceries. I wanted to go because I needed time alone with her to talk about my situation. Uncle Owen and Emily were coming to visit on Saturday, and I knew there might not be a chance to share my news—that I'd missed three monthlies. I harkened back to the night with Charlie at the Queen's Inn, when he'd said *I'll take care of you* and I'd felt a warmth I'd never experienced wash over my body.

Rose was the only person I could tell or talk to. As we rode along, I listened to the cadence of the horse's hooves on the gravel road and silently practiced the words I'd say.

"You're quiet this morning."

I stared ahead at the swaying rump of Dusty, Earl's fine Clydesdale, watching his ears flick and flitter as he trotted. "Rose, I've missed my monthlies since February. Could that mean…?"

"Whoa up there, Dusty." Rose pulled up on the reins, and Dusty stood still. I waited. Could she be angry, ask me to leave? Could she boot me out of the wagon, make me find my own way back to Kingston?

"Martha." She set the reins in her lap and turned toward me. "I've been wondering what happened when you and Charlie went back to Kingston. You haven't talked much except to say you had a fine dinner and that Emily and Owen liked Charlie. Martha? Were you and Charlie alone for a while?"

Before I answered I sat and watched my fingers weave one over the other. But then, the words tumbled. "We went to an inn after we had dinner with Emily and Owen. When we left, they thought Charlie was going back to Barriefield and I was catching the late train home."

I'd sat with the fear and the shame since the time I'd known something was going on—since I'd begun to realize that I might be expecting a baby, Charlie's baby.

Rose's questions penetrated fearful places. I was already feeling sick most days, and now I'd wrecked my life and maybe Charlie's. Where will I go? Who would take me in? Questions tumbled over fears while Rose sat and watched me struggle.

When she spoke, her voice was almost a whisper. "Are you expecting a child, Martha? Charlie's child?" That's the moment my tears flowed.

Dusty who'd been standing still shook his head and started to move forward.

"Whoa, Dusty, whoa back." Rose grasped the reins with one hand, her other hand grasped mine.

I sobbed.

"Oh, Rosie, I'm so ashamed. I've wrecked everything."

"Martha, look at me."

My eyes still shut, tears dripping off my chin, I lifted my head.

"Please open your eyes and look at me."

In the time it took to turn and face Rose, she took both my hands and held them against my growing stomach. "First of all, we needed some good news, and I guess this'll have to do. And next, well, listen to me, Martha. I was once where you are. Charlie came along very soon after Earl and I married and after we moved to the farm. We had to leave town because our parents felt we'd shamed them. My father ordered me out of the house. Do you understand what I'm saying, Martha?"

I nodded a confused yes. "You mean you and Earl...?"

She paused and I looked into her face.

"Yes. When we married, I was expecting Charlie, and I was probably about where you are now, so why would I judge you? I have a friend who is a midwife in Kingston. I can take you to her and we'll be sure that what you think is happening is indeed true. And we'll see this through together. There's only one person we must not tell right away and that's Charlie. I'm not sure if he's ready to know he's going to be a father. Maybe he just needs to deal with being a soldier right now."

I stopped at that but let it pass for now.

"What about Emily? What about Owen?"

"I'll go with you when you tell them. If you are expecting, you're carrying my grandchild. And if there is a chance—and I pray not—but if there is a chance Charlie doesn't come back..." Her words drifted, her eyes clouded. "We'll need to be a family."

◆

There was a scent of spring newness in the air as we rode home later that afternoon, Dusty trotting with that horse's inborn knowledge of the way home. Groceries were piled in the back of the wagon. Rose and I sat in the silence of a new kinship.

All of these moments changed in an instant.

When we drove up to the house, Earl was standing on the steps of the front veranda, a paper in his hand. A telegram. We sat at the supper table that night, Earl, Rose, Ryan, and I, food on our plates uneaten. Even Ryan's favorite, mashed potatoes with cream, was untouched. He reached over and touched my arm, his tears streaking his cheeks through the day's dirt. We hadn't the heart to tell him to wash his face before dinner.

"I don't understand. Is Charlie dead?" Earl, whose only words since handing us the telegram were "Charlie's wounded," answered in a whisper. "No, son, Charlie's been hurt. We'll hear more soon, I'm sure."

Rose left the table and walked to her chair by the woodstove. She sat, her hands folded in her lap, her face drained of color, staring at the door as though she hoped Charlie might walk into the room. No one spoke or moved.

She looked at the telegram in my lap. "Read it to us, Martha," she said.

I exhaled the breath I'd been holding in my chest, took the paper and spread it on the table. My voice was steady. Fear sometimes could do that to me. I read slowly.

> *We sincerely regret to inform you that 450655 Private Earl Charles Sloan infantry officially reported dangerously ill. Transported to Orpington Military Hospital England. Shrapnel wounds back, right shoulder. Will send further particulars when received.*
>
> *Officer in charge records office.*

No one spoke. The fire crackled in the stove. A log fell.

"Read it again," Rose said.

# Chapter Eighteen

*Is this joy? To be doubtless alive again,*
*And the others dead? Will your nostrils gladly savour*
*the fragrance, always new, of a first hedge-rose?*
*Will your ears be charmed by the thrush's melody*
*sung as though he had himself devised it?*

—Robert Graves, "The Survivor"

### July 1917 ◆ Kingston, Ontario ◆ Martha

We stood on the train platform, waiting. Straining to hear the rattle of wheels on the tracks or the shrill whistle. Earl stood at attention dressed in his dark blue suit, the stiff collar of his shirt grazing his chin. Rose fingered the top button of her best black suit jacket while she held one hand pressed against her chest. Ryan hopped from one foot to another, his short gray pants and scratchy black knee socks rough against his skin. He'd polished his boots to a mirror sheen. "Charlie's boots'll be shiny," he'd told me.

And me. I wore a white blouse and navy wool skirt, a gift from Anna before she'd left for France, an outfit I treasured. Emily had given me one of her sweater shawls that covered the small bump of my stomach. No one spoke. A car horn blared. They'd come! I'd not heard back from them when I sent the letter telling them that Charlie would be arriving home close to the end of June.

"Rose, it's Owen and Emily! They're here!"

Her face lit with a Rose smile that told me she knew something I hadn't known.

"Did you write to Emily?" I pointed to Rose, as I mouthed the words.

Strange and wonderful happenings had occurred since the day Rose and I took the train to visit with Owen and Emily—the day I told Emily I was expecting Charlie's baby—the day I'd dreaded and the day that turned on its head. When I gave her the news, she'd whispered, "I'm here if you need me." Something had shifted in her.

Today, nothing could daunt me. Charlie was coming home. I'd saved so much of life to tell him. My daydreams about looking after the farm together as Rose and Earl get older, about making Ryan an official brother for our new baby. Still, though, I held a quiet fear. Should I have told him before today?

My mind was charged with hopes threaded with doubts, thoughts chasing one another like Jake, Charlie and Ryan's dog, when he pursued a squirrel.

Charlie's last letter from Orpington, the convalescent hospital, lay folded in the pocket of my skirt, the letter the nurse had written for him when he knew he'd be coming home.

I ran to Uncle Owen, who was unfolding himself from his Model T.

His face brightened as I slowed to greet him, my hand outstretched. He took me into his arms and held on. It wasn't like him. His wool jacket brushed against my cheek and caught my tears like dew on his collar.

"You came, you came." The jitters I felt about Charlie's arrival collected in my throat, and for a moment I wondered if I was still that girl who'd stood sobbing in the front hall of Uncle Owen's house years ago. Emily's small hand on my back drew me away from his shoulder. Her arms reached for me in an awkward hug.

"Martha," she whispered into my ear, "if only Anna were getting off the train with Charlie." I froze into a straight-backed dismissal of what she'd said. How could she think of anything other than Charlie's arrival right now? But Emily could still find the injured places in me, those raw spots of old hurt. When I pulled away from her, I saw something new. I saw my mother's eyes in Emily's, and possibly hope for forgiveness.

A train whistled and the clacking of wheels echoed down the tracks.

Women, mothers, sisters, lovers, daughters, emerged from the tiny station. Men, brothers, fathers, sons, stood at the side of the platform, some at attention, some saluting.

I ran from Owen and Emily to the platform in time to see Ryan jumping and yelling. Fearing he might fall under the wheels that were screeching to a halt, I grasped his hand and intertwined his fingers in mine.

A crowd gathered around where we all thought the boys would appear. When the conductor let down the train steps, no one pushed, no one shoved. There was an unspoken bond among us. An energy of expectation held us together. Everyone in that crowd hoped for a miracle and feared the worst. What if their soldier was broken beyond repair?

A young man guided by a tall, angular soldier in khaki appeared at the top of the steps. His eyes were covered with a bandage that circled his head. He didn't see the mother who rushed to him from the midst of the crowd. Behind him, a soldier moved carefully step by step; he too leaned on the railing. A tin plate covered the half of his face that had been blown away.

A woman reached her hand out to him, her voice thick with tears. "Johnny, you're home." His was a crooked smile, but a smile nevertheless.

The war for them was over. For me, time slowed down. I waited. I watched other people gather at the foot of the steps. More passengers descended. People dispersed

I placed one foot on the bottom step. "I have to find Charlie," I said to no one in particular. And there he was. He sat in a wheelchair, arms folded across his chest. Behind him a young man in civilian clothes beckoned to me. "Come on up," the young man said.

"Mart?" Charlie lifted an arm to me, while the other fell to his lap.

I reached up to his hand and felt the roughness of his skin, the grasp that I remembered.

"Told you I'd be back. At least some of me."

What a sight we were, me halfway up the steps into the small entrance of the train car, Charlie trying to lean forward while the young man held his shoulders. Something in the set of his face, shadows beneath his eyes, undid Charlie's cheery words.

"Sergeant Sloan, I'll need to get help to lift you and the chair down the stairs. Ma'am, you'll need to stand away."

I grabbed the railing and backed down to the platform, not taking my eyes off Charlie's face. Earl, Rose, and Ryan were crowding around me. Uncle Owen and Emily stood back.

"Here!" Earl cried out. "I can help. You, young man, hold Charlie's chair where you are and I'll grab the front wheels." Carefully, gingerly, they lowered Charlie down to the platform. Earl held the arms of the chair and backed down the steps. This was his boy, home now. He'd take care of him. He'd be sure he landed safely on Canadian soil.

"Gentle, now. Gentle," Earl murmured as he might have when he'd picked up a young Charlie after a fall.

Charlie's face crumpled for a second and I knew he felt the pain of the movement. On the platform he rearranged the blanket that covered his knees and, when he was ready, looked up at all of us. A young Charlie had left to fight a war—an older, battered Charlie returned.

I could not wait another moment. "Charlie Sloan, welcome home." With that I broke ranks from the family, took his rough hand, and held it to my cheek. There would be no more hanging back for decorous reasons, or what might be considered proper. He was back, he needed me, and I needed to tell him we were soon to be a family.

◆

THE MORNING AFTER HE ARRIVED HOME, I SAT ON THE porch with my tea. I wore my yellow flowered apron over my blue cotton dress. My hair was tied back with a white ribbon I'd once found among Ma's belongings. I felt a glow on my cheeks that translated into sweaty palms. I waited for Earl, who'd said he'd bring Charlie out in his wheelchair. Everyone seemed anxious about my decision to tell the father of my child about our baby. Rose worried that it might be too soon. "He's just home, Martha, doesn't he need time to be back?" Earl was concerned that Charlie might, "You know, that thing the doctors say—relapse." I wasn't sure if Earl knew what that meant, but I had faith that Charlie would take the news well, and happily.

"She's a determined girl," I'd overheard Earl say to Rose as I'd left the kitchen after supper the night before to go into the back room where I slept.

And I was. Determined. How long could I walk around carrying our baby and say nothing? If for no other reason, it felt shameful.

The screen door squeaked and protested while Earl maneuvered Charlie and the wheelchair out onto the porch. "Mart. You are a sight for sore eyes."

I waited for a moment. He looked pale. His eyes, which I remembered as always bright and dancing, were dull. Like the flame in a kerosene lamp that had flickered and died. His body slumped into the chair as I hesitated. *Oh, Charlie*, I wondered, *where are you in there?* I touched my fingers to his. Earl crept back into the kitchen.

"Charlie Sloan…" I gathered myself to tell him about our baby. I put my hand in his and sat beside him. He closed his eyes, held my hand.

"I've not known peace for a long time," he said.

The moment to speak vanished.

We sat in the morning sun, silent and together.

"Maybe tomorrow." I thought.

◆

Nights were the worst.

Charlie slept in his old room, in his bed he'd had since he was a boy. Earl helped him when he needed to move down the hall, or go out to the privy. The Charlie I experienced during those first days was not the Charlie I'd known before. That hopeful, sunny young man was lost somewhere out in the trenches of Vimy Ridge in France. There was a sadness about him that crept into his face and his body. He'd be there, talking, and without warning his eyes shadowed, his shoulders sagged, and he'd sometimes rock in his chair, as though he wanted to dislodge an unwelcome phantom.

Some nights when I heard his moans, I'd creep up the stairs and slip into his room. There I'd pull his old wooden chair to the bed and sit. He should not be alone, I thought. I'd pull back the curtains to let moonlight fall across his bed. Some nights I sang a song I'd sung to Ma when the consumption overtook her.

> *Over in Killarney*
> *Many years ago,*
> *Me Mither sang a song to me*
> *In tones so sweet and low.*
> *Just a simple little ditty,*
> *In her good ould Irish way,*
> *And I'd give the world if she could sing*
> *That song to me this day*
> *Too-ra-loo-ra-loo-ral, Too-ra-loo-ra-li*

If my throat tightened with my sadness, I'd stop singing. But Charlie, eyes closed, would murmur, "Don't go away," as though I might be some sort of dream and he, back in the trenches, was reaching up to me.

The nightmares left him perspiring and breathless. He'd call out orders, "Over we go lads, over! Take cover!" One night I crawled up beside him, put my head on his chest, and listened to his heart race. I thought surely he would die, but when his breathing slowed, his body relaxed into the softness of the flannel sheets. Like a child, he was asleep in an instant.

◆

ONLY AT NIGHT WERE WE ALONE, YET IN ALL THE DAYS he'd been home, we'd not spent time just us. It could have been that Earl and Rose were protecting him from the news I held. Or Charlie himself was locking his spirit away from me. Whatever he was feeling, whatever sadness had overtaken him, he was not ready yet to take me in.

Earl would help him down the stairs to the kitchen, where we'd have breakfast, all of us. On the good days, Charlie would ask to be wheeled out to the barn where he'd give orders to Ryan about milking and tossing hay, to the joy of the boy.

On the rough days, Charlie would shut himself away in the parlor with pen and paper, where he'd write letters to the families of young men he'd served with. I knew because he asked me to take the letters into town to the postmaster. I never asked what he'd written.

◆

WE'D NOT BEEN ALONE FOR WEEKS.

Then, finally. He'd know soon. My bump was no longer small, but Rose and Earl had continued to ask me to give him more time. "Wait till he's feeling strong again." For me, their hesitation was no longer so important.

I'd been up early, put on my overalls, and sat on the porch until the sun rose. This is the day, I said aloud. I will tell him. I no longer listened to Rose or Earl, and even Emily, who all thought he needed time. No, we, Charlie and I, needed time together to take in how our lives had changed. We were no longer two young people—we were going to be parents.

I knocked on his door as the sun was rising. "Charlie?" I whispered. "Can I come in?"

"You know you don't need to ask." I found him sitting on the edge of the bed, his legs stretched in front of him.

He was dressed. A plaid work shirt, overalls, straps hanging. Bare feet hung below his pants. He reached for his wheelchair.

"Charlie? How did you get dressed?" From the other side of his bed, near the wall, I heard a small chuckle.

"Ryan MacDougall, how did you get in here?"

A tousled head popped from under the comforter. "I'm helping Charlie." My temptation to leave and let the two enjoy their time slowed my resolve, but I'd practiced what I needed to say to Charlie. He was the father of our child—denying that was wrong. "Papa Earl is downstairs having his breakfast, Ryan. He needs you to help with the cows. So, scoot."

A nod from Charlie and the boy was out the door and down the stairs.

For the first time since Charlie had arrived home, I felt a rush of shyness. There he was, straps of his overalls hanging loose, his feet bare. I remembered his body.

"You look like you're ready for work. Are you milking this morning?" I asked.

"Mart?" He reached over to me, placed his large hand on my rising stomach and looked up at me. I let a breath seep from my lips, felt the soft air up into my nose.

He said nothing. I inhaled another breath. With one hand on my chest, I placed my other over his hand that sat motionless upon my stomach. His mouth was a straight line, the edges of his eyes were creased into tiny wrinkles I'd not noticed before.

I froze. "Charlie. You're a dad," I whispered.

"Ah, fuck, Mart. I don't know what to say. I know I asked you to marry me. But not like this." He pointed over to the wheelchair by the window, his legs hanging over the edge of the bed. "What have we done? What have we done?" he muttered.

I took my hand from his and turned to get to the door. I was Martha that young girl, ready to run, ready to escape the next torment. Before I could get away, he grabbed my arm.

"Mart! Don't run away on me. It's a shock, yeah, and I need time, we need time. C'mere, sit." He pulled himself along the bed to make room for me to sit. He groaned.

"Mart?"

I couldn't answer him. My voice was frozen.

All I could hear was Charlie's *What have we done?*

All I could think was *What have I done?*

# Chapter Nineteen

*I move in the descent of days*
*From what was dreamed*
*To what remains.*

—Wendell Berry, "Boone"

### July 1917 ◆ Orpington Hospital, Kent, England ◆ Anna

I CAME OFF DUTY FOR THE SECOND TIME LATE THAT afternoon and was checking out for the night, but first I needed to speak to Matron about one of my patients, who I believed was experiencing serious shell shock. As I neared the room where the nurses wrote their records for the day, I saw Matron at the large window where she watched over the ward. She held up what looked like a packet of letters tied together and beckoned me to come in.

Our Matron took care of us on this ward, patients and nurses alike. She noticed when we did a few extra hours on a shift, as I'd done today, and she took care to listen carefully to our thoughts and observations about the young men under our care in the ward.

Forty-six beds, forty-six soldiers who'd experienced grave horrors. Men whose lives were forever marked. As I walked among the beds on my way off duty, I took hold of hands and smiled, I leaned down to some boys whose heads were bandaged and I whispered gentle good nights, especially for those I knew could not hear me. I placed my cool hand on foreheads that burned with fever.

Matron smiled as I walked into her office. "Sister, there's a package of letters for you. It's a large one so I suggested to the young man from the postal depot that he leave it here with me." Sometimes her care for us was like a mother's curiosity. She was waiting for my reaction.

I saw the return address and name as I took the packet from her hand:

Dr. Andrew Wilson, Etaples, France. This same address was written across three other letters; the fourth was also from Andrew but addressed only from France, no town or place name. Matron took my hand and asked, "Is this the doctor you've been telling me about?" I couldn't speak, I was so afraid I might weep with relief. It seemed a long time since I'd had any news from him.

I nodded.

"And the other two, are they from the doctor as well?"

I hadn't looked further on within the packet but there were two more letters, and these brought me relief and joy as well. They were from Martha.

Matron took me by the shoulders and turned me toward the door. "Go now, go to your room. Make a cup of tea, wrap yourself in a blanket, and read your letters, soak in every word. I will try not to call you in for duty until morning."

We'd had word that a major battle was being fought near Ypres, and we knew the hospital would soon be taking wounded from hospital ships sailing from Le Havre to Southampton. Everyone here at Orpington was on high alert, waiting and wondering when the convoys of wounded would descend, and sleep would become a luxury.

Matron, in her quiet way, was telling me to be still, at least for the night.

◆

BACK IN MY ROOM IN THE NURSES' HUT, I HUNG MY BLUE uniform and placed my bloodied white apron into the laundry box. I took a clean apron, folded it, and placed it on the trunk at the end of my cot. With a sigh, I took my boots off and placed them under my one chair and hung my stockings over the back of it. Too tired to even walk to the bathroom down the hallway, I slipped into my flannel gown, promising myself I'd go later and wash my face.

I knew the days of resisting Andrew's offer of marriage were about over. During this time we'd been separated, and not having word from him since February, I'd realized how important he was to me. His attention to my well-being when I became ill, and his concern that I take time to "battle my demons," as he called my recovery, took on another layer of meaning as I gained strength and renewed belief in myself. Maybe he'd been compassionately right to have me sent to Orpington Hospital.

He'd blocked my return to France by organizing my placement at Orpington, and for a time I'd resented his interference in my life.

I stretched out on my cot with one of Andrew's letters and began to read by flashlight.

MARCH 1917

*Dearest Anna,*

*I'm at Remy Siding, having found myself placed here after returning from you at Margate. Please know*

> *I wanted nothing more than to stay with you and see you through the pain of your shell shock. I was grateful to the powers that be who gave me furlough.*
>
> *You have cared for the wounded and heartsick almost since the beginning of this awful war. I'm worried that you'd feel I might have left you there without a thought—nothing could be further from the truth.*
>
> *Forgive me if you've felt shunted aside. It was never my intention.*

I lay the letter across my chest and closed my eyes. I remembered how he'd stayed with me in my room at Margate when the hallucinations overtook me, how he held me in his arms. Somewhere within my tortured soul, I'd felt loved. I remembered how that felt.

I turned the letter and picked it up to return to reading.

> *One day, it is my hope you will see your way clear to reconsider my offer of marriage.*
>
> *The matron on your ward at Orpington has let me know what a boon you have become there. That does not surprise me. Please consider the possibility of staying there—this war cannot go on much longer and I believe you've done your part over here in France.*
>
> *We've had some rough times with constant shelling and men being brought in from casualty stations, some who don't make it to a bed before they die. The nurses are working steadily to tend to the wounded, even some who've been on their feet for 24 hours. I know it's not fair that I tell you these things, Anna, but you were always the one I could talk with.*

*I'll stop here—a commotion going on outside my tent, or maybe that's the rain.*

*I look forward to your letters.*

*I'll keep writing. Please think of me and the possibility of being together when all this is over.*

With my fondest regards,
Andrew

I wasn't sure if his insistence was concern for my well-being, or that marrying me would send me back to Canada, back to safety. The thought didn't call up annoyance as it once had. Something had shifted in me, my heart was opening.

Still, I hadn't finished my work in France.

What if I could find wherever he was and ask to be sent there?

I sat up suddenly, sending the other letters flying to the floor. When I reached down I grasped the one with a recent postmark, the one that said "somewhere in France."

With his letter in hand, I walked over to my small desk, lit a candle, and sat down to write.

*Dear Andrew:*

*Whatever has happened to our mail? I have just received four letters from you and two from my dear friend Martha.*

*Your letter written in March I read immediately, and so glad I did. You must be wondering what has happened because I haven't written to you for months.*

*To put your mind (and heart) at rest, I believe Orpington is wonderful, and much as my pride was hurt, I need to tell you, coming here to work after my* convalescence was a wise decision. Did you know, I expect you did, that this is an Ontario Military Hospital? Such a stack of supplies and beautifully equipped. When the wounded men arrive, we feel so sad for them, mangled as they are, bullets or shrapnel lodged in bodies, battered, smashed…some hardly recognizable. Yet, Andrew, when we come to know each one on a ward, when we first hear one laugh, or someone tells me about his family (I've even met some men from Kingston), we come to care about them.

I feel as though I've been working with some of the best doctors and nurses around, and I feel revitalized and ready to return to France.

Yes, Andrew, I am still determined to return to the front—my work there is not finished. Even though I know there are nurses and soldiers yearning to go back home, I want to go where I can continue to offer my help. That's where I need to be.

And now to your words: "I hope you will see your way clear to reconsider my offer of marriage." I have thought about you, how you have cared for me, and something has shifted, for me. Andrew, I want to be your wife.

Would you agree to marry when this war has ended?

And more, if I can manage it, to be placed with you, might we work together once again?

I won't know where you are unless I ask the powers that be. I'm sure Matron here will help. She is such a good woman.

My eyes are closing.

> Tomorrow, I will read another of your letters, and I will begin working on my transfer back to the front, and to you.
>
> Fondly,
> Anna

I crawled into my bed, pulled the flannel quilt up to my chin, and lay with images floating: Andrew reading my letter, a broad smile lighting his face, the moment I walk into his arms. I let myself imagine what it could be like back in Canada, introducing him to Martha, my dad, and Emily. I drifted into a welcome sleep.

◆

It was an insistent knocking. "Sister, Sister, we need you!"

A convoy of ambulances was pulling up to the hospital.

A battle had begun near a place called Passchendaele.

My intentions were to get to France as soon as possible, and my other letters would have to wait.

◆

### July 30, 1917

My diary:

*They came in waves. They came by ambulance trains. They came reaching out for morphine. They came moaning. They came bleeding. They came eyes still wide with fear. They came asking for a cigarette. They came and they kept coming.*

"You're the good sister, aren't you?" His name was Ronnie. He died before we put him into a bed. A young man reached from his stretcher to take my hand. His throat bandaged, his voice a whisper. "How are you today?" he breathed. He died last night.

An officer, both legs wounded, shrapnel in his back, tried to salute as I walked over to him. I smiled. He wept.

It's been a very bad day. I'm wondering if I should leave Orpington yet. But I promised Andrew, I promised I would find him.

Oh, God, keep him safe.

◆

TONIGHT, I WALKED TO MY HUT IN A DAZE.

When I walked along the corridor to my room, I saw Matron sitting at a desk in the writing room, pen in hand poised above a paper. I tried to walk by without disturbing her, but unsuccessfully.

"Oh. Sister…Anna. I need to speak with you. Could you come and sit? I know you must be exhausted, but I think you might be pleased with my news. I only wish I were."

With those words, I knew. Somehow, someway, I was going back to France. The room was illuminated by a green banker's lamp on the desk, which threw a surprisingly bright light across Matron's face. Her smile was tentative, her eyes shadowed with regret.

"You and I have talked at length about your request to go back to France. I have some understanding of your desire to return. I have said little to you about it because I wanted you to have more time to consider and reconsider."

I was by now twisting my fingers in my lap. I wished only that she'd say what it was she needed to say. Had my request been quashed altogether? Would I have to find some other way to travel back to France, back to Andrew?

Matron took what appeared to be an official notification from a folder on the desk. "Here you are, Anna, here's your way back to France." She handed me the letter, and as I scanned it, I felt that someone somewhere had heard me.

CANADIAN ARMY MEDICAL CORE: ASSISTANT DIRECTOR MEDICAL SERVICES: Reinforcements needed for No. 4 Canadian Casualty Clearing Station St Omer. Please send additional nurses. 10 Sisters if possible.

"Does this mean…?"

"Yes, Anna, I've sent along your name in company with four other nurses currently working here in our ward. I believe one might be a friend, Margaret Anderson?"

"Maggie! Maggie has requested a transfer?"

"Yes, she has. This is all I can say right now, except No. 4 CCC Station needs you soon, so you'd best begin preparing. There is a hospital ship leaving quite soon from Calais to sail to Dover. It's a yacht actually, commissioned as a hospital ship. Possibly you'll be asked to assist with the wounded when you dock back in France. From there, you and the other nurses will travel with an escort to Longuenesse. I wish you well, Sister, and I pray you arrive safely. You're a skilled operating room nurse and we cannot afford to lose the likes of you. Godspeed."

With what seemed final words she handed me other papers, which officially documented my transfer. As I rose to walk away, I turned to her, "Matron, I am ever grateful for your wise guidance…"

For a moment she removed the veil of her official capacity, stood, and put her hand on my shoulder. "Anna, please know this, you have made a remarkable recovery, and in that, you have been extraordinary with shell-shocked men here. I admire your courage and your determination." She dropped her hand from my shoulder and turned back to the desk.

I was dismissed.

# Chapter Twenty

*Over and over again I have been thrown to the ground.*
*Over and over again I have risen up.*
—Wendell Berry, "Let Us Hear From You"

### September 1917 ◆ Frontenac County ◆ Martha

I decided to leave. To go back to Kingston, back to Emily and Owen.

Ryan, dear Ryan, had held back tears when I bent down clumsily to kiss him on each cheek. "Why are you leaving? Did I say something to upset you?" One tear had begun to make its way through the smudges of dirt on his cheek. What could I explain to him, how could I make him understand?

I'd looked over to Rose and whispered, "Will you try to explain to Ryan why I'm leaving? He thinks he's done something."

Rose said nothing to me, but bent down and put an arm around Ryan, "You've done nothing wrong at all, Ryan, in fact, you may be the best of all of us."

As Ryan walked away from us, his shoulders rounded in a slump, I thanked Rose for her help.

"And Charlie? What do I say to him?" Her gaze penetrated me. When she turned on her heel and left me standing, cloth bag at my feet, I felt like Lot's wife, turned to stone.

◆

Charlie had become more and more remote. I'd wheel him out onto the porch, where he'd sit and stare out over the lawn and the fields beyond. When I encouraged him to stand and try to walk out to the barn with my help, he'd look away and shake his head no. Eventually, he ignored my presence. I felt as though I was invisible to him. Once when I asked him what he'd like to do that morning, he'd said, "I'd like to be left alone."

How much breakage does a heart allow before it crumbles? My heart felt like glass splinters were tearing it apart bit by bit.

Rose would watch him as he descended into his own hell. I wondered if she blamed me for being unable to help him. I wanted to yell, "I don't know what to do! I don't know what to do!"

Charlie and I continued this morning routine until I couldn't anymore. He was sinking. Sinking into a somber mood where he'd convinced himself that his life was over, that he'd never walk again, and that he was useless. The doctors at Orpington Hospital in England had sent a report along with him, which Rose and Earl shared with doctors in Kingston. Everyone was puzzled and worried. Charlie still had a piece of shrapnel in his back, yet the doctors said it should not be paralyzing him. It was as though he'd persuaded himself that he couldn't walk. *He's given over to despair*, the doctor's report stated, in unusually non-medical terms.

Whenever I tried to ask him about the war, he'd turn his head like a child not wanting his porridge.

Eventually, he refused to talk to me at all.

And that was when I decided it might be best for all if I left him with his parents and Ryan. I decided on my own that his brand of hell was my fault. I represented pain to him, not solace. I'd let Charlie down, just like I had let down Ma. I still held the thoughts of Ma dying with no one to comfort her—not even her daughter there to send her on her way. Here I was again, helpless and useless.

He'd be better here without me.

I'd tried to talk with Charlie about the possibility of me going to stay with Emily and Owen. I used the reason that it would be a better place to have the baby. He looked at me as though he'd forgotten that there was a baby and the possibility of a life together. The Charlie I had known was no more—those years before the war, us, were gone. Maybe he'd left me behind in France with all his memories of what used to be.

An old voice broke into my despair—Ma's voice. *"Emily is family. She'll know what to do."* The next day I packed.

Rose's voice, like a chorus, joined Ma's in my imagination: *"What do I tell my son?"*

I spoke to my bedroom walls, to Ma's image and Rose's face in my mind.

"He needs help, and right now, I don't know how to do that."

◆

THE NEXT WEEK, IN THE QUIET OF MY OLD ROOM IN Kingston, I decided to talk with Emily. My old experiences cried out against confiding in her, but my hope and Ma's voice won the day. And I wrote to Anna. It seemed to me I was calling in the troops.

◆

Morning sun glazed the countertop in the familiar kitchen. Emily sat in her usual place at the table, her newspaper spread before her. Headlines called out the latest news about the war. She was so intent, her finger following along under each line, she didn't notice me standing in the doorway.

"Emily?"

I realized she'd been searching the pages.

"Oh, Martha, I didn't hear you come downstairs." Immediately she pushed the paper away and folded it up like a person caught reading something she shouldn't. "What would you like for breakfast?"

My hands were sweating. I could feel the redness creeping up the back of my neck. *What now? Where do we go now, Aunt Emily? Should I be here in your kitchen?*

"Martha? Are you all right?" She smiled. Emily actually smiled. "Your cheeks are a bit flushed. Are you ill?" I held the back of a chair and waited for words to form.

"Um, no, Aunt Emily. I guess I'm feeling a little out of sorts."

"Not the baby, is it, dear?"

Dear. Emily called me "dear." *Don't trust her.*

"I'm sure it's not. I guess I'm kind of out of sorts. Charlie and all." How I wanted her to come over to me, arms outstretched, the way Ma would have. We stood, two hesitant people, me wanting to weep, and Emily watching. But the air between us felt different. Was her face softer?

Did I see Ma in her eyes?

When she had agreed without pause that I come and stay with Owen and her, I knew something was different.

OUT OF PLACE                    181

Maybe seeing what the war had wrought in Charlie's life, and thus in mine, had given her new perspective on what mattered. Maybe concern about Anna. It seemed wrong to grasp onto ancient hurts while Anna lived with human destruction and Charlie had returned, a lost soul.

I gathered myself from my thoughts and headed over to the stove to get the kettle.

"I think I'll have tea and a biscuit." Memories of making tea for Ma stopped my hand as I picked up the kettle. I took a breath and leaned on the edge of the counter.

"Martha? Are you all right?" I heard footsteps and felt her hand on my back. My chin lowered, my eyes closed. Four years ago, Emily probably would have left me standing alone rather than acknowledge me. Today she cared. As I turned to face her the baby kicked against my stomach. I smiled and realized tears were on their way. Tears for Charlie, for Anna, for all whose lives were ever changed by a war none of us understood.

"I left him, Emily. I left him. He's hurting, and I left him."

Her arms reached around me as far as she could, her mouth touched my ear, her voice a whisper, "Maybe he needs to be there at home knowing you will be cared for here. While he does what he needs to do to find his way back."

"I don't understand, Emily. Why wouldn't he need me there to help him?"

"Oh dear, dear girl. Can you know how sometimes we turn away from those who love us when we feel helpless? Charlie feels helpless. He promised you the world, he gave you a baby, and now he's lost. Now he's lost." I heard such desolation in her last words. I reached over my shoulder and grasped her hand. We sat there in the kitchen that morning.

I told Emily my fears, and I told her my hopes for Charlie and me. I told her how lost I felt too.

◆

I'D BEEN WITH EMILY AND OWEN FOR MORE THAN TWO weeks when I finally took paper and pen and began a letter to Anna. It was late afternoon. Emily was napping on the couch and Owen was at the university. I went to the desk in his library, a place that felt safe and welcome.

I wasn't even sure where to send a letter, but I needed to feel her there in the room. If she were here, Anna would be sitting in the large leather chair worn with the years of Owen's contemplative moments—reading students' mathematical creations and, these days, remembering the young men who'd written brilliant theorems, young men now dead.

For a few moments, I closed my eyes and imagined Anna curled in that chair, hand on her cheek, elbow resting on the faded armrest, her attention wholeheartedly fixed on my words.

I leaned into the glow from the desk lamp.

*Dear Anna,*

*How are you?*

*I need to begin there because I think of you every day. Sometimes when I wake up, there you are.*

*All that time you spent with me those years ago is the reason that I'm comfortable with this pen in my hand, letting the words form under my fingers. How much you have taught me. I haven't been back to the high school in Kingston since I moved to the farm, but*

*Rose, and now Emily (and, of course, Uncle Owen) give me lots of chances to read and write. You gave me such confidence in myself.*

I remembered the times Anna and I had laid on the floor in the parlor reading together, laughing together. What a grand teacher she had been.

*I'm writing to you now, Anna, because I want you to know how life is here. And I don't want you to worry. More than anything, though, I want you to know how we pray for your safe return.*

*There are times when I'm not sure where to start when I write to you, which may be a reason that I haven't sent you letters in the last while. I know that Uncle Owen writes to you faithfully, and I've discovered that Emily sends you packages. Cakes. Doesn't she make the best war cakes? All that brown sugar, nutmeg, and ginger.*

*I guess you know I'm about to give birth…I talked about that when last I wrote, but I'm afraid I was not in good shape at the time. Charlie hadn't arrived home yet, and I was so worried about him. He's here now, but he's not himself. Don't think I'm terrible but I've come to live here with Emily and Owen till the baby comes.*

*I feel as though I've abandoned him, and I guess in a way I have.*

*Lately I've tried to be with him, to sit on the porch, to wheel him out to the barn, and sometimes to read his favorite stories. But over time, Anna, he's not wanted me to talk. Once, he took a book from my hand and threw it on the ground. He's so angry with* me, not with Ryan, or Rose, or his Dad, but with me.

It's as though he wishes I weren't having a baby. At least that's how I feel.

His mom and dad have taken him to doctors in Kingston at the military hospital there at Queen's University. Uncle Owen has helped so much, connecting Charlie with doctors there.

May I tell you what one doctor has said? He feels that Charlie is suffering the results of not only the horror of guns and trenches, but the shock of everything that happened after he was hit—he was taken by stretcher along the trenches, and he was wet and cold, and exhausted. I know they'd try to give him morphine, wouldn't they Anna? The pieces of shrapnel in his back must have shifted. I can't imagine how painful it was. And, his nightmares awaken him shouting. He talks to his dad about watching his men mowed down by artillery and machine guns. And he cries.

He seemed so glad to be home when he first arrived. The doctors at the military hospital in Kingston remarked on his spirit. But he became a haunted man, and I'm afraid it got worse after he found out about the baby. Am I imagining?

Speaking of the baby, he or she—I'm not sure who I hope for—is very active this evening.

I'll sign off for now, dear Anna.

If you get a chance, could you let me know where you are now? Can you? Are you allowed?

I dropped the pen across the page and crumpled over with a dull cramp. Water dripped from me onto the floor.

Everything became a blur. Flashes of faces appeared. Once I was sure that Charlie was in the room. Emily spoke to someone, a midwife. "She's almost there." The pain became all I knew. Until another voice, another face, appeared. Ma floated where I could see her.

Then nothing. Until the cry.

◆

I HADN'T KNOWN IT WAS POSSIBLE TO LOVE SO DEEPLY and completely. Nothing and no one had ever grasped my heart like this wee babe who lay in a wicker bassinette by my bed. Everything between sitting at Uncle Owen's desk watching a puddle of water drip to the floor to this moment was a blur. Voices murmured from a far-off place outside the closed door. I let my gaze wander about the room and realized I was in the front bedroom downstairs, Anna's old room. Pain was still holding me, yet I felt detached from it. A tap at the door. A whisper. "Martha?"

Someone I didn't know rose from the chair by the window, someone who rustled as she walked, like Anna had when she came to say good morning on her way to an early shift.

"She's just coming around." An unfamiliar voice, gentle like Anna's.

Another whispered question brushed past me. The words were like branches rustling in the breeze outside my window. I slept.

◆

"MARTHA, DEAR, YOU NEED TO WAKE UP." A VOICE FROM a distance, a gentle touch on my forehead. As I opened my eyes, I let the scene dissolve and clear, dissolve again, clear. Aunt Emily stood by my bed. At her side stood a woman in a crisp, white uniform, cap atop her dark hair.

"Martha? Can you hear me?" Emily whispered. But it was the sound of a soft whimpering that opened my eyes and cleared my head. My baby, my girl. I struggled to sit up.

"No, wait a moment, give yourself a chance to come back," said the woman in white.

*Come back? Come back from where?*

I felt like I'd been away for a very long time, and now I settled back into my body and a new life.

Like a light from somewhere, I remembered my baby. I pushed my hands down onto the mattress and leaned against the pillows piled at my head. Emily reached around and grasped me just the way Ma would when she picked me up from my bed.

"Here, Martha, let me help."

As soon as I sat against the pillow, I reached my arms toward the midwife who stood holding my girl. She placed her in my arms, a little person folded into a flannel blanket. Love radiated from my body. I felt a kind of warmth I'd never experienced before. Life became something new.

I placed my finger on her chin, and her tongue played against her lips.

Throughout those minutes as I fed her, I promised I would protect her for always. I heard a sniffle and looked up. Emily was wiping her eyes. "Oh, Martha. She's beautiful." I closed my eyes for an instant and reached a hand to Emily. "Do you have a name?" she asked.

Before I could begin to answer, I heard the front door open, and a commotion in the hall outside my room. Uncle Owen's voice greeting someone in a loud stage whisper, "You came." A rattle and squeak, as though something was being moved or wheeled.

The midwife turned to leave, to see what was happening, but Emily stopped her.

"Not to worry, Miss Agnew, I'll tend to this," as though she knew, maybe possibly planned it? I held my baby close to my body and watched the door close behind Emily.

I didn't move. I sat staring at the door. The midwife had slipped from the room. All seemed quiet for a moment, my girl falling asleep in my arms. Then another commotion at the door. Someone who sounded like Ryan spoke, "No, please, I can do this." I heard a soft chuckle that I could swear was Charlie's. My heart began to pound; my breath escaped in what felt like giggles.

Rose backed through the door, bent over, leaning on something. "Be careful, please, don't hit the wall."

When she stepped aside to hold the door open, she smiled over at me.

Charlie in his wheelchair sat in the doorway, Ryan at the helm behind him.

"Now, now? Can I now?" Ryan shifted one foot to another. Charlie lifted his hand as though to say, wait. His face bore the remains of scars he'd brought home, but his eyes, oh his eyes. There was a crinkle there I remembered, an upturn at the corners of his mouth.

He beckoned Ryan to wheel him in and over to my bed. No one spoke. At the side of the bed he reached toward his baby, still wrapped in her flannel blanket, her eyes fluttering in a dreamlike sleep. I put her into Charlie's arms.

Explanations, expectations of what lay next in the hours to come, could wait. For now, in this moment, we three were home.

War not only destroys bodies. It takes the souls of those who've fought and shatters them into fragments like the pieces of shrapnel in Charlie's back. What had happened to his body would eventually be set right and what had happened to his soul was possibly beyond repair, but we set out, all of us, to walk that path with him. We began that day.

I watched how Charlie held his girl. He placed her in the crook of his arm, moved the corner of the blanket from her face, and looked down at her.

"Ah, Mart. She's beautiful."

Rose beckoned to Ryan to follow her from the room. She'd done her work, so I discovered. I moved closer to the edge of the bed, letting my legs dangle. I felt like that girl who'd sat on the edge of her mother's bed, not knowing how to help.

Without taking his eyes off his girl, he began to talk to me.

"Mart, I'm scared. The war isn't anything like people here think."

I took a breath and held it, so afraid was I to break into the moment. He sat so still I wondered if he was all right. When he shifted in his chair, I exhaled and the baby whimpered.

"Let's put her in the bassinette." I stood for the first time in hours and felt the room sway for a second. The dizziness passed, and I reached for her.

I sat back on the bed, my feet in between Charlie's on the footrest of his chair. He put his hands on my knees and looked at me full in the face.

"I can't talk about the war, but I can tell you this—I want to go back to the military hospital here in Kingston. A doctor there said he could take some of the shrapnel from my back—he's worked over in France and he knows his stuff. They have people there too who can get me walking again."

"How do you know all this, Charlie?" I couldn't keep the doubt at bay. My voice quavered. What if I started hoping again?

"When you left the farm, I spent a week letting Ryan wheel me to the barn, where I'd watch him lift hay for the horses, milk cows, sweep out the floor, and the whole time he talked to me about how much he wanted to stay with all of us. '*For the rest of me life!*'"

I couldn't help but laugh at Charlie's imitation of Ryan's high Irish voice when he was excited.

Charlie's eyes clouded. "And Mart. I thought about everything life has done to Ryan, what the streets of Dublin tossed at him, being homeless, the beatings he took, sent to a country to live with strangers. And…I thought about you…and your life…."

He stopped and looked away.

When he came back, he took my hand and enveloped it in his rough fingers.

"I can't guarantee who I am anymore, I can't even say I'm Charlie, and maybe someday I can tell you what happened over there. I have a screaming voice in my head some days. Mart, I need your help."

I think I stopped breathing. Charlie needed my help. The helpless, useless me was no more.

That night I lay in my bed, Charlie beside me, my head on his chest. Earl and Owen had lifted him from his chair.

The next day he'd go to Queen's Military Hospital.

That night, our girl became Sarah Rose.

# Chapter Twenty-One

*"You are just the nurse to help them return to life."*

—Matron

*"I wasn't too sure how I could do something for a wounded soldier, that I thought I'd never be able to do for myself."*

—Anna

### June 1918 ◆ Étaples, France ◆ Anna's Diary

A MONTH HAS PASSED. HOW COULD THAT BE?

It's my last day at Étaples. This place where I found beauty in the midst of abomination.

Last May 19th I lost a friend.

Last May 19th I lost Andrew, the man I'd come to love.

I'm struck with how deep my grief is, and yet I move through the days, doing what needs to be done, being the woman I have become. How I do this remains a mystery. Maybe someday when I'm back home, I'll figure it out. I sound like Andrew. He often said that to me. "We'll figure it out." Oh, Andrew, I found you just in time to lose you, forever.

On May 19th a terrible air raid lasting for almost three hours brought horrors to Étaples, particularly our No. 1 Canadian General Hospital. Patients died, a Nursing Sister was killed, I knew her, we'd worked together in surgery. Two others were wounded and have since died. I wonder at myself and how matter of fact it is to say it. Is this what happens after *years of witnessing death and destruction of human bodies and souls? Have I become immune? Why am I still alive?*

*Why am I alive and Andrew is dead?*

I lifted my pen and set my diary aside on the bed. When I lifted my feet and legs to lie back, I felt the strangeness of normalcy. Here I was lying on a bed in a hut, one of the ones not hit. Almost a month ago, I'd been on shift staying with patients as bombs exploded. Why I was still living was a miracle to me. If I'd gone back to the nurse's quarters at the end of my shift, I'd probably be dead too. They'd taken a direct hit.

Now the quiet that surrounded me was a combination of strange and comforting. Morning was approaching and the prospect of my last day here at Étaples rose up. I'd decided to take Matron's advice and a word from my good nursing friend Jennie to leave Étaples. I'd been posted, with the gentle counsel from Matron, back to No. 16 Canadian General Hospital, back to Orpington Hospital, back to the place where I rediscovered my soul. Matron and Jennie were the only ones who'd seen my anguish when Andrew succumbed to his wounds the night the bombs fell. For protocol reasons, I'd said very little about the plans Andrew and I were making.

I remembered how each of those women had cared for me the day after the bombing. They'd taken moments to hold me as I cried for the future I'd lost, like all the men and women dead because of that awful night.

◆

### May 20, 1918

"I'VE MADE A POT OF TEA, ANNA. COULD I GIVE YOU A cup?" Sister Jennie sat on the floor of one of the wards that had not been hit. I sat on a bed just above her. We two, in company with other nurses, had volunteered to take over shifts and responsibilities for the nurses who'd been wounded.

During the night of the bombing, one of the orderlies who'd been helping at a makeshift operating theatre was brought in, blood everywhere. A gaping wound across his chest. From his stretcher, he'd beckoned to Jennie and me and in a raspy whisper told us, "Dr. Wilson was hit…"

Jennie grasped my arm as I started to run to the door.

"No. Anna. You mustn't go out. There are men out there who are rescuing the wounded. They'll bring Dr. Wilson in. We'll attend to him right away."

But I knew as soon as the stretcher-bearers brought him into the ward and placed him on a cot. I knew there was nothing more to do.

Now on this day after the bombing's crescendo and the barrage of artillery, the guns had silenced. Jennie sat at my feet. I sat motionless on my bed.

I tried to lift the weight of grief from my chest, but my body felt dismembered, my hands and my arms numb. I wanted to rush back to the ward, to go to where Andrew had been placed. I needed to put my hands on his bloodied face and plead with him to come back. But Andrew was gone.

Through a mist, I heard Jennie speaking soft words. "Anna, would you talk to me, tell me again how you found Andrew when you returned?"

"How can I say his name?" I called out. For the first time, I let sobs caught in my throat become an animal cry. I wailed and pounded the bed, I stuffed my fist into my mouth. Never in my life, not even when my dad told me my mother had died, had I given rein to grief's brutality.

She sat, Jennie did, holding my feet nestled in her lap, and rocked with the rhythm of my pain. While my body softened, I closed my eyes and began to tell Jennie the story of how I found my way back to Andrew, those weeks ago that now felt like years. The words soothed.

◆

"It wasn't that difficult to find him, Jennie. Dr. Andrew Wilson, a surgeon from Kingston, Ontario, was famous in the Canadian Army Medical Corps." For a moment a smile escaped my lips. I took the handkerchief that Jennie handed up to me and wiped both cheeks and the corners of my mouth as I warmed to the memory. I paused long enough to wonder at the depth of my sadness for a man I'd known for such a short time. Later I'd realize I was also weeping for a future lost.

"I thought I knew where he was posted. But because of the censors, he couldn't tell me exactly what town. So, when I arrived in St. Omer in France, I spoke to the Matron there who used her own communication system—matron to matron, captain to captain, doctor to doctor—to follow his trail. To find him.

"When he left me at Orpington Hospital in England, he'd gone back to a Canadian Casualty Clearing Station in Étaples, one of the postings he'd requested in France. There, I guess, he'd created a bit of a name for himself with the military, outspoken as he could be about sending men back to the front when they were not fully recovered. Doctors, nurses, orderlies, and patients admired him. Some even loved him. I was among those. But the military world was not happy with what some called 'insubordination.'"

I wrapped a gray army blanket around my shoulders

and let my feet settle into Jennie's lap. Telling the story gave a softness to my grief. Misty eyes blurred the edges of it. "And me? Shortly after arriving at CCS at St. Omer, I was sent to Longuenesse where they'd asked for replacements, and from there, in a few days, I was sent on to Étaples.

"You know how that goes, don't you Jennie? Sometimes you arrive at a posting, you'll be there for two days and then be told you're moving again. St. Omer was shelled and bombed on May 12, which could be why I was moved on so quickly, only to come here and be bombed."

Jennie nodded. "Oh, yeah, I know about moving. I was sent to Salonika on the Mediterranean Front and had hardly put my bag down before I was sent back here."

Her words sounded distant. *How am I having a conversation? How could I be telling this story?* I felt another strange moment of normalcy. *Everything will be all right. We'll figure it out.* And the realization dropped again like a shadowed cloak. He was gone.

I felt Jennie's hands rubbing my feet, and I inhaled just to know that I could. "Keep going, Anna. Tell me about finding him."

I blew air between my lips and tugged the army blanket tight around my shoulders. *If I keep breathing, if I keep talking, I'll feel my body.* I looked around at the familiar, the photograph of Dad and Emily, Rose and Earl, and Ryan and Martha all standing straight, Martha's hand on Charlie's shoulder. Charlie sat in an old leather chair, and he held the wee girl, Sarah Rose.

Something about that photograph urged me on. I tumbled back into the story of Andrew and me. "I boarded an ambulance train and took care of the wounded men while I traveled to Étaples. That trip is a blur, but what I remember most, as I sit here now, is the look on his face when I arrived with those wounded men."

"Did he know you were coming?"

"No. I just took my orders, packed my kit, and left Longuenesse. When he saw me, neither of us moved, neither of us said a word."

I knew I was approaching the end of my story, but I needed to tell Jennie what Andrew and I had talked about, and what we'd hoped for. I slid off the bed onto the floor beside her. I took the army blanket and covered our knees. I closed my eyes.

"'We'll go home together,' he said to me when I walked up to him that day. We just stood and looked at each other. He spoke with such assurance I knew he'd figured it out. All we had to do now was wait out the war. I believed him."

Jennie was quiet for a moment, then she took a breath and asked me, "Did you and Andrew have any time, just the two of you?"

"These days, when the next day or the next hour could be our last, the world wasn't clean-cut. Life was grasped by many men and women. The present moment. But Andrew and I, for some inexplicable reason, had felt indestructible. We had held onto the possibility of intimate moments somewhere far from the war. We spent those hours we had together in operating tents, which in some ways were our intimate moments. Our work together was magical, people said. My memories of him will forever be how he worked to save a life. How he was always the last person around an operating room to give up. After those hours, we'd go to his hut and lie down together and hold one another."

"Anna? What are you remembering now, today?"

I leaned my head back against the cot and closed my eyes.

"I remember how soft his voice was when he'd be talking with a patient, particularly young boys who came in on the verge of dying. I remember how gentle his touch was even as he operated. And oh, I remember how we sat in the early hours of a morning when the artillery had become quiet and the silence seemed to hold us in a kind of limbo. Some nights when we'd walk back to our huts, we'd talk about the soldier whose life we'd just saved. Andrew always wanted one of us to write to the family even though we knew the military had a protocol. Once a patient, lying there on the table, asked Andrew if he had a sweetheart back home, and he answered, 'Nope, she's right here. Standing beside me.' I'd grinned, mostly because we weren't supposed to fraternize. But we lived our lifetimes in the middle of a war."

I opened my eyes and caught Jennie wiping her cheeks on the scratchy, wool blanket.

"Thank you, Jennie, you are a good friend. And when I leave for England tomorrow you get to keep my army blanket."

For the first time in what seemed a long time, we giggled a little.

◆

ANOTHER KIT BAG PACKED. ANOTHER SERIES OF GOODbyes. A train pulling from another station.

Matron had asked me to take time on the trip back to England to rest, to sit quietly.

"There are enough other Nursing Sisters on board this train and on the hospital ship who are signed on to take care of the patients. You will not begin your duties till you're back at Orpington. Do you hear what I am saying? Or do I have to order you?"

I smiled and reached my hand to her, and for an extra moment we stood in a firm handclasp. "Take care of yourself, Sister Anna. You have brought honor to all the nurses. Where you are going will not be easy, tending to men who are in constant pain or who may never walk again. But you are just the nurse to help them return to life."

I wasn't too sure how I could do something for a wounded soldier that I thought I'd never be able to do for myself, but I smiled my gratitude, let my hand drop, picked up my bag, and climbed onto the train.

◆

## Orpington Canadian Military Hospital

How could it be?

My days at Orpington were restoring my broken spirit.

All those months ago I had come here, irritated and unsettled because I wanted to go back to France, and Andrew, in what I considered a Machiavellian manner, had me sent to this place. How he'd done that he'd never revealed to me, then or even after we found each other in Étaples.

Now I was back at No. 16 Canadian General Hospital, and in some mystical way it had been Andrew's doing. Andrew's death dropped me into dark places, yet with Jennie and Matron's help, I found my way back, back to this hospital—and it was here I began to reclaim parts of myself I thought I'd lost forever. Parts reclaimed, yet changed.

During my off hours I'd walk the roads, and I'd breathe in the scent of the hedgerows fragrant with the cream of hawthorn blossoms. It was as though Andrew had once again spirited me to a healing place.

And it was here as well, over the thousands of miles between us, that Martha and I began to construct a plan that bonded us more than we'd ever imagined could be possible. A bond that took us into our shared future.

◆

I'D BEEN ASSIGNED TO THE PSYCHIATRIC WARD SHORTLY after I arrived at No. 16 Canadian, where I was attending patients who were going to be transferred back to Canada. They were neurasthenic, some of them forever mentally wounded. When Matron here at the hospital read my records and discovered my convalescent time at Margate, she'd sat me down in her office for a heart-to-heart talk. I remember my anxiety that day as I sat opposite her, wondering why I'd been called in.

"Sister Anna, did you choose to go back to France after your convalescence and your work here at Orpington?"

I wasn't sure if she was puzzled or if she thought I might be a bit bonkers.

"Yes, Matron, I did. I asked for a posting back in France and I was intent on returning."

"What moved you to go back when many would have welcomed the option to stay here or be moved to a hospital in Canada?"

I didn't answer right away. A breeze caught the curtain at the open window and lessened the heat of an unusually warm July day in Kent. Matron sat erect.

Using her official rank, I began, "Captain…" She smiled and shook her head with a slow back and forth.

"No, Anna, this is not an official discussion. Your records contain descriptions of your spirit and determination throughout this war, even when you yourself succumbed to what some military people want to call nerves. I do not choose that word. I rather think you became tired of the horror. And…you chose to go back there. Why?"

My shoulders rested, and my starched apron settled under my folded hands.

My voice was strong when I replied, "Because I wanted to finish what I started all those years ago, and because I needed to find my friend."

"Have you finished?"

"Not till this war is over."

"You are unique among us all, do you know that?"

"I don't think so, Matron. I've met and worked with many more like me…nurses and doctors." It was here my voice broke. She waited and asked for no more explanation. I received my assignment for the rest of my posting at No. 16 to work with the boys in the psychiatric ward.

Throughout my next days and nights, I sat with those who had slogged through mud to their knees, who'd endured shells and shock from blast after blast after blast. It was as though some dark force had passed through the air and through their brains, yet leaving no sign of injury. I'd found a calling, so Matron said.

One day I came off duty, weary from hours of staying with Eddie, who wanted more than anything to have me place a pillow over his face…hours of quiet talk…hours of listening as he told me about watching his buddy get decapitated…a story he needed to tell again and again until he took his sleeping draught.

Back in my room I sank into a lovely leather chair, one donated by some kind person in Ontario. The chair brought the image of my father into the room, how I'd sit in his old leather wingback chair in his office while he told me student stories. *How was he?* I realized I missed him very much that night.

I spied a letter that sat on the desk there at the bottom of my bed.

The handwriting was Emily's.

# Chapter Twenty-Two

*Let each man be judged*
*By his deeds.*
*I have paid my price to live with myself on the terms*
*That I willed.*

—Rudyard Kipling, "The Refined Man"

## October 1918 ◆ Kingston, Ontario ◆ Martha

THE TRAIN ROUNDED THE CURVE, STEAM ANNOUNCING her return. I stood once again on the wooden platform waiting to greet someone I loved, someone returning from the war.

Charlie stood at my side, leaning on his cane. Emily and Owen had opted to stay sitting in his Ford parked by the station.

Rose and Earl had said they felt only Anna's family need be there to greet her. "It's an important occasion," Rose had said as she stood facing me and shifted the sweater coat upon my shoulders for the third time. "This is for family. We'll see Anna later when she's home and settled."

One other waited for Anna. Sarah Rose, dressed in the yellow sweater and bonnet that Emily had knit for her, leaned into me, her plump hands grasping at my hair. I'd wondered about bringing her to the station with the noise and crowds, but she laughed and clapped her hands as the train pulled in. Sarah Rose was afraid of no one and nothing. She'd wanted to stand between the two of us; she knew something special was about to happen, but I felt better holding her in my arms. She'd discovered running before walking, so we knew our girl would be off in an instant chasing after the train.

Could she be a reason Charlie had made attempts, every so often, to walk out to the barn? The two of them were a sight—he, limping, dragging one foot, she pulling at his hand. Today he'd walked with his cane from the car to the train platform.

Ryan was Charlie's other miracle worker. Ryan, who was now my height, knew every cow in the barn and knew how to grow and harvest his own vegetable garden, which flourished and fed us with carrots, lettuce, beans, and my favorite, tomatoes. I could almost believe we were a family, that all was well.

Yet, as I stood beside Charlie, I felt the shadow of his distance from me. Something was still broken inside him. I couldn't get in there to help him. He wouldn't let me.

The whistle of the train, the grinding of its wheels, shook me from the dark places that lingered, and I let the excitement of seeing Anna overtake me. I gathered Sarah into my arms as she bounced and kicked against me. "Down, down," she commanded. Charlie lifted his arm and patted her back, a smile creasing his face. "Hey, Duffer, your Auntie Anna's on that train. Be good, now."

People on the platform moved in clusters to the steps as the conductor lowered them. He stood for a moment, hand on the railing, and surveyed the sky over our heads. "Kingston," he called out. As he stepped to the platform he turned, his arm stretched up to a hand reaching down. He took a cloth bag from the hand, a faded worn valise that looked like it had traveled many miles.

"There she is!" I hollered. "Anna! Anna!" Sarah Rose jounced and bounced in my arms as I ran through the crowd toward her. Laughter burbled from my chest to my throat. I heard myself hooting. Sarah Rose put her hands over her ears. "Mama, Mama!" she called with a grin, catching my joy. In seconds, running as I was, Anna and I were two steps apart. A sob like an exclamation escaped—I wasn't sure if it was hers or mine. Sarah Rose grasped her arms around my neck at the same time that I threw one arm around Anna's shoulders.

"Martha, Martha, dear, dear Martha." All those years. We held the moment until a small hand patted and pushed against my face. "Mama?" And all three of us laughed.

A hand clasped my back, another outstretched to Anna, "Boy, Martha has sure missed you." Charlie was behind me, reaching around to introduce himself.

What was I doing? "Anna, you've not met Charlie."

When I pulled away from her, she moved toward him and grasped his hand, a slow smile trained upon his face. "Oh yes, I've met you, Charlie. Hundreds of times. All those boys I cared for—you are forever them."

His eyes shadowed for an instant. I wondered if he might begrudge her assumption that she knew about horror, his brand of horror. A smile tried and played around his lips but was gone. "Pleased to meet you, Anna." He reached a hand to her.

Anna was nonplussed throughout the few seconds. Her hand enclosed his. The depot, the people greeting others from the train, swirled around us like a mist. Within another moment I realized Emily was standing there. She'd moved a measured step at a time from the car over to Anna and the rest of us. Owen chose to wait until we beckoned him to come over. The crowd dispersed as the train pulled away, some women holding the arm of a soldier, some wiping their eyes, some laughing. We stood in silence, the six of us. The sound of the train dwindled down the tracks.

"Charlie, take her." I held Sarah out to Charlie, and she giggled as she reached for her dad. Emily whispered to Anna, "Thank you for coming home." I barely heard but I saw her eyes shine.

In the pocket of my dress, I held the last letter I'd received from Anna. She'd written:

> *I'm coming home, Martha. Matron said, "You're going home, Sister." Of all the people who'll wait for me, I want you to know I'm coming home and please be there when I arrive. I'm excited, I'm terrified, and I'm grateful. So many cannot say "I'm coming home." Young boys and Sisters who were my friends—they will stay here in French soil, forever.*
>
> *Matron-in-Chief MacDonald has given the word that this is not a furlough, this is the end of the war for me. I've fought it in my way, we all have, doctors, nurses, soldiers who've died, and those coming home. Loss is everywhere and a part of me remains in France buried in a grave in Étaples. My heart has been ripped to pieces. Now I want to put myself back together. Will you help me? Word is around and about that we could be nearing the final days of this war but I'm tired—I can't wait—I can't look into those boys' eyes any longer—soldiers whose lives are forever shattered.*
>
> *I received a letter from you and one from Emily. Those two letters brought me home. What you and*

*Emily say concerns me, believing I might be able to help Charlie, so, my dear cousin, we'll do this, you and I together. If he is in deep despair as you've described, he's going to need gentle care. I've seen so many Charlies—he is a lucky man to have his family gather around him. I will be there, and I will do what I can.*

I held her letter there in my pocket like a kind of talisman, like the shamrock I'd pressed into the pages of my Bible before I'd crossed the Atlantic. Anna's words were a promise and a hope. Now she was home, but something about the Anna I knew was missing. Her eyes were clouded. Maybe she was tired. She was thinner than I remembered. Her navy blue uniform, buttons shining on her jacket, her brimmed hat covering her hair, which she'd pulled into a bun, all gave her distinction, but her spirit…no, her spirit had dulled.

I reached for her cloth bag, but she stopped my hand in midair. "I'll get that, Martha. I've carried it across the ocean. I'm kind of attached to it now."

"Do you have other bags?" Charlie asked. He knew the rigorous details of coming home.

"They'll be on their way sometime soon, I expect. For now, I'm traveling light. You remember that, eh, Charlie? Traveling light?" A glimmer of a smile played at the corners of her mouth.

He spoke, an edge of bitter memory staining his words. "Yeah. Brit Lee-Enfield gun, a bayonet, a knife, maybe a couple of grenades." He shifted Sarah Rose from one hip to the other. "Dragging around a lot more weight now carrying my Duffer here." His eyes lightened. Anna smiled at him. She knew exactly what he was describing.

"What's a Brit Lee-Enfield?" I'd watched the two of them make what seemed like an immediate connection. They held a shared story, one I couldn't relate to. I wanted to know all that he'd kept so secretive from me. What and why was he hiding out in his experiences, not letting me in? Maybe Anna could help him disentangle his pain. I'd not yet seen a way through to discover what we might have been.

"It's what kept me alive sometimes, Mart." He let Sarah Rose down to the platform and offered his oversized hand. She wobbled and grasped his fingers, gaining her balance. There was a catch in my throat. I watched them turn and walk toward Emily and Owen, who were making their way to the car.

"Tell Mart what a Lee-Enfield is, Anna," he called over his shoulder.

"It's the rifle he carried. But he'd probably rather forget it altogether."

I hesitated there on the platform. Anna, who seemed to be off somewhere, didn't move or try to follow the others, now standing by their cars. That's when I saw her waver. I reached for her hand. "Anna?" She turned away from the curious eyes of our family, put her hand over her mouth. Her shoulders shook. When she dropped her hand and looked over to me, her eyes were bleak, her forehead creased with lines I hadn't noticed until now. We were two women changed by a war that had rocked each of our worlds. Neither of us spoke, until Anna. "None of this place feels real, Martha. I understand how Charlie might feel. Where do I go now? What do I do?"

I wanted to answer her. I wanted to say "Come with us. Come with me. Come to the farm." But I hadn't the courage. Anna had always been the brave one, the one who knew what to do. She'd been so assured for that instant when she connected with Charlie. Now she appeared fragile, like a bruised animal. I fumbled with her coat buttons like a mother who wanted to comfort her child but not knowing how.

Something dropped inside me that felt like my heart opening. A fierce caring. "I know where you belong at least today, maybe tomorrow." I felt like the keeper of the watch for Anna. "And I'll take care of you." The words tumbled from my mouth. "Why don't you come home with Charlie, Sarah, and me? It'll be noisy and a bit chaotic."

Anna's face crumpled before she took a breath. Something told me she needed the innocent noise of Sarah's gleeful shouts when Ryan took her on his shoulders and twirled. She needed the lilt of Rose's song while she baked, and Jake's bark as he announced his entrance accompanied by Earl, both back from bringing the cows home. Each and every sound life-giving.

She said nothing. I swallowed several times, to keep from yelling out at her, "Let me help you. Charlie won't let me help him. Please let me help you."

"You see…" She clenched my arm with a grip that dug into my skin. "I'm scared, Martha. I'm scared." That was my prompt. Everyone had moved away to their cars and stood in a silent pause. They were waiting for me to say what was next. I held the answer for Anna.

I called over to Emily and Owen, "Could you come over here for just a moment?"

"Anna?" Owen reached his hand to her as he approached. Emily looked to me. I shook my head to caution her. "Uncle Owen, I think…" Anna's hand still clung to my arm. "I think Anna…" Anna dropped her hand from my arm and stepped to her father.

"Dad, I'm not good. Would you understand if I went along with Martha for a couple of days? When I've sorted myself, I'll take the train back home to you?" I saw a woman and her father making room for the changes wrought by a war. I wondered if I'd been able to do that for Charlie.

Uncle Owen stepped back, slanting his head to his shoulder, and a puzzled frown crossed his face for a second. I wanted to cheer for him and his goodness. He placed both hands, one on each of Anna's shoulders. If I hadn't known any better, I'd swear he was blessing her.

"Remember what I'd say to you, Anna, when you were a girl and the world was too confusing?"

"I don't remember," she whispered.

"I'd say, 'Anna, girl, go to a place where people are laughing, and where you feel safe.'"

For the first time that day, Anna's face lit. "I do remember that. I'd go find my friend Ruby—remember how many brothers she had? They always seemed to be laughing."

Her voice dropped away. I smiled over at Uncle Owen and mouthed the words. "Thank you."

◆

THE FARM WELCOMED US BACK. ANNA UNPACKED SOME of her belongings, then sat in the kitchen with me. We breathed in the scent of Rose's apple pies and butter tarts.

I'd sat quietly throughout the trip back from Kingston, a two-hour ride with sporadic clusters of conversation. Sarah Rose had slept in my lap. Charlie had driven with that driver's face intent on the road. Anna had closed her eyes every so often. I was unsettled. I was glad I'd asked Anna to come with us, and I admit I was feeling a small sense of pride that I'd been the one to step forth and untangle a bewildering moment for Anna and everyone. Now what? Was I to hand over my confusion about Charlie? Say, "Here Anna, you fix him?" What if she could help where I'd been helpless?

I didn't know what to do from here. What now?

◆

I heard Earl's shouts from the barn all the way into the kitchen. "Ryan's fallen. I need some help out here!"

Charlie, who'd been putting Sarah Rose down for her late afternoon nap, came down the stairs, moving faster than I had seen since he'd arrived home. He clung to the railing all the way down, but he moved like a storm gathering.

Anna and I had been peeling potatoes for supper. She was first to jump up, as though ready for a convoy of wounded soldiers. "On my way, Earl," she called as she dashed for the door, with Charlie at her heels. The door flung back on its hinges as she called over her shoulder, "Martha, get that wool blanket that's on the chesterfield. Rose, get some…"

"Got it," said Rose, throwing chopped ice from the icebox into a pan.

Charlie and Anna were heroes that day, both pulling on their wartime be-at-the-ready training. They worked like a well-oiled team, Anna charging everyone to leave Ryan on the haymow without moving him.

"I need to be sure he's not broken anything."

Ryan, who kept trying to stand up, received Anna's best lieutenant voice: "Stay still, Ryan!"

Charlie climbed to the haymow with Anna, and the two, with occasional quiet comments to each other, determined Ryan was all in one piece, nothing broken or twisted.

I stood watching them work together with mixed feelings of admiration for their resourcefulness and envy at the shared way they took on a crisis. Somewhere in me I wanted to be the person Charlie could turn to, as he did with Anna. When I moved that shadow part of me aside, I was more grateful to Anna than I was envious. And I saw the possibility of mutual respect emerging between them.

We'd been right to urge Anna to come home with us. She and Charlie could help each other return from their mutual hells. My *"What now?"* had an answer. Anna would help me get my Charlie back, and she would become an important part of this family, forever. And Ryan survived his fall, which he admitted later wasn't the first tumble he'd had from the loft.

# Chapter Twenty-Three

*Who shall we follow next?*
*Who shall we kill next time?*

—William Stafford, "At the Grave of
My Brother: Bomber Pilot"

## Martha

Three days later, Charlie took the horse Dusty and the buggy to collect the rest of Anna's luggage from the train station in Athens. He'd arranged with the station master to take it off the train in Kingston and send it along on the rural train through the northern part of the county. Anna rode with him.

"They need more time alone," I'd told Earl, who'd offered to drive them. What we'd all seen in the midst of the flurry of activity around Ryan was a subtle shift in Charlie. Ryan's fall had triggered some kind of clearing in Charlie's brain. He'd watched Anna carefully as she ensured that the boy bore no broken bones or sprained joints.

◆

"You've had a nasty fall this time, Ryan, so lie still while Sister tends to you," he'd said. I noticed how Charlie automatically called her "Sister," as he would have when the noise of artillery filled his senses. Anna had swooped into full nursing mode when she ordered Ryan to lie still on the haymow where he'd fallen.

I'd listened and watched. "All right, Ryan. Tell me where it hurts," she'd ordered as she sat down in the haymow beside him. Charlie, behind me, stood watching Ryan's expression. He knew physical pain and the face of it. He knew, too, that with Ryan's life experiences back on the streets of Dublin, he'd go into that dark place where it was dangerous to admit weakness. Charlie knew all about that.

As I saw Charlie and Anna working like a medical team seasoned by years of carnage, I sensed a bond beginning to weave between them. Two damaged people worked in sync to ensure that Ryan was all right, just as Anna would have done every day in some hospital, and Charlie in some trench.

"What do you think, Charlie? You know Ryan. Is he trying to be a hero?"

"Gee, I don't know, Sister Anna. He looks kinda pale to me."

She put her hand under Ryan's leg, and I was moved by her gentle motion as she lifted it. "Does this hurt, Ryan?" she asked.

"Nope."

Each time she tried a different joint his answer remained the same, with only a slight wince when she lifted his ankle.

"Ryan, bud, are you telling Sister the truth?" Again, Charlie referred to Anna as Sister, just as he might were he in a Casualty Clearing Station assisting with a wounded soldier.

"Yep," Ryan answered.

As she sat back and settled into the haymow, she spoke to Charlie and smiled down at Ryan.

"I think he may have a slight sprain in one ankle. What do you think, Sergeant Sloan?"

OUT OF PLACE 213

"Brave soldier he is, Sister."

Charlie and Anna helped Ryan to his feet and encouraged him to lean against them.

"We'll go to the house, Ryan." I thought I could hear the tone of her best Sister Lieutenant voice. "But you mustn't put your weight on that foot yet. Lean on Charlie."

"You sound like you've given orders before, Sister." Charlie gave her a nod as he started back to the house, his arm a support for Ryan. Before he'd gone far, Anna called out to him.

"Will you drop the 'Sister,' Charlie? I'm no longer a lieutenant or even a Nursing Sister. I'm just Anna."

Something inside me felt a moment of irritation, like jealousy. Was I envious of their banter? I wasn't sure what this might be about.

"That'll be a hard one for me, not to call you Sister. I look at you now, I watched you with my boy," he flicked the runaway piece of hair on Ryan's forehead "and I see those faces of nurses who were always there, especially when I'd given up."

"When I'd given up." I heard him admit right then that he'd almost given in. But that world he'd opened to Anna. Not to me.

The feeling caught my chest—*Why not me, Charlie, why not me?* I knew that soldiers who held their pain close often couldn't tell someone in a family, even someone who loved them. Someone like me. He'd declared his anguish to Anna, not me.

But, then…Ryan, as Ryan could, dropped the heart of the story into the midst of us. With a hop, he faced Charlie. "Are you gonna tell Anna stories of your war? She was at the same war as you, ya know."

All of us—me, Charlie, and Anna—sucked in a breath. I wasn't sure whether to laugh, snort, or grab Ryan by his ear.

The air hung on a breeze and waited. Charlie turned back to us and put his arm across Ryan's shoulder. Charlie's eyes were brighter. Still, his shoulders slumped.

"Nah, Ryan, Anna's seen it all. She doesn't need to hear my tales."

At this moment Anna stood and brushed the hay from her skirt. A pigeon flew across the upper reaches of the barn roof and lit on a beam just above Charlie's head. Anna walked to Charlie and trained that determined gaze of hers on his face.

"There. See?" She pointed at the bird. "Even the pigeons want to know your story."

She beckoned me over to Charlie and Ryan. "Martha, why don't you help Ryan back to the house. Charlie, I need to tell you a bit of what happened to me…I haven't really told anyone here except letters to Martha. Would you hear me out?"

Charlie nodded.

"What do you think, Martha, if Charlie and I share war stories while you take Ryan to the house?" I took a second to answer, but I knew, without a doubt now, this is what Charlie needed, what Anna needed, and what I needed.

"Okay, Ryan." I took his arm from Charlie's shoulder and placed it in the crook of my elbow. "Let's you and I go find some ice and get Ma Rose to work her magic."

We left Charlie and Anna, who'd dropped onto the haymow that had cushioned Ryan's fall.

As I opened the door I heard them begin to talk.

"So, Vimy? What a feat that was. Which Canadian division were you with, Charlie?"

I slid the door shut, walked Ryan out into the autumn air, and left the two damaged souls to begin repairing each other.

# Chapter Twenty-Four

**Anna**

Dusty flicked his tail as he ambled. Dusty would go from a trot to a stroll, depending on Charlie's urgings, or his contemplative moments.

It was during one of those moments that he pulled back on the reins and Dusty halted. When Charlie turned to face me directly, I knew the question was on its way.

"So, why are you home?"

Elbows on my knees, my hands clasped together, I studied my shiny black boots.

Without looking up, I spoke my truth and the family's.

"I was tired. Wounded men kept coming. Lives and minds shattered. Some days all I could do was hold a hand," I said. "And, I left my future buried in Étaples."

Charlie put his hand over my clasped fists and held it there.

"I know about your doctor, Anna. I'm really sorry."

I thought I was done with crying but sitting in that wagon—Dusty's tail flipping back and forth, Charlie's sorrow—wetness blurred my vision. I wiped my face with my sleeve.

"I need to find my way back to life," I said. "And you do too, I suspect."

He picked up the reins, stared at Dusty's rump, and clicked his tongue. We moved a few feet and stopped. Dusty turned his head and looked at Charlie as though to say, *Are we going forward or not!*

"So where will we start?" he asked.

"At the beginning," I said, and listened.

Charlie held the reins tight. "Vimy was a mountain of mud that April. Colder than hell, if you can imagine hell freezing. I think it must have been the coldest spring in a long time. We sat in trenches, waiting. I'd just finished a week in the rear trenches and I was back in the front line. Easter Sunday—waiting for the storm to begin. Imagine if you can…"

For a moment I thought he'd become lost in the memory of the place, of the horror. He sat with the reins in his hands staring off beyond Dusty, beyond the road ahead—to the shouting and the screaming and the smoke, the twisted wire, the men hanging on the barbed wire…

I waited. My inclination was to tell him I understood, that I knew the picture well that he was painting. Instead, I let the silence be. I watched him bow his head for a second, and then lift his face to the sky. Was he even breathing? But he let a breath flow between his lips, as he might have done while waiting, waiting in that trench.

"…in those trenches men smoked and talked—some just sat on ammunition boxes and leaned against the chalk walls. We could hear the Canadian artillery—and somewhere inside I think we hoped they'd finish the Fritzes before we had to go over the top. Geez, Anna, a friend of mine down a ways from me was sprawled on his behind writing a letter to his girlfriend in Toronto. It was the last letter he wrote." I wondered if he'd go silent again. Was this a bad idea?

"Charlie? You don't have to." I knew how painful it would be for him to find the words, but I hadn't realized how deeply sad I'd feel, how desolate. The two of us were joined together in images of sounds, mud, and frozen fear.

The quiet surrounded us. Off in the distance I could see the train station and I wondered whether Charlie had reached some place in his memory that was closing down again. Shutting us out. But as we made our way where the road narrowed into a dirt square, Charlie gave a flick of the reins and Dusty guided the wagon right to the station platform. He placed the reins on my lap.

"What's this?" I'd not driven a horse since a stint with the ambulance drivers at Étaples. "You want me to drive?"

"Yep," he answered, as he clambered down to the ground. "I'll get your luggage, put it in the back, and while you drive us home, I'll spit up the rest of what brews inside me."

A bit shocked at his words and the prospect of driving back, I protested.

"No, Charlie, I'm not sure I'm any good—why don't I just sit and listen?"

"You'll be fine. I know you've driven ambulances, Martha told me. And I need to talk. I really need to talk." When he turned back to me, he was already standing on the train platform, his eyes brimming. "Please."

When my two cases were stowed in the back, he climbed up beside me, rested his boot on the foot rail, and stared ahead. "Let's go home, Anna. I have more to say, so take 'er slow."

By the time we turned into the lane to the farmhouse, my chest held the heaviness of his loathing for war, for images that would not be erased: one minute talking to the man next to him, the next watching a bullet take off the top of his head.

There beside me, Charlie became a man living a hell he'd not been able to share with anyone—I'd seen what he'd seen. I knew every story.

Men with legs blown off, lying in the mud, dying.

A man who'd begged Charlie to shoot him.

The roll call in the days following Vimy, when more often than not a name was called with only silence responding.

Shell holes filled with bloody water.

The dead left, because stretcher-bearers hunted for the living.

The smell of lime, spread to keep disease at bay.

The ungodly, ear-splitting, never-ending roar.

His last sentence as we pulled up to the barn was strangely remote, almost as though he was speaking from a view far above the carnage.

"The ninth of April was a hell of a long day."

I jumped down from the wagon and decided to leave Charlie there until he felt ready to come in. But then I stalled midstep, walked around the wagon and put my hand on Charlie's knee. He was weeping silent tears. "I lived…why?" he whispered. I stood waiting.

When he dropped down from the wagon, I reached my arms up to him and buried his face into my shoulder. We stood like that for a few moments. As I let go I heard a small "Thank you."

I walked to the house and didn't look back. They greeted me at the door, Martha and Sarah Rose.

I looked into Martha's eyes, "He's going to be okay. Go marry him." And I walked into the house.

# Chapter Twenty-Five

November 11, 1918 ♦ Martha

"Be sure that you stay here in your room." Anna grinned as she walked to my bedroom door. "Don't even consider coming out to look over the railing. You need to come down those stairs like a woman they've never seen before. Wait until you hear Rose playing the wedding march. Promise?"

"I promise." I knew I was blushing, which gave me an effervescent feeling, as though I'd already had champagne.

In about an hour, Charlie and I would be husband and wife. Here I was, a bride ready to give my heart to Charlie Sloan, father of our daughter Sarah Rose, son of Earl and Rose, soldier and hero to all of us, particularly Ryan. Miracles had occurred in the past few weeks—the world had shifted on its axis and righted itself. Whatever happened between Anna and Charlie that day in October, and whatever continued to unfold over the two weeks she decided to stay with us, she'd helped Charlie search out his soul.

One evening out in the barn, the two of us, Charlie and I, sat on hay bales. There I saw a glimmer of him coming back to me. He took my hand and with a funny grin said, "Mart, I just want you to be ready because at supper tonight, I have a question for you."

And he did.

That night he reached over as we finished our stew and apple pie, took my hand, and there in front of everyone, with Ryan giggling and Sarah Rose blowing bubbles, he asked me to be his wife. Anna, Earl, and Rose clapped their hands. Sarah thought it was a party and joined in the applause. Ryan grinned. For the first time, possibly in my life, I was mute.

Now, today, dressed in a cream silk gown fashioned and sewn by Rose, I sat on my bed, waiting. I fingered the fringe on the cape she'd given me, the yellow cape she'd worn when she and Earl were married.

I could hear the commotion down in the front hallway. Voices floated up through the vent. I heard Ryan's attempt at whispering, Sarah Rose's squeaky laugh, and Earl's deep chuckle.

"They're here," I heard Rose call out.

I made my way over to the window. Below on the circle drive were Owen and Emily, Ryan tripping over his feet to offer his arm. I wondered and hoped there might be a place in my body where I could hold and keep this dancing delight, hold it and come back to it someday when I might need it.

Something more was happening. Owen was waving a newspaper and laughing. I couldn't make out his words.

Charlie's tenor in full voice rose from the living room where we were to be married any minute. Rose was at the piano, but she wasn't playing the wedding march. It sounded like the song "Tipperary," loud and raucous.

Earl yelled up from the bottom of the stairs, "Come on down, Martha, come on, sing with us. It's a celebration."

I grabbed the hem of my dress and ran to the top of the stairs. "Earl! What's going on? What's happening down there?"

Owen, who came through the open door, stopped beside Earl and held up a newspaper for me. I could see the headlines:

FRANCO-BRITISH SWEEP ON WIDE FRONT:
CANADIANS PLAY PART IN GREAT VICTORY.

The war was over. We'd all found our way through to the end. I felt a calm like none I could remember for a long time. Anna was here, home, safe. Charlie was home, and I knew that, somehow, he'd be all right. Down below, with the singing and the laughter, the world seemed a possible place to live in once again.

"Martha, Anna. Come down. Come down. It's over. The war, it's over!" I wasn't sure but I thought I could see tears on Earl's face when he hollered up the stairs to Anna and me.

Anna stood by me, her hand in mine. Her eyes shone with some memory that I might never understand. She dropped down and sat on the top stair. I folded my wedding silk and touched down beside her. "Martha, it's done. It's over." I felt she'd left us for just a few seconds and gone back there to Andrew, to her friend Jennie, to Matron, and to all those boys she'd cared for.

She laughed, lifted herself, and turned to face me. "Wait here! I'm going down there. We have a wedding ready to start and a new world to welcome in the door. Don't move till I call you." She actually skipped down the stairs.

By the time I followed and arrived at the archway into the living room, everyone was standing in front of the fire that Charlie had built in the old stone fireplace. Ryan, Earl, Emily, and Owen were gathered beside him. I swallowed my surprise and delight to see Charlie in his dress uniform—crisp khakis, shining brown belt, and three chevrons sewed onto his sleeve. Sarah Rose stood holding his hand.

Rose at the piano began to play, then nodded over at Charlie, who turned to watch as I followed Anna into my new life. Without another breath, he began to sing. There would be no wedding march at our ceremony—he sang for all of us, and for those friends whom he knew would not be coming home.

*Keep the home fires burning, till the boys come home.*

While he sang, I walked up to him and took his hand. All of us joined in.

"Repeat after me, Charlie," the pastor said.

But before he could begin the familiar phrases, Charlie placed the ring on my finger, bent down, lifted Sarah Rose, and held her between us while he turned to face me.

We held a collective breath.

"Martha McGrath, Sarah Rose Sloan," he began. "I promise to take care of you, to keep you safe from harm, and…" He paused and squeezed my hand. "And, I will stay by you as long as the world lasts. Or longer."

I felt a smile that began in my eyes and traveled to my lips. It was like the brush of a white feather. Sarah Rose sat back in Charlie's arms, her eyes intent on his face. I wondered if she knew this was a moment she'd want to keep safe within her blossoming memory. With our own words and thoughts winging to everyone around us, Charlie, Sarah Rose, and I became a family.

"You may kiss the bride." Pastor smiled. As Charlie leaned into me, still holding Sarah Rose, she, little as she was, placed her hand on my cheek, "Here, Daddy. Here," she said.

Laughter unfolded like ripples across the room.

"Time for dancing" Earl exclaimed. Rose played her favorite songs, Earl brought out his fiddle, and Owen sang in that deep baritone we loved to hear.

And Emily? Emily danced an Irish jig.

Later that night, after we'd eaten too much food, gobbled too much cake, sang until we were hoarse, Charlie and I clambered into Earl's Ford and set off down the lane, me waving, he honking the horn until we disappeared around the curve. For a few minutes I sat in the quiet of our newness, Charlie driving with one hand, his other in mine. I let myself remember the afternoon, the fireplace, the good wishes, the laughter. Yet somewhere within a flash of a memory, an image crossed my view—one that stood still for just a moment: Anna standing back from the family, her arms crossed, hands cresting on the crook of her elbows. She'd looked distant, detached from the frivolity, a smile playing lightly on her lips. Where is she, I wondered. But then Charlie slowed the car, pulled to the side of the road, took both my hands, and kissed them.

"I love you, Mrs. Sloan."

Anna drifted from my mind.

# Part Four

## The Rescue ◆ 1938

# Chapter Twenty-Six

*That failed hope doesn't prove the failure of hope is a comfort of sorts.*
—Wendell Berry, "The Handing Down"

### June 1938 ◆ Berlin

Dear Owen (Dr. Johnson),

I am writing to you as my dear colleague and friend. The events here in Germany have become increasingly frightening. I'm not sure what is being printed in Canadian newspapers. I won't elaborate except to say the German Jewish population is in grave danger.

Jewish professors have been dismissed from their university posts and I have lost my teaching role at the University of Berlin. I do have another source of income, which I cannot divulge right now. Only to say it is a private contract and could cause me some difficulty later on.

I have had many unexpected and horrid experiences over the past few years, but nothing compares to the growing fear I'm experiencing as I see Jewish businesses destroyed, synagogues ransacked. We've had to register all our assets with the Nazi government—many of my friends and colleagues are fleeing the country. Some say this will blow over, but I disagree. Just the other day, when I was bringing my girls home from school, we barely avoided a vicious mob.

My sorrow is doubly profound. My wife, Berta, had a serious heart condition, which worsened after Ilse's birth, and to which she succumbed when Olivia, our eldest daughter, was only three years old. If Berta were with me now, I know she would find a way to leave this country and take the girls to safety. Now it's up to me. I need to get my beloved Ilse (11 years) and Olivia (14 years) out of Germany. I fear the winds of war are fast approaching and I want to ensure that they're able to leave Europe. I need to know that they will be safe where none of this horror can touch them. This is why I write to you today.

Do you recall that Berta had a sister in a town very near your town of Kingston? I remember how we talked about that coincidence when we attended the conference in Hamburg in 1935. Sigrid, who is Berta's sister, has agreed in letters back and forth to take in Ilse and Olivia. However, she is not able to make the trip to get them to Canada. Owen, I'm asking if there is any way you might rescue my girls. I'd not be asking you to assume such a monumental task if I were able to do any of this myself. I've tried to renew my own passport and was turned down by the Nazi government. I was able to acquire passports for the girls, even though they now have red Js on them, which identify them as Jewish. I'll try again to get permission to leave; however, there are some bureaucratic reasons, I'm afraid, for which the Nazi government does not want me to leave the country.

*I'm taking this letter to a Canadian Trade Commission in Berlin where I'll ask them to put it in their mail. My plan is to send Ilse and Olivia to England where I hope you might meet them and take them to Canada.*

*So many of us are desperate to find ways to send our children away. When I first had this conversation with a colleague from the university, I couldn't believe that he was suggesting I send the girls away from Germany, and Europe. But now I see it as the only way.*

*There are no words to express how grateful I'll be if you see a way clear to help me rescue Ilse and Olivia.*

*Your colleague and friend,*
*Simon Lansky*

◆

### July 1938 ◆ Kingston, Ontario ◆ Anna

THE LIGHT OVER THE BACK DOOR SHONE A WELCOME AS it had for these past few years when I'd arrive home from duty at the Kingston Asylum. It had been a tough night at the hospital, and I needed the warmth of the familiar limestone walls and dormer windows watching from the roof over the street below. I sat with my hands on the steering wheel and gazed over at the shrub roses Emily had coaxed into masses of glorious yellow, roses that she and Martha had planted together. I missed Martha, I missed her wisdom and her way of calming my soul when my sorrow for my patients in the hospital overwhelmed me. She always knew when I needed her, and she'd come.

One of our patients had been agitated most of the night. He was one of the sorrow-ridden soldiers who'd come home from the Great War later than most and had been directly admitted into the Kingston Asylum. My heart was heavy for him. His family had gradually stopped coming to see him, which in a way I understood, as he became more psychotic and less like himself. Life had ended for him when shell shock set in and lucidity disappeared.

Now, at seven-thirty in the morning, I was home from my night shift, and I looked forward to the quiet and a peaceful sleep. A smile played at the corners of my lips, the first in many hours. My coupe still had that new car scent, which reminded me how lucky I felt to have resources, friends, and family all around me. And a brand-new red Ford coupe! The Great Depression throughout this decade had created so many sad stories. Dad had offered to help with my payments, but since being promoted to supervisor of a ward at the hospital, I felt sure I could afford this luxury. I was grateful to have a home with Dad and Emily. Living together was a boon to all of us, especially since Emily had had her stroke and Dad was finally slowing down.

I noticed a light in the kitchen window as I got out of my car, and I knew that Dad was up making his first cup of coffee and Emily's tea. The streets were silent on this summer morning, and I thought that Dad would be setting out to walk across the campus to his office at the university. It would be fruitless to try to persuade him to let me drive him over a couple of streets away. He, still the professor even though soon to retire, insisted on taking himself there even when there were no classes.

"Some student might need to talk to me," he'd argue.

My thoughts leaped over one another—the sadness at the hospital, my good fortune to be climbing the familiar steps of home, the bed that awaited. It wasn't until I'd come into the kitchen from the back hallway that I saw Dad sitting at the table. He was still dressed in his blue, striped pajamas, his tattered slippers barely covering his feet. My father never appeared in what he considered an undignified state of undress. What alarmed me most, though, was his apparent despondency, elbows balanced on the oilcloth covering, his hands over his face, his shoulders hunched.

The morning newspaper lay open beside him.

"Dad?"

When he looked up at me, his eyes were sad. I dropped my nurse's bag onto the floor, grasped a chair, and slid it over beside him.

"What is it? Is Emily all right?" When I put my arm across his shoulder, he reached for my hand.

"It's Simon, my friend in Germany. I just never believed…" The newspaper headlines brought my recent coffee gurgling into my throat.

*Not again, world. Please, not again.*

Synagogues vandalized in Berlin. Jewish businesses closed.

"What's going on, Dad? Has something happened to Dr. Lansky?" I watched as he straightened himself in his chair. His eyes cleared. His lips disappeared into a tight frown of determination.

As he rose from his chair, he reached down to take my hand. I had a flashing image of him bending down and lifting me to his knee, the day my mother died.

"A letter arrived from my friend Simon Lansky in Berlin. He was so good to me at that conference in Germany. Do you remember?"

"Of course I do, Dad. He almost persuaded you to stay and join the mathematics faculty there. What's happened?"

"Here, Anna." He handed me a letter. "This is what's happened."

Exhaustion spread through my body after I read the letter. I felt as I'd often had in France when life was sorrow and futility. "Oh, Dad. It's all happening again."

We sat, the two of us, and stared out the window, our helplessness on our shoulders like a familiar cloak.

"There's nothing I can do, Anna. I have no idea how I…me…fast becoming an old man…I'm not sure Simon knows how I've aged since last we saw one another…he's ten years younger. How soon could I get a passport?" He paused and rubbed his hands across his forehead, "Or am I just a coward who makes excuses?"

I understood his confusion because I'd known this sense of inadequacy. I saw the light of morning throw beams across the floor, and I heard the faint sound of Andrew's voice still echoing: *What do you think, Anna? What now?*

"I'll go, Dad. I'll find the girls." And I'd take Martha with me.

◆

## Louise Basin Docks, Quebec ◆ Martha

"Anna? Do you remember?"

I stood staring out at the huge side of the ship that we'd board in just a few moments.

I grasped and held onto her hand just the way I had twenty-five years ago. My life again offered adventure; this time I was aware that my decision to travel to England with Anna affected others. That fifteen-year-old girl in 1913 had been on her own traveling to a new life and a new country. I was a mother and a wife now, and I was responsible for helping run a farm that had become prosperous in spite of the Great Depression. Charlie's words were still vibrating: "Mart, do you have any idea how dangerous this whole journey might be? Anyhow, what do the lives of two little Jewish girls have to do with you?" We were out in the barn away from curious ears. I was glad no one else was around to hear his words.

"Charlie Sloan! I'm going to pretend I didn't hear you say that." I'd folded my arms and walked to the sliding door and put my hand on it to push when I felt his hand on my back.

"Mart, come back. Sit down. I'm sorry."

He'd known how that remark cut into the core of me. I'd been a lost child just as these girls were. I knew how agonizing this rupture was going to be for Ilse and Olivia because I shared their story. Carrying a sense of kinship, Anna and I were on our way to Southampton.

◆

THAT NIGHT I STOOD AT THE RAILING AND WATCHED THE stars lighting the dark sky as far as I could see. I'd left Anna asleep in her lower berth when I decided to take a stroll up top. Sleep was going to be elusive for me.

A man stood at the railing a few feet from me. His navy blue jacket and cream wool pants gave him the jaunty air of someone on a carefree cruise. We all knew better. Many passengers, I noticed on board this ship, avoided eye contact, each seeming in his or her own troubled world. Were they going to England to stay, or, like us, hoping to bring someone to safety? I tried not to stare, but he looked out of place on this tourist deck.

Suddenly, the ship zigged to one side and followed a different course. I grabbed the railing, afraid that something might be wrong.

"It's all right, ma'am." He'd moved down the railing and was a few feet from me. "There'll be a lot of zigging and zagging as we cross. The captain is being extra cautious."

"Why is that?" I asked. Afraid of the answer.

"Oh, there's been some nasty news coming out of Germany, particularly since their invasion into Austria last March."

"But what does that have to do with us going to England?" I was beginning to wish I hadn't come up on top.

"Being a former Navy man, I understand caution." He smiled, but I saw hesitation in his eyes. I began to wish I hadn't persuaded Charlie to stay home.

"Don't you worry, ma'am, I can't imagine that Fritz wants to take on Canada, which would mean Britain. By the way, how long will you be staying over there in England? Not long, I hope."

"Oh, not long." I turned. "Excuse me, sir. I need to check on my friend."

As I walked away. I could feel him watching. I opened the door into the outer hallway leading to the stairs down to our cabin. I felt my breath quicken as I walked along the corridor and felt the movement and the vibration of the ship's progress under my feet. I needed to remember—Anna had been very clear we were to say nothing about our reason for sailing to England. When I tiptoed into the room, Anna lay on her side asleep as though she were beginning an uneventful cruise. I wondered if she might have been so familiar with the unknown, she felt comfortable with it. Only another adventure.

I pulled my blanket from the top berth and crept back to the door. Anna murmured, sighed, and slept.

I made my way along the corridor to the tourist lounge

where I found a chair I could curl into under the cover of my blanket. I closed my eyes to discourage any passenger from approaching for conversation. A couple had pulled two chairs up to a small table and were involved in a game of chess. I was grateful for the quiet.

I wanted time on my own away from anyone, even Anna, to consider what lay ahead of us. Uncle Owen's concerns and his misgivings lay tucked in a part of my brain that alerted me to possibilities. Had we thought everything through?

The official papers that would allow the girls into Canada were in a leather folder. Uncle Owen had contacted two government friends who had signed permission for the girls to enter Canada…after he'd expressed his hesitation. Our passports were up to date…a letter from Ilse and Olivia's aunt declaring her guardianship. And a letter Anna had written that declared she would take care of and support the girls if anything happened to Aunt Sigrid.

When I asked, "Are you sure, Anna?" I received what the family called "the Anna Stare."

I pulled the wool blanket up under my chin. I imagined how it must have been for Miss Ashcroft when she shepherded all those Home Children and me from Liverpool to Quebec. No one was lost. What a miracle that was! As I drifted to sleep, I mulled over all the plans again.

The zigzagging of the ship lulled me like a rocker. I slept.

# Chapter Twenty-Seven

*It is a serious thing*
*Just to be alive*
*On this fresh morning*
*In this broken world.*

—Mary Oliver, "Invitation"

### August 1938 ◆ Berlin ◆ Olivia Lansky

I LAY ON MY BED, MY HEAD PROPPED UP ON TWO PILLOWS. My sister across the room was trying to stuff her overflowing suitcase. She pushed three of her dolls in among her favorite sweaters. "Aaargh." Frustration sounded like a gargle in the back of her throat.

"Ilse, you can't take three dolls to Canada. Papa said we each can have one suitcase. If you take three dolls, you'll have no room for clothes!"

I tried to sound like Mama. If only she were here. She'd be organizing us all, telling us to move slowly and think through everything we needed to take. Her gentle way of telling us what to do was a voice in my head. What we had to do today and for the next months, maybe years, Papa had told me quietly, was the most important thing we'd ever done. I wondered if he might have talked to the spirit of Mama about Ilse and me leaving our home.

*Mama, help me to be brave. Help me to take care of Ilse.*

"Ilse, please hurry, Frau Vogel will be here soon, and we

must be ready." I sounded impatient, and right away I was sorry. My sister scrunched her face, which usually made me laugh, but today I wanted to take her in my arms and tell her everything would be all right. But I couldn't. I didn't know what to say.

"I'm scared, Olivia." She stood in the middle of our tiny bedroom, her one bag on the floor. I'd watched as she'd stuffed and pushed a doll, a sweater, a dress, a pair of shoes, and her favorite book until the cloth sides bulged.

*What would Mama do? She'd get down on her knees and hold Ilse close.* It felt very strange for a moment as I walked over to my sister. She wasn't much shorter than me, so I held out my arms to her. Her head landed just under my chin. My arms circled her. I could feel her breath against my chest, her short sniffs damp with tears.

"Ilse, come sit with me." I took her by the hand, and with a few steps we flopped onto the bed. I let her have a few more sniffs. I waited as I sent a silent prayer to Mama.

*Help me do what you would do, say what you would say.*

I straightened my back, took Ilse's hand in mine, and turned to her. Mama had taught us to breathe before we said anything that might be difficult or hurtful, especially if we didn't know what to say or if we were scared.

"A long breath lets you think better," she'd say.

"Let's do this together now, Ilsy. Let's take a couple of really long breaths and let's talk about what Papa has told us to do. I think that'll help, don't you?" She wiped her fist across her eyes and nodded yes.

"All right, I'll start." I inhaled an extra-long breath that became a bit of a gasp, and Ilse giggled.

"It's going to be a great adventure…"

Ilse pursed her mouth the way she often did when I

tried to boss her.

"No, Ilse, it will be! We're going to a new country, and we're going to live with a family who knows Papa and who knew Mama, so they're not really strangers."

"Olivia." She sat up straight and looked me in the eye. "It's an adventure, but I know it's dangerous. Papa told us, and I want Papa to come with us!"

"You know he can't."

When Papa told us we were going to travel to Canada, he'd been honest. We knew there could be no arguing. Ilse and I could no longer go to our school, because we were Jewish. Papa had lost his job at the university, but for some reason he wouldn't be able to join us. That scared me, but I didn't tell him or Ilse that I was afraid about what might happen to him. Rumors flew around the community about families disappearing, and I had a good friend whom I'd not seen for days.

Mr. Schneider, who owned a grocery store around the corner, had come one morning to open up and found the windows smashed, and a huge black "J" written across the door.

"I know, I'd like Papa to come with us too, but he promised he'd come as soon as he could. For now, we need to do everything he says. Frau Vogel will be arriving soon, and we must be ready."

Ilse leaned forward and rested her elbow on one knee, her chin balanced on her fist. She scrunched her forehead again, as though considering what I'd just said. "Olivia? What did Papa mean when he said Frau Vogel could be in mortal danger? I don't know what that means…"

Papa had been so serious when he told us about Frau Vogel that I felt a place in my stomach turn to water, the way it would when I had to go to the bathroom.

"Frau Vogel," he'd said, "is a German who hates the Nazis. And that must forever be our secret. She knows we are Jewish—in fact, she came to me, I didn't go to her. She wants to help us. After I decided I could trust her I told her about sending you girls to Canada. By the way, she wants to go there soon too. I don't know how long she can carry on with what she's been doing."

"Why, Papa?" Ilse had asked.

"Because what she's doing, helping Jewish people..." Papa had stopped for a moment and put his hand over his mouth. "...is dangerous."

That's when I asked him.

"If she gets caught, Papa, what could happen to her?" I knew the answer. He'd said nothing in reply.

◆

"Olivia, Ilse, we need to hurry along. Frau Vogel will be at our door in half an hour. We need to be packed and ready." I heard Papa's call from the kitchen.

It all seemed normal, Ilse and I bickering, Papa hurrying us along, but nothing about what we were about to do was ordinary.

"It's a great adventure," he tried to tell us once again.

But right now, it all felt frightening, and I wasn't sure how I'd feel when we waved good-bye.

"Girls, can you bring your suitcases out to me? I have something I want to put in each of them." Grumbling and mumbling, Ilse shuffled out to the kitchen, dragged her suitcase across the floor, dropped it down, and sat on it. "Papa, Olivia is so mean."

"Ilse." I watched from the doorway of our room while he lifted her to his knee and wrapped his arms across her narrow chest. "How many dolls do you think you'll need in Canada? I am sure they have dolls in that country. Maybe there might be one waiting for you?"

"A Canadian doll, Papa?" She turned and looked into his eyes with a gaze that could have ripped his heart from his chest. But instead, he hugged her.

"Tante Anna and Tante Martha know all about dolls. They were little girls like you once." I didn't know these women, Tante Anna and Tante Martha, yet Papa trusted them to take us to a safe place. He'd been telling us stories about Anna and Martha since arrangements and plans had been put in place for the journey. In my own head, I tried not to think about how far away we'd be from him. "At least," he'd said, "I know where you'll be and who is taking care of you."

A quiet knock at the door startled me. "Should I answer it, Papa?"

"It's all right, Olivia, it's all right." He let Ilse jump down from his knee and stood up. "It might be Frau Vogel, she's early."

A knot collected in my chest as I walked to the door. The knocking sounded again, this time more insistent.

When I opened the door, Frau Vogel leaned in and grasped my wrist.

"Olivia. We need to go. We need to go now," her whisper hoarse and urgent. "Police are going into apartments across the city. Friends are telling me about people being brought out into the street and loaded into trucks." Her cheeks were flushed, and tendrils of hair had loosened from her braid. When I saw the fear in her eyes, I knew a kind of danger that weakened my knees.

Frau Vogel was a friend, a courageous friend who was putting her life in jeopardy. For us. "We must take the girls and go to the train station now. I have a car downstairs," she said.

I beckoned to Ilse, who was grasping Papa's hand.

"Come over here by me." I took her hand. I could feel my heart rushing the blood to my brain. My throat was raw from trying not to cry. Still holding Ilse's hand, I brought Frau Vogel into our apartment and closed the door.

"Where are they now, do you know? Where are the police?" Papa asked.

"I'm not sure, but I think we can't wait for a later train. We must go."

Frau Vogel picked up Ilse's suitcase. I dropped my sister's hand and picked up my cloth bag, room enough for sweaters, a dress, shoes, my hairbrush, underwear, and two books, one to read and one for writing my stories.

When Papa came to us his eyes were windows of tears. He held his arms out and enfolded us into his body. He kissed the tops of our heads, and for a few seconds we stood motionless.

I reached up to place my hand on his cheek. "We'll put a candle in the window every night for you, Papa. Just the way we always did when you'd be away." His arms dropped to his sides, yet I could feel him trembling. He put his hands on both our shoulders and steadied himself.

"Olivia, Ilse, here's what I need you to do. Go now with Frau Vogel. Do everything she tells you to do. Do not stray from her. When you are finally on the train, stay close by each other, hold hands. Talk to no one. Remember everything we talked about when we were planning. Look for the train to Cologne and when you reach the border …"

I looked over to Frau Vogel, who by now stood at the door, one foot already in motion.

"We've gone over this, Simon. I'll be sure they arrive safely. And we know what to do at the border, don't we? I will not leave them until I put them into the hands of Anna and Martha. We have to go. Now."

"We will do this, Papa, because you've taught us how to be brave." These were the only words I had left.

"And Papa…" Ilse's small voice had taken on a new confidence. "I don't need three dolls, I'll take Marianne."

"Simon?" Frau Vogel, hand on the door latch, looked to me, her mouth forming the words, "Say good-bye."

"Ich liebe dich," he whispered.

In the hallway, I heard the click of the latch.

Ilse, Frau Vogel, and I stepped toward the stairway and headed down.

◆

FRAU VOGEL HAD SAT QUIETLY ON THE TRAIN FROM Berlin most of the way to Belgium. Ilse and I kept our books on our laps, heads down, eyes on the print, but neither of us read. Every so often we'd steal a glance at other passengers who were preoccupied, we hoped, with their own journeys. There were other children and I wondered if they were like us, escaping to a safer place. At one point a man, dressed in a black uniform from head to toe, walked slowly through the train car, staring down at the faces of the passengers as though he were looking for someone.

When he left our train car and moved on to the next, I exhaled a long, slow sigh and realized I was squeezing Ilse's hand. Time moved slowly, even though the rattle of the train wheels and the squeals around curves told me we were speeding our way to the border.

Frau broke her silence when the train began to slow down and the screeching of steel on steel announced we'd soon be at the border. She spoke quietly. "Ilse, Olivia. I know your Papa talked with you about what happens when we cross the border. We'll soon be going into Belgium. Be sure your papers are all in order and ready."

I reached inside my cloth bag for the small pouch where Papa had stowed both our papers, the ones he'd had forged. My fingers trembled as I grasped the folder that held these passports. My knuckles turned pale, the color of my face, I was sure.

Frau Vogel, sitting opposite Ilse and me, rummaged in her needlepoint bag. She was now our Tante Alice. Papa had coached us and coached us to call her Tante Alice—whatever happened, we needed to have a believable story. I'd rehearsed it again and again with Ilse.

Frau Vogel was Tante Alice who was taking us to Calais for a last holiday before school started again in September. I was nervous, but I knew how important it could be for all of us—Ilse, Papa, Frau Vogel, and me—that I do exactly as we'd planned.

Each of us on this train had a part to play. According to our forged passports my name was Emma Fischer, Ilse's was Lara Fischer, and Tante Alice was our mother's sister. Frau Vogel had thought it best that we didn't travel as Jewish girls. So much of what could happen depended upon the border guards. I took a long breath and squeezed Ilse's hand again.

When the guard approached, he stood, his hand outstretched,

"Ausweiss, bitte." (*Identity card, please.*)

I gave him our papers. My hand was steady.

"I am Emma Fischer. My sister is Lara."

# Chapter Twenty-Eight

### September 1938 ♦ Irish Sea ♦ Martha

A BREEZE FLOATED ACROSS THE DECK AS THE SHIP GATHered speed. I leaned across the rail and let the wind blow against my face. How many years had it been since I stood at a ship's rail and watched the land disappear from sight? Liverpool, 1913, that's how long ago. A mere girl who thought she might never see British soil again. I watched the distance gather as we sailed from Liverpool, my yearnings for that other time and place beginning to fade like the mists. Home? Was I leaving again? No. Home was far off the bow of this ship. But old memories were following me like the sea gulls circling as we sailed on. 1913. I was a fifteen-year-old girl leaving behind a life that held sadness and loss. *I did what I could, Ma.*

A gentle swell rocked the ship. *I did what I could. I did what I could.* Was I still holding the melancholy of an orphan child? Was I mourning Ma after all these years? Those children, those Home Children who'd sailed with me from Liverpool to Quebec in 1913...Where were they all now? Had they found peace? Had they found place?

My place now lay beyond the waves and the ocean. Charlie, Sarah Rose, Owen, Emily, Rose, Earl, Ryan. I counted them off in my head like those family pictures that had accumulated on the mantelpiece at the farm. I was part of them.

I knew that soon I'd need to go back inside. Anna was

having breakfast with the girls. We'd decided that it would be best if they spent time with her because we were prepared for the possibility their Aunt Sigrid might not take them in. For now, Olivia and Ilse would be living on King Street with Owen, Emily, and Anna.

I'd not mentioned to her that I'd been having second thoughts. Maybe the girls needed a bigger family, others closer to their age, like Sarah Rose. It was a conversation we needed to have, Anna and me.

Another swell, a larger one this time, rolled and rocked the ship defiantly. I wondered if we might be entering some weather.

"Tante Martha?" A small voice, a gentle pull on my sleeve. What was Ilse doing out here on the deck by herself? When I turned, she held out her hand the way Sarah Rose might on those times she needed me to come with her.

"Oh, Ilse, whatever are you doing out here by yourself!"

"I'm not by myself. Tante Anna and Olivia are just inside." She pointed at the doors into the dining room. "They're sitting at the breakfast table. When we saw you through the windows, I said I'd come get you." Again, she lifted her hand to mine. She seemed so much older than her eleven years. Her eyes entered my gaze and stayed steady, a practice she'd possibly learned to stare down the German guards. But the black circles spoke to me—a girl, just past her eleventh birthday, living unimaginable upheaval. I'd been struck at how confident the girls were when they spoke English—Simon had been working with them for months. Their ease with a second language reflected self-assurance. I wondered about that. Was it partly bravado and determination not to disappoint Papa? Or had they learned their escape strategies well? I'd been watching for signs of crumbling into despair, but what Anna and I saw was sapping fatigue.

Ilse and Olivia had been so tired when they arrived at Calais, they'd collapsed into the nearest chairs on the middeck of the ferry and stayed there for the hour and a half across the Dover Straits. There'd been little time for talk or the story of their ride through Germany and Belgium. When Anna and I described the rest of the journey we'd be taking to arrive at the ship in Liverpool, we watched for tears and waited for pleas to go back to Germany. Neither happened. They were like two girls walking through a dream. Every so often Ilse asked, "Are we near Canada yet?" Olivia shushed her, saying something in German that either reassured her or chastised her, we couldn't tell. Even though we knew they both spoke English, they chatted with each other in German. Anna and I agreed they needed to do whatever felt like comfort. Speaking their own language, we believed, gave them a faint sense of the familiar. Changes were happening fast around them, like the rattling wheels of the train that carried us from Dover to London and on to Liverpool. Like the hubbub and commotion of boarding the ship at Liverpool. Like the experienced movements of the crew as they lifted the ship's ropes from the bollards on the pier. Like the disappearance of land as we sailed out into the Irish Sea.

"I know and I remember all about trying to find something familiar," I'd said to Anna while we stood outside the bathroom on the train on our way to Liverpool, waiting for the girls to finish.

"As do I," she'd nodded. "But can you even begin to imagine what this might be like for them?"

I'd paused a moment before I answered. "I know what this is like."

Just at that moment, both girls opened the folding door and greeted us with, "We're done!" It was the first time we'd heard them giggle.

I remembered Miss Ashcroft when I, a young Irish orphan, first crossed the Atlantic, without family, without place. She'd looked out for me as Anna and I were doing for the girls—as she stood by bathroom doors onboard ship, as she pointed out stars at night while we stood by the ship's railing. Now, here, on the first morning of our journey, Ilse stood beside me on the deck. Strands of her hair, loosened from her braids, floated with the wind. Her face was directed toward the bow of the ship and her future. I let the enormity of our responsibility for and to these girls sink into my shoulders. I stood beside Ilse, my hand light on her shoulder.

"Come on, Ilse. Let's go have breakfast."

◆

OLIVIA AND ANNA WERE SITTING OVER NEAR THE WALL by a small window. The tourist dining room accommodated several passengers; however, many had not appeared for breakfast that morning. Something about the movement of the ship made breakfast less then appetizing for those not so seagoing. Not only was it rolling and rocking, it was zigzagging. I still wasn't sure why the zigging and zagging, but I made a note to myself to ask Anna what she thought.

Now, for us, it was breakfast time. "Good morning, you two." Anna was playing her brisk everything-is-fine nurse role. I imagined her walking into a ward of wounded men, a breakfast tray in hand, her smile at the ready.

"We missed you, Martha. When we woke up you weren't in the cabin, so we sent Ilse to gather you up when we spotted you out there at the rail."

I slipped into the armchair at the table and beckoned Ilse to come sit beside me. No sooner had we sat than a steward, dressed in his black morning uniform, brass buttons shining, arrived by our sides. Ilse's eyes widened, her cheeks paled. She grasped the arms of the chair, her knuckles white. Olivia whispered across to her, *"Es ist in Ordnung, Ilsy. Er ist unser Kellner. Er ist kein Wächter."*

I glanced over at Anna, who was sipping her coffee.

"What's troubling you, Ilse, Olivia?" I asked.

Olivia stirred her cereal around in the bowl. "Guard. She thinks he might be a guard."

Ilse's hands grasped the arms of the chair while she watched the steward pour her orange juice. I looked up to him and smiled. "Excuse me, sir, is it possible for us to know your name?" Miss Ashcroft had taught me to talk about what I feared when we made that 1913 crossing together. There was so much that had been unfamiliar then, and now her spirit was there coaching me today with Ilse and Olivia.

"Certainly, ma'am. It's Samuel." We caught his lovely Scottish brogue.

"Where are you from, Samuel?"

"Ah, ma'am, I'm from Glasgow." He said this with a wink and a smile for the girls.

I watched Ilse out of the corner of my eye and saw color return to her cheeks and a small smile shimmer at the corner of her lips. The waiter placed a bowl of cereal in front of Ilse, handed her a spoon, and left.

"See, Ilsy, he's not a guard." Her older sister whispered, this time in English.

"Did you think he might have been a guard, like a border guard in Germany?" I waited until Samuel had moved farther across the dining room. Ilse fingered the edge of the tablecloth, her eyes cast down.

Then she straightened in her chair, looked over at Anna and Olivia, and turned to me. "I was very frightened when we had to get off the train and board another one. I was scared they might be sending us back."

The girls allowed us a glimpse of their story, but only a brief one, while we breakfasted on our poached eggs and bacon. Olivia sat for a few seconds, a piece of egg perched on the edge of her toast, her napkin twisted around one finger ready to dab leftover yolk from the edges of her mouth. Anna and I gave her those silent pauses because we knew stories needed time to tell—it was a family watchword for all of us. Wait for the story to be told.

Olivia looked across the table to Ilse, who had put her fork on her plate and sat back. Her color had returned, but she seemed reluctant to say anything more.

"It's all right, Ilsy. I was scared too. I thought if we stayed a moment longer with those border guards going up and down the aisle…well…I thought I'd be sick. We were near the rear of the car, so we had to watch them while they quizzed all those sitting in front of us. Three people were taken off the train before we were told to board another train."

"Could you tell why?" Anna asked, her words hushed.

"Not really, though one of the women told to leave started to cry."

"What did Frau Vogel do? Did she say anything to you this whole time?" I wondered now how these two girls could appear to be so calm as they'd left the train at Calais.

Ilse picked a piece of toast from her plate, crunched on it, and ignored her sister's disapproving stare. Not proper behavior, *"you're chewing too loud, manners,"* seemed to be the message. How tense they were, how eager to please. When her slice of toast disappeared, she wiped her hands on her napkin.

"Frau Vogel," she said, "is the bravest lady I know."

Olivia nodded and lingered over her breakfast. Her voice was barely a whisper when she spoke. "Yes, Ilse is right. I'm worried what might happen to Frau Vogel if war comes their way. Papa said it might. She's very angry…"

Ilse dropped her fork onto her plate and wiped her napkin across her eyes.

"Ah, Ilse. I'm so sorry." I reached across the arm of the chair and drew her to me. "Maybe we'll talk about all this another time."

Anna shook her head no. "Um, I think maybe…they want to talk about Frau Vogel now. What do you think, Olivia?"

Once again Olivia became the big sister as, with evident self-possession, she reached over to Ilse. "I'm sorry, Ilsy, I didn't mean to upset you."

I knew at that moment Olivia had learned, as I had at her age, that she was meant to be bold and resolute.

Anna picked up her cup of tea from its saucer and leaned back into her chair. No one spoke for a moment. Until Anna. "Ilse, Olivia. We didn't have long to get to know Frau Vogel. What she has done for you and for your papa, and for us, is extraordinary. And I understand why you are worried."

Whatever lay ahead for us, for these girls, we needed to face it head-on without pretense or delusion. Their lives were changed. They might never see their papa again. They might never see home again. Frau Vogel herself could be in danger—maybe even by now she was in trouble.

Anna placed her teacup back onto its saucer with a gentle gesture of resolution. I smiled over at Olivia and took Ilse's hand. "I have a sense that Tante Anna is about to say something important. I've learned to listen when she does." I grinned over at her.

"Important? I don't know, but something Tante Martha and I want you both to know. We think you are the bravest young women we've known for a long time. What you've set out to do, what you are doing for your papa, and, may I say, for our family is remarkable. Do you understand?"

Olivia nodded, " Thank…" But before she could finish, Ilse's face began to crumple.

"Oh, Ilse, stop." Olivia's face reddened and she became the older, impatient sister. "Crying doesn't help."

Ilse tossed her napkin onto the table and, for a moment, I thought she might slip off her chair and stomp off. She dug her fingers into the arms of the chair and in a louder than usual voice, said, "You always say that, always…that's because you never cry about anything."

Tears brimmed. The overflow coursed down her cheeks.

What did I do when Sarah Rose wept? I did exactly that—turned my chair to Ilse and drew her onto my knee, and opened my arms to invite Olivia, who didn't hesitate. I thought possibly I felt a sob or two escape her lips. Both buried their faces into my wool sweater, and I held them with the strength of all my past sorrows.

Looking over their heads I saw Anna nodding her head and smiling.

"Your Tante Martha is a good lady. She'll take care of you."

◆

LATER THAT AFTERNOON, OLIVIA AND ILSE ASKED IF

they might write a letter to their papa. We were sitting in the ship's library, enjoying the gentle pitch and roll of the ship, without feeling queasy. "I'm sure he'd be very happy to hear from you," I offered, even though I wasn't sure any letters would get to him. "We'll mail your letters to the Canadian Trade Commission, the same place your papa sent his letters to us."

"Do you think he might not get mail, as soon as the Nazis find we're gone?" Olivia asked. Ilse was sitting by a porthole. She was folded into a chair that enveloped her and was caught up in one of Sarah Rose's old books we'd brought along. Anna, ever the adventurer and the explorer, was sitting with a map of our crossing. At Olivia's question she raised her head.

"We'll stay in touch with your papa. You know that my dad—remember he's the one your papa wrote to—my dad will write to him, too. And he'll work on bringing your papa to Canada, as will I."

I wondered if Anna's words might give Olivia false hope. From all we had heard and knew about what was happening in Germany, there was much to fear for Simon Lansky. Yet, she seemed content right now to accept Anna's encouragement and left her chair to walk over to a desk, where she took the ship's paper and pen. With her chin resting on cupped hand, she began to write.

Anna and I sat quietly for a few moments. The girls seemed settled, for now.

We were sailing through St. George's Channel into the Celtic Sea, on out to the Atlantic. At our top speed and without the danger of storms, we'd be at least five more days at sea. Maybe in that time we might strengthen the girls' spirits, and help them begin to move into their new lives.

Possibly we'd start by encouraging them to tell us their fears.

◆

THAT NIGHT THE SEAS WERE CALM. THE CAPTAIN HAD welcomed us all at dinner and assured us that we'd have a safe crossing. Why was he reassuring us?

I asked Anna the question after we'd tucked the girls into their bunks in our cabin. We stood for a while at the door to the cabin, making sure all was quiet. When we heard their regular breathing in finally restful sleep we slipped out, walked to a small lounge just by the passageway to our cabin, and dropped into soft chairs with rounded arms and high backs. Both of us sighed in unison.

"Have you been holding your breath, waiting for something to happen?" I asked.

"Probably since we stood waiting for them to arrive in Calais."

"Why do you think the captain was assuring us we'd have a safe crossing?" I sat feeling the rhythm of the ship, lulled by the grumble of the ship's engines far below.

Anna sat, her legs curled beneath her, a book open on her lap.

"I expect with all that's going on in Europe and especially Germany—there's always the possibility of danger."

"Danger of what?"

"Well, the Lusitania in 1915. That surprised a lot of people, when a German submarine torpedoed a passenger ship."

"But we're not at war with Germany. And wasn't the Lusitania carrying weapons from New York to Britain? Didn't Germany declare the waters around Britain a war zone?"

Anna looked over at me, her eyes narrowed into a curious stare. "How do you know all this?"

"Charlie," I said, grinning.

"Oh. Well, maybe our captain knows all about those submarine stories, too, and is being extra cautious."

"This is a conversation we'll not have with the girls." I paused for a moment. "Anna?"

"Mmmm." She'd gone back to her book.

"God. They must be so scared and sad. I just remember how I was twenty-five years ago with all those Home Children, all of us crossing to another country.

"I think they need…" As if on cue, we heard a shriek from our cabin, just four doors down from the lounge. I was on my feet and running, with Anna at my heels.

As we reached our cabin door, I fumbled for the key I'd slipped into my change purse. Anna had the palm of her hand against the door, ready to push.

Sobbing filled the room.

Ilse was sitting straight up in her bunk, Olivia at her side, arms about Ilse's body,

" Shhh…shh…it's all right, Ilsy. I'm here. It's all right."

Ilse's eyes were round and black, and her body shook as though some chill had captured her. She seemed in a trance.

"Hold her, Olivia, keep holding her. Talk to her. Don't try to wake her. She's having a bad dream and she's still in it. I've seen young soldier boys who were like this," Anna said.

With that, she sat behind Ilse and began to stroke her back with a soft touch. I poured a glass of water from the pitcher on the bedside table. Soon her sobs lessened, her shoulders and her back softened, murmurs became whiffs of breath from her lips.

Olivia whispered, "Ilsy. It's me, Via. Tante Martha's here, Tante Anna's behind you. We're all here."

A tentative knock at the door broke into the silence.

I opened it a mere crack and found a young steward there, his face pale.

"Is everything all right, ma'am? I heard some screams while I was checking the passageway."

"A bad dream, sir. We are fine, but thank you for checking."

He nodded, turned, walked away, and looked back. "Everyone is fine?" he asked again.

"Yes. Everyone is fine. Thank you." I closed the door with a promise that all would be well.

When I returned to the bunk, Ilse was curled up, her head in Anna's lap. Olivia lay beside her sister.

Tomorrow we'd begin again.

# Chapter Twenty-Nine

*"I want to think again of dangerous and noble things.
I want to be light and frolicsome.
I want to be improbably beautiful and afraid of nothing,
as though I had wings."*

—Mary Oliver, *Owls and Other Fantasies*

### September 10, 1938 ◆ Frontenac County ◆ Charlie

THE AIR IN THE KITCHEN SIMMERED. THE ANTICIPATION of the train arriving midafternoon was like a firefly darting around the room. Ma busied herself washing lunch dishes, walking from dishpan to cupboard, drying a cup with a fierceness that could erase the painted bird on the side. Dad sat with his tea, blowing on the surface absentmindedly. It would soon be not just cooled, but cold. And Sarah, so like her mother. She was antsy and restless, pacing around the kitchen, down the hallway, back to the kitchen. I saw Martha in our daughter when something needed attention, like meeting a train on time, particularly this train. She was in the hallway, almost at the front door, when she turned back. "Dad? It's almost twelve-thirty. Don't you think we need to get going?"

She trotted back into the kitchen and stood at the table, bouncing from one foot to the other foot, as though she believed she might propel me from my chair if she kept moving. I pushed away from the table, stuffed the last of the ham sandwich into my mouth, and stood.

"Might as well be on your way, she ain't gonna stand still till you go." Dad held his cup out to Ma. "Another cup, Mother?"

I paused at the door, my hand on the brass knob, and looked over to Ma. "I think we'll set off."

Ma stood by the table in the kitchen pouring Dad's second cup of tea. Her hand shook with an old tremor. It crossed my mind they might be feeling left out of all the excitement.

"Are you sure you and Dad don't want to come with us to meet Mart, Anna, and the girls?" She placed the teapot down with a slow deliberate move, turned to me, and in that way of hers that telegraphed *"there'll be no more discussion,"* she folded her arms across her chest.

"Charlie, those young girls don't need a crowd of people rushing up to them. It's proper for Owen to go as he's a friend of their father, and Emily will go if she feels up to it." She paused for a moment. "And Ryan."

"Does he want to go?"

"He does, but he has duty at the air base tonight and in the morning. He said he'd try to get over later tomorrow."

Ryan had joined the Royal Canadian Air Force the day he'd turned twenty-one. He'd flown forest fire watches and mail runs. Any chance to fly, he took it. He was that boy who'd run through fields, jumped over fences, and chased cows into the barn. Now we all wondered what might lie ahead for our dashing Irish-Canadian flyboy.

"Dad? We gotta go!" A call to "be ready and be there" rebounded from the laneway and through the open screen door. We'd taught her well—Martha, Anna, me, and the military.

I grinned back at Ma, who shook her head. "Better go, Charlie, or she'll be back in here draggin' ya by the collar."

With a kiss on the top of my mom's head and a wave to my dad, I trotted out to the Ford where Sarah Rose sat in the driver's seat. No sense in arguing about who'd drive. She was the new generation. She'd been driving tractors since her twelfth birthday and hounded me for driving lessons until she finally got her license. There wasn't much that could hold this girl back, no adventure too risky. That's what scared me. The threat of war and all.

We rode down the lane, leaving a dusty cloud floating across the fields behind us, stopped at the road, and turned toward Kingston. The ride would take some time, so I settled back, took a cigarette from the package in my shirt pocket, lit it with a casual flare, blew the smoke out the window, and watched the fence posts drift by. A sense of relief loosened the knot that had taken root in my neck since Martha and Anna had sailed to England. They were home. They were safe.

There'd been many nights throughout the past month that I'd lain awake imagining what could go wrong. How could I have agreed to let them go?

Martha had assured me, over and over again, that they'd be nowhere near harm's way.

"And...Anna can handle almost anything!" She was right, but nothing Martha said could extinguish my anxiety.

One night, as we were on the verge of sleeping, I uttered another plea. "Please promise me the two of you won't try to do something foolhardy, like meeting the girls in Belgium at the German border." Martha had turned, then looked away and pulled the cover to her chin. The pause said volumes. They *had* talked about traveling to the border.

"Martha?"

"I promise, Charlie. I promise," she'd said.

I worried every day they were gone until we received the call that they were on the train from Montreal to Kingston. It was the first time I felt a true breath in my chest since they'd left.

As we turned the corner onto King Street, I spotted Owen and Emily standing in the driveway, Owen with one arm around Emily's waist. She leaned into him. I wondered if the stroke a few weeks ago had, as Martha might say, "taken the stuffing out" of Emily. Her face drooped severely to one side and her right foot dragged.

Sarah pulled into the drive, stopped the car, and turned the engine off. "Wait here," I called over my shoulder as I jumped out. I wanted to help, but Emily raised up a hand to stop me.

She'd been a feisty woman since the day Martha had introduced her to me, but there was something else buried in her manner. There was a stone wall between us. I'd asked Martha if she knew anything. Had I said something that insulted Emily? I did have a way of thinking I was being funny with offhand remarks, yet throughout all the years Martha and I'd been married, Emily remained only courteous and cool toward me.

"That's the way Emily is," Martha had said while she waved her hand to brush away my doubts. But I didn't see her coolness with Rose and Earl, or with Ryan. She'd hugged him and teased him about his hair till he was well into his teens. She'd held Sarah Rose and sung to her when she was a babe and read her stories whenever we visited. Never calling her "Sarah." She was always "Rosie" to Emily.

Eventually, over the years, I found reasons to go for family visits less frequently.

Today I watched Emily struggle to slide into Owen's Chevy, refusing my hand. A strange woman. Her stepdaughter and her niece were coming home, safe from harm. They were remarkable women who'd accomplished something extraordinary. My wife was one of those women.

Seemed to me that Emily held some kind of a grudge. Right now, though, I didn't want to deal with whatever pique might be needling her. I only wanted to celebrate my wife's and Anna's return.

Owen called to me as he put one foot on the running board of the car, "Charlie, will you be sure to bring Anna and Martha and the two girls over to the car when they arrive, I don't believe we'll get out to greet them." He leaned into the car. "Will we, Emily?" She shook her head no.

I beckoned over to Sarah Rose, who'd been leaning against our car, her ankles crossed, her arms folded. She walked to the Chevy, where she sat down on her haunches by the passenger open door.

"Excited, Aunt Em?"

For the first time since we'd arrived, Emily tried a droopy smile.

"Yesh."

"Are you looking forward to meeting Olivia and Ilse?" Sarah took both Emily's hands. "They'll have a story to tell us, won't they? Just like you and Mom and your stories."

I beckoned over to Sarah.

"Sarah Rose, I think we'd better be on our way. Owen, we'll see you at the train. Emily? You can be proud of those women of yours." I needed to say how I felt in spite of the strain between us.

I started to walk away with Sarah Rose.

"And you too…Shharlie…" Her whisper followed me to the car.

◆

Paper streamers colored the white linen tablecloth in the Johnsons' King Street dining room, crisscrossed pink, red, blue, orange. Plates of food—schnitzel, German potato salad, Mom's ambrosia with fruits and cream—all wove themselves in among the streamers. My mother was the best cook I knew. She'd found recipes for German dishes, and I discovered why she declined the invitation to the train station. She and Dad had planned a celebration.

When we'd arrived at the Johnsons from the station late that afternoon, Owen was right there on the porch to welcome the girls to his home.

My feelings of anxiety had dissolved. I stood apart and watched Anna and Martha take Olivia and Ilse's hands to walk with them across the lawn and up the steps to greet Owen. I felt a throat-catching pride. What brave women, all four of them.

Owen greeted them with his broad smile. "Olivia, Ilse, your papa and I have been friends for a long time, and having you come into our family makes us as happy as the day Martha joined us. She was just your age, Olivia." With that he beamed over at Martha, whose eyes were suspiciously glistening.

I watched from a distance as Olivia stepped up to Owen and reached her hand into his. Could I have been this composed?

"Thank you, Mr. Johnson. Ilse and I appreciate that you have offered us your home."

I could imagine Simon practicing their English with them. No child that I knew, or at least any I'd met, would use words like "offered us your home." They were living between their worlds and easing their way into the unaccustomed. Could I know what they might be experiencing? Could any of us? Martha. Anna coming back from the war. Me returning from France.

◆

It didn't take Sarah Rose long to introduce Olivia and Ilse to Gran Rose and Grandpa Earl, who'd been closeting themselves in Emily's kitchen. The girls tried out the words "Gran" and "Grandpa," but soon were calling them "Oma" and "Opa." Possibly we were all trying a bit too hard, yet a sense of family pervaded the walls.

When the celebratory meal became empty plates and bowls scraped clean, I caught Martha's eye. Beckoned to her. "Time to slip away maybe? Let everybody settle?"

"Not yet."

And that's when she told me. Out in the kitchen, she and I volunteered to do dishes, just the two of us. Or, more correctly, Martha volunteered us. Sarah Rose had gone into the parlor to read to Nan Emily. Owen, Anna, Ilse, and Olivia had gone into his study, the door shut.

Martha, hands in a soapy dishpan, stared out the kitchen window. For the first time that afternoon, she showed her fatigue and worry.

"Charlie, Anna and I talked about where the girls should live."

"I thought you'd decided they'd be best here with Anna, since their aunt can't take them." I slid the tea towel over the plate and waited.

"Anna's nursing at the psychiatric hospital, Owen still has students at Queens, and Emily is in no condition to care for two teenage girls."

"No one thought this through before you set off for Europe?" I could hear an edginess in my voice. I didn't want an argument—she'd been away for almost a month, and I'd missed her. But what the hell was she proposing?

When she turned to me, I saw a steady determination in the set of her mouth and the flash of her eyes. She folded her arms across her chest. This decision was made. "We think that Olivia and Ilse need to come to the farm to live with us, at least for now."

I dropped the tea towel down onto the counter and stood with my hands on my head.

Reasons why not hurtled from one to the next to the next: "Where will they go to school out there? What about synagogue? Where will they sleep? Have you really thought this through? Couldn't we all just talk about it? I'm feeling a little pushed here, Mart." I turned around, leaned on the counter, and folded my arms.

Martha stood rigidly at the sink, her head down. Her knuckles were white.

"Mart? Are these girls those Home Children you couldn't rescue?"

The nod of her head was almost undetectable. Her face bore the sadness she held apart from me. "The girls need a home, Charlie. That's all I can say. We can give them that."

I reached across and took her chin. "You're a good woman, Martha Sloan." There'd be no more to say.

The next day, Dad and I went to the lumber mill to buy wood for the room we'd build onto the back of the house at the farm.

# Chapter Thirty

*Someone I loved once gave me
a box full of darkness.
It took me years to understand
that this, too, was a gift.*

—Mary Oliver, "The Uses of Sorrow"

### July 6, 1939 ♦ Kingston, Ontario ♦ Anna

"Martha, I think you need to come. It's about Emily."

Nothing had prepared us for Emily's decision to give up. With no word from Simon, and war rumors flying about, we were caught up in our own anxieties. None of us realized how much she had weakened. She talked little. She complained not at all. I cooked on the days I worked regular hours at the hospital. Dad carried on with his custom of taking tea to her in the morning, and often found her still in bed when he arrived home from his morning walk through the campus. Still, we chose to believe that she was recovering. The doctor had told us she needed rest and recuperation. Her dizzy spells had gotten more frequent. She'd grab the edge of a table sometimes, or pause on the stairway, her hand grasping the railing. But Emily refused to let anyone fuss.

Earlier in the week, I'd taken time from my work at the hospital and planned to drive the hour and a half to the farm to visit with Olivia and Ilse. Martha had asked if I could come, and if Owen and Emily might come as well. We'd said yes, and asked Emily if she'd like a drive and time away from the house. She'd become a shut-in, or as she referred to herself, "an old lady."

"I think I'd rather just stay home, Anna." That was the end of it. Owen was not convinced.

"Em, you need to get out of the house. You haven't been out for ages. I know the girls would like to see you," he said, though the girls had hardly had a chance to get to know her. He said his piece and dropped onto the chesterfield where Emily sat, her head against the back of the sofa, her eyes closed. She spoke like someone distant from us, the words an effort. "You decide what you're going to do. I'm just going to stay here."

We didn't go to visit with the girls. That night, after supper, she stood up from the table and said, "Goodnight, all. I'm tired."

I looked over at Owen, who rose up from the table to help her. She waved him back down.

"Finish your tea. Leave me be. I'll see you in the morning." And, leaning on her cane, she left.

When Owen sat down, his shoulders sagged. "Do you think she's worse?"

"I can ask the doctor to come out. She does seem weaker." I'd seen sickness and death. I knew she was tired to the bone.

In the middle of the night, Owen woke to her gasps.

She was gone in minutes.

◆

Emily's memorial was three days later.

I walked with Dad behind Emily's coffin at the cemetery. Martha, Charlie, Rose, Earl, Ryan, and Sarah followed.

Sarah had come to be with Martha because she knew how painful this would be. Although Martha's face was a mask and her shoulders rigid as she walked to the grave, I remembered her at the service the moment the pallbearers wheeled the coffin down the church aisle. As she stood, she'd grabbed for Charlie's arm, her face crumbling. Sarah had put an arm around her mother's waist to steady her.

"Mom. I'm here. Dad is here. We're all here."

As I heard Sarah's words, I wondered if she thought that Martha was reliving her own mother's death, when she was only a girl herself.

"Anna, I wouldn't have believed that I'd miss her," Martha had said when we returned from the church. "It's as though I've lost Ma all over again."

She grasped Charlie's hand and let a guttural sob escape from her throat.

"A few weeks ago, Anna..." her voice broke into a sob. "She baked oatmeal cookies and sent them out to me, with Sarah Rose. In a note she..." Martha put her hand across her chest. "In a note, she wrote *These were your mother's favorite.*"

A sense of regret sat like a stone in my chest as I listened to Martha, a sorrow for Emily and me. We'd not allowed ourselves to cross the boundary of stepmother and stepchild. I'd never seen the loving Emily. I wondered to myself, how many other people had I left behind? How many had given up trying to find my heart?

Was that what made Andrew so dear to me? He'd not given up, even when I tried to keep a distance.

After the funeral, when all had left the wake, I opened the door into Emily's sewing room, breathed in the scent of crisply folded cottons, and walked over to her sewing machine. I ran my hand along the smooth wood of the table, sank into her cushioned straight-back chair, and wept.

◆

## September 10, 1939

I'D GAINED A PROMOTION AT THE KINGSTON ASYLUM, where I now supervised a total ward. Many of our patients were older men who'd served in the Great War. After all these years, the painful experiences for some had destroyed their lives. I felt a calling to go back to help. But right now, I felt an overwhelming fatigue. With the funeral, and wanting to take care of Dad and Martha, coupled with the intensity of every day at the hospital, I needed respite.

I was sitting at the kitchen table, having just finished the last notes of appreciation to all those who'd written their condolences.

Friends and colleagues had written kind words to both Dad and me. Notes expressed sadness for losing a wife and a mother. Here we were once again, the two of us, mourning. He more than me, I surmised, something I regretted. But there were other messages attached to a few of the notes, particularly from Dad's colleagues. Men writing from the Canadian government. I'd wondered. Each day he'd been retreating to his study. Whenever I inquired, he'd tell me I needn't worry myself. "I'm doing what I need to do, Anna."

Had he had taken on some government work? Clandestine work? The mood of the times, with suspicion of foreigners rampant and our shared worry about Simon and war pounding at our country's doorstep, all had left me wary, even of my own father's activities.

What had been the relationship between him and Professor Lansky? Why would he have felt such a strong bond with my father, one that gave him the trust to give up his girls to Dad's care? I'd asked these questions of myself and shared them with Martha, but never had I received a straight answer from Dad. Now, with Emily gone, had he retreated into a kind of shadow world? I had to shake myself every so often because I couldn't be persuaded that Dad was involved in covert activities.

Maybe I'd worked too long with shell-shocked men, whose hallucinations of spies and informers often left me wondering whose world was real, theirs or mine.

Lost in my thoughts, weighing deliberations, I jumped when Dad yelled out from his study. I pushed back the chair and ran down the hallway. "Anna! Anna! Come here!"

"Dad? Are you all right?" Dressed as I was in my starched white uniform, I rustled and crackled as I moved toward his door. He flung it open. Disheveled, sweater vest buttoned wrong, beginnings of a beard—so not my father. He stood in the middle of his study, seeming to sway. I grabbed his arm, fearful he might be having some kind of attack. I held him around the waist to steady him.

"Oh, for God's sake, Anna, I'm not one of your patients. Stop hovering."

"Well, you just yelled as though you were having some kind of attack, Dad."

"I yelled because our country's at war again."

His words caused me to freeze in place. "Oh, God, no."

A chair by his desk barely caught me as I dropped down. Dad flopped into his large wingchair there beside me and took my hand. "We knew this was inevitable, Anna. Britain declared war just a week ago—the headlines have been full of war-mongering stories for weeks. Look at this."

He passed the newspaper to me.

OTTAWA, Sept. 10—Extra edition of the Canada Gazette declaring a state of war exists between Canada and Germany.

A horrible thought occurred to me. "What about Simon?"
"I've heard nothing from him. Nothing for weeks."
"Can you contact the trade commission in Berlin?"
"There'll be no way now that we're at war."
"Dad? What do we tell the girls?"
His chin sank onto his chest, and he shook his head back and forth.
"The truth."

◆

I CALLED MARTHA LATER THAT EVENING, AFTER I returned home from the hospital. She answered on the second ring. "Martha, it's Anna." In the background, I could hear laughter and the deep rumble of Ryan's voice.
"Hi, Anna, have you heard?"
"That's why I'm calling you. Can you talk privately? I need to ask you about the girls and their father."
"Not really, everyone's collected in the kitchen. Ryan has weekend leave so he's here entertaining us with his stories. I'm really worried that he'll go over to Britain and join the RAF."
"I wonder if you and I might meet somewhere. Maybe tomorrow morning? I have the Monday off this week."
"You sound as though something's wrong."
"Something wrong? Other than the fact we're at war again? Martha, think about it. War. We're at war. Again."

"Hey, don't snap at me. I didn't start this war."

"I'm worried about everybody—the girls, Dad, us, the country. I've seen it, Mart. I know what this means."

"We all know what this means. What if I come there? I could stay overnight."

"Yes," I said. I needed Martha, her practicality. "Let's be together."

◆

## September 11, 1939

"I brought some of Rose's biscuits for Owen. How is he?" Martha set a box filled to the brim with the tea biscuits Rose had baked that morning.

"You must have broken the speed limit to get here." The cuckoo clock on the wall by the kitchen door chimed out half-past ten.

"Not really. I left just after Charlie drove the girls to school, and that was about eight o'clock. Even took my time enjoying the quiet." Her eyes wrinkled into a smile. Two teenage girls and the occasional visit from Sarah Rose home from nurses' training at Kingston General did not contribute to a quiet household. But I knew she delighted in the sounds of a family.

"Owen is grieving. He's so puzzling. I don't think I knew how he had come to depend on Emily over the years."

I poured a strong cup of coffee to take to Owen, just the way he liked it. "Come with me while I take this to him. He's in his study. As far as I can tell he's been in there all night."

Sounds of static and faint voices greeted us as we opened his door. Owen sat in his chair still in his dressing gown, his hair tousled, which told me maybe he had rested.

He sat twirling knobs on the console radio we'd all gone

together to buy him for his birthday, just the week before Emily died. She loved the music. Now he searched for news as we stood waiting.

"Dad? We've brought you a bit of breakfast. Martha's here."

He waved his hand, without looking back at us, his way of telling us to be quiet. "I'm listening to the news. Special bulletins." A newspaper lay across his desk with headlines about Canada entering another war. He turned back toward us, away from fiddling radio knobs.

"Martha! What a nice surprise."

"Dad, I told you."

"Good to see you too, Owen. Horrific news about the war."

"Inevitable, my girl, inevitable. It had to happen. I've thought this ever since that maniac Hitler rose to power. Now you tell that husband of yours not to get any ideas about going, and talk some sense into Ryan if you can."

"I'm trying, Owen. But there's more we need to think about. Anna and I need to talk about what to say to the girls about their father. If we've heard nothing, then do we assume the worst and start to prepare, or do we wait? I'm not sure what's best."

I sat in the leather chair over by the window and watched two red squirrels scamper across the lawn toward the old maple tree that I'd climbed, and fallen from, more than once.

"Anna, did you hear what Owen just said? He has a letter from Simon."

"Forgive me," I said. "Lots on my mind these days."

"What could be more important than this?"

Owen, ever the peacemaker, interrupted. "The letter says little, but yes, it is important to know he's alive."

Martha's sigh resounded like a call to arms. "Yes, it is

important. But what do we do? We can't just sit here. There's a letter from Simon, the girl's father. Shouldn't they know that?" Owen was quiet for a moment. As he spoke, I was sure he'd weighed his thoughts like the thinker he was.

"Simon's letter only said he had a plan. Didn't give any clue what that might be. But, of course, he's not going to write anything in a letter, nor did he sound confident—just that he knew he had to do something. He couldn't wait." Owen paused, then looked past us, out at the squirrels. "We tell them."

# Chapter Thirty-One

*"Those who have a 'why' to live,
can bear with almost any 'how.'"*
—Viktor E. Frankl, *Man's Search for Meaning*

### 1939 ◆ Berlin ◆ Simon Lansky

*My darling girls and the extraordinary family of Owen Johnson.*

*This could be my last letter to you for a while. Possibly a long while.*

WHEN I BEGAN TO WRITE THAT LETTER, IT WAS THE DAY after Kristallnacht, 1938, when the Nazi's paramilitary went mad. I knew if I were to keep my promise to the girls, I would have to take action. How could I think I might survive what horrors were already happening? I listened each day to the wail of sirens. I watched from my window as friends emerged from apartments down the way and climbed into the rear of trucks. Some people were pushed and shoved by the German soldiers, soldiers whom I used to think were my countrymen. I had to take action. I couldn't give up on my girls. What was the alternative? I began to plan.

I knew the government had knowledge and records of my work since I'd been a small part of the birth of rocketry in Germany. Professor Hermann Oberth had been a hero of mine since the early 1930s. At the beginning, I believed his work was never intended to be used for military purposes, but there were rumors. Within the community of mathematicians and physicists, word spread that Von Braun, a young member of the Society for Space Travel, had accepted an invitation to take charge of a newly created missile development lab of the German Army in 1932. Many of us who were part of the Society objected, but to no avail. Being one of those who objected, and being Jewish, I was sure I'd be on their watch list. Fear had become my friend. She sniffed out danger. She became my protector, my guiding spirit, and my cunning. I seldom went out, or if I did, I skirted busy streets, away from crowds, away from gatherings.

Eventually, I spent little time with others. I became cautious even with those I once had trusted. The word was, those you think are your friends could be the ones who might betray you. I was unfaltering. I would not become one of them—one of those rounded up by the police. I would survive.

My plan unfolded with the very people who managed the building where I lived. I placed my trust and my life in their hands. Miss Vogel and her father, Otto.

She'd rescued my girls and lived to tell me of their journey. I remember, when they left, that I'd imagined how dangerous an odyssey they'd undertaken. How could I have thought they'd arrive safely in Canada? What could I have been thinking?

What if Olivia, in her impetuous way, spoke out to a border guard?

What if they let their false identities slip? It could happen. What if fatigue clouded their responses to the German guards?

What if Ilse's tendency to wander off sent her in the wrong direction? Olivia had promised to keep her always at her side.

What if they were separated?

What if I'd wrongly trusted Miss Vogel?

What if they'd been held at the border?

The day Miss Vogel brought the letter from the Canadian Trade Commission, the letter telling me they were safe with my friend Owen, I wept just as I had when they'd left.

"Thank you," I'd whispered before my legs gave out. She guided me to my old leather chair where the girls had sat with me so often.

"They are safe, Professor. Soon you will go too."

◆

JOHANNA VOGEL WAS THE DAUGHTER OF OTTO VOGEL, the German superintendent of the apartment building I'd been sent to when we were forced out of our home. They were Quakers, part of a small group carrying on dangerous work. Otto hid Jewish people for short periods of time in his basement; Johanna arranged to transport them in plain sight to the French border. I'd never met anyone like her. I saw little of her until it was time to go.

My beard had grown into long gray tufts over time since the girls had left. My hair, with Johanna's help, was now white. The chemicals from the dye turned my black strands into the blanched alabaster of an old man. My eyebrows, which had always been bushy and dark, were now white and trimmed back. Gone was my professorial vest and starched shirt. I wore Otto's flannel sweater, gray and faded. I felt older than my years from the outside in and the inside out. I learned to shuffle and hunch my shoulders. Simon Lansky, Professor of Mathematics, was gone.

◆

"Professor Lansky. Can you hear me?" A voice sounded beyond the brick wall that separated me from the basement of our apartment building, a place where I'd been living for the past few days. When I decided to place my trust in this man and his daughter, I did all they asked me to do. They were in danger, too, of a police raid. I needed to hide until they had a plan for me to leave.

Remnants of food on plates were scattered on the dirt floor, left from however long ago it had been since Otto Vogel took out the loose bricks to hand me bread and cheese.

But I had to leave, and soon. It had become too dangerous to stay in this hiding place, and Otto would have to make a report on the number of Jews still in his building. The plan he and his daughter had hatched was to report he'd found me dead in my bed and beginning to smell, which was why he'd called the funeral director. We all hoped the Nazis wouldn't do their spot checks on that day. The day they removed my body.

I waited until I heard Otto's voice and the scraping of the trowel against the brick wall. The air had become stale and foul, even though Otto had created a breathing space just under the stairs where I was hidden. I welcomed the air flowing in from the basement.

"Come," he whispered.

I adjusted my eyes to the dim light before I began to follow Otto up the stairs. All I had were the clothes on my back. Otto's clothes.

Johanna stood at the top of the stairs, an older man at her side. His black suit, white shirt, and slicked back, dark hair startled me. "The funeral director," Johanna whispered.

"He will take you in the hearse to the next contact. You need to lie down so we can wrap you in canvas."

There, on the kitchen floor, laid out by the back door, was a canvas tarpaulin.

I dropped to my knees and let myself be rolled into the rough sailcloth. My head was strategically placed under a badly patched hole, which allowed enough air for breathing. I wondered for how long. Before they could tie me in, I reached for Johanna's hand.

"Godspeed," she whispered, and the canvas fell over my face.

# Chapter Thirty-Two

*"Before you know what kindness really is, you must lose things, feel the future dissolve in a moment like salt in a weakened broth."*

—Naomi Shihab Nye

### November 1939 ♦ Frontenac County ♦ Martha

Earl had surprised us all, even Rose, who vowed nothing Earl did could ever surprise her. He'd driven off last Saturday. "I'll be back later this afternoon. Don't hold dinner," he'd called out as he'd swung open the kitchen door. Even Charlie, who tracked the whereabouts of all of us diligently, hadn't known what his dad was planning. We knew he'd gone into Kingston, that was all. And that he'd taken his Ford pickup. Late that afternoon, the dust rose as his truck bumped its way down our lane. Ilse was out the door first to greet him, followed in close chase by Olivia.

In one year, both girls had taken a shine to Earl. The day we decided the girls needed to come here to live, Earl had been hesitant. "What'll the neighbors say," he'd muttered. "Us having Germans here!" In fact, those were the words written by Simon's sister-in-law when she sent her last letter.

*I've decided it best not to bring Simon's daughters here. There's an anti-German feeling in this town. I've managed to get through that and have created a place for myself over the years.*

We sent a note to her to say the girls were getting on fine with us. We never heard from her again.

We'd weathered those first rough days after they arrived because we felt protective, and we all knew how it felt to say good-bye to someone we loved. I knew what kind of grief Olivia and Ilse were experiencing. Rose and Earl had watched their son leave for a horrific war thousands of miles away and welcomed home a stranger who was unwilling to talk about his terrors. Loss and despair were not foreign to any of us. "All the more reason," I said to Charlie, "to offer kindnesses where we can."

And over the year, Earl begrudgingly admitted pleasure in having "young ones" around the farm again. None of us dared broach the subject that possibly the girls might not intend to live on the farm forever, but we accepted without argument that Olivia and Ilse had managed to fill the spaces that Ryan and Sarah had created when they left. Ryan had been gone for a while since he'd joined the Royal Canadian Air Force. He was flying coastal patrols on the East Coast, yet I knew from his letters he was itching to get over to England. Sarah was in her last year of nursing school at Kingston General Hospital. She'd learned to avoid the subject of following in her Aunt Anna's footsteps, at least within earshot of me. I'd overheard her one Sunday when she'd come home for a good chicken dinner. She and Charlie had just arrived from their drive back from Kingston. All I heard as they walked into the kitchen was, "They're going to need nurses over in England, and some of us are even talking of applying to go on hospital ships. They're going to need us, and soon."

"No," I'd said, and slammed the oven door, which rattled the dishes warming on the top of the new electric stove. "I could not handle giving my daughter to another war. It's bad enough Ryan's gone."

The conversation ended abruptly there, but it was not over. I knew.

As Sarah left that night to go back to the hospital, I whispered into her ear, "I love you. Please think about what you're doing."

I received her kiss on my cheek as a signal she knew my fears, but she'd do what she wanted regardless.

◆

LATER THAT AFTERNOON, WHEN WE HEARD EARL'S pickup bouncing and rattling down the lane, Ilse and Olivia appeared from the back kitchen where they'd been peeling apples for Rose's apple jam. They were dressed in the heavy Irish-like sweaters I'd knit for them—the temperature having dropped like a stone the night before and the back kitchen being our cold storage place. How they heard Earl's arrival, none of us knew; nevertheless, they materialized through the doorway, across the kitchen, and out to the porch, just as Earl pulled up.

By the time Rose, Charlie, and I stepped out onto the porch, the girls were already running back, whooping and hollering like the fulsome Canadian teenagers they'd become. "Martha, Oma, Charlie, you should see what Opa brought home." They bounced onto the porch with a force that set the white rocker rocking. "You should see. You should see."

Charlie stepped off the porch and headed for his dad, who was sitting in the pickup and taking the last long puff on his cigar.

"Look in the back of the truck. Take off the packing

paper," Earl rolled down the window and called out to Charlie.

Rose, Olivia, Ilse, and I stood on the porch and watched as Charlie ripped away at the brown, heavy paper, gradually revealing a shiny wooden floor radio.

"It's a radio? Dad, a radio?"

"Not just any old radio. It's a Philco," Earl called as he climbed down from the truck. He walked back to Charlie, a kind of swagger in his step.

"Here, don't just stand there, help me get it down and in the house."

None of us spoke for a moment, all wondering why we now owned a *new* radio when we had a perfectly good one sitting on the side table in the sitting room.

Earl read our minds.

"Hey, everyone. We need a radio that will broadcast up-to-the-minute news about the war without all the static and interference. Anyway, that old radio must have come from Marconi himself. It's that old." Earl and his jokes.

In a few moments, a handsome wooden floor radio stood on our porch. Olivia and Ilse held themselves at the door, jumping from one foot to the other, side by side like two eager colts.

"Will we be able talk to Papa?" Ilse called over to us.

I knew immediately what they were thinking. Their papa had owned a ham radio until the Nazis had confiscated it. He'd been able to listen to broadcasts from France and England.

While Earl and Charlie struggled to get the radio through the door, I drew Ilse over to me. "Olivia, hold the door for Papa Earl, and go in with Rose to show them where to put it."

My hand in hers, I led Ilse to the steps and beckoned her to sit beside me. I placed my hand on her shoulder to try to still her squirming.

"Ilse, this is a radio, but it doesn't transmit like your papa's did."

"But it looks a little like Papa's."

She looked so crestfallen, I wondered if Earl had told her he was getting her a magic box, a story Charlie had heard as a boy from his dad. Grandpa Earl did like to spin tales, especially for Ilse.

"So, you mean we only listen?"

"That's the idea. But, if this is the kind of radio I think it might be, we can listen to people from as far away as England."

Later, I'd regret those words.

◆

EARL AND CHARLIE HAD SET THE RADIO IN THE SITTING room and rearranged the furniture so everyone could listen close by. That afternoon, Rose had called Owen and Anna to come out for dinner and listen to the broadcasts. When they arrived, I was shocked to see an old man alight from his car. Owen moved slowly along the path to the house, Anna at his side. I wondered at how much he'd aged over the past few months since Emily's death. I still puzzled over his intense grieving—whomever she had been to him, he looked like a man who'd lost his rudder. His face brightened as Olivia and Ilse ran down the steps to meet him. I knew they brought light into his life.

"Papa Owen. We are glad to see you," Olivia said as she reached out to take his arm. "And I you, young ladies, I you."

Anna stepped back so the girls could take both arms

and walk with him into the house.

"How is he, Anna?" I slowed to leave time for them to move through the door. "He seems to be aging a lot since Emily died."

Anna stopped midway up the walk to the house and put her hand on my arm.

"Yes, he misses her, but he is also very worried about Simon. We haven't heard from him except that last letter." She let a long sigh escape. "Martha. I need to go back. Back to…"

"To where? To Europe? Anna, no." Within the short space of only a few days, I had had a visceral reaction to the possibility of losing two women I loved. "Why do you always need to plunge into the unknown?" I could feel tears smarting at the corners of my eyes.

"What do you mean, always? Where have I been for the last twenty-some years? Here in Kingston, doing what a dutiful daughter does."

Her face flushed the instant the words escaped her mouth. She held her hand to her throat and looked beyond me. "Mart. I wish. I…"

"Anna, I jumped. I'm so damn afraid of losing you." I saw a small grin play at her lips.

"Damn, Mart? Damn? You just said 'damn.' Anyhow, I made it through one war. And. I'm not the stay-at-home woman you are."

"Hey, while you're in your fine house back there in Kingston or trekking off to some war, I'm out here trying to learn how to run a bloody farm."

Anna grabbed my arm and dragged me to the door. "And a fine farm it is. Enough. Now let's go inside and the two of us listen to that bloody radio."

# Chapter Thirty-Three

*Tell me, what is it you plan to do*
*With your one wild and precious life?*

—Mary Oliver, "The Summer Day"

### November 1939 ◆ Frontenac County ◆ Anna

News blared from the radio. Everyone was clustered around the shiny wooden box like chicks at feeding time. Earl had dragged his rocker directly in front of the radio and set about twirling dials and adjusting volume until Rose said, "Enough." We sat in a circle, Charlie on the cushioned stool, leaning into the sound of the commentator, as though he could see the soldiers marching through the streets as he had done years before.

Olivia and Ilse were cross-legged on the carpet, their faces alight with anticipation. I worried that they still believed news of their father or people like him might be broadcast for all those on this side of the ocean, who waited with glimmering hope to hear something good, anything. No one looked up, so intent were they on the deep, sonorous voice of Winston Churchill, not yet prime minister, making one of his first broadcasts of the war.

When I looked over at Martha, who'd chosen to stand, her eyes were closed and her mouth a firm line. I wondered if she might be ready to weep. I beckoned her to come upstairs, away from everyone for a while. No one questioned us as we climbed the stairs away from Churchill's words:

> "Ah, the Nazi menace, it is the U-boats that are feeling the weather and not the Royal Navy—but we must be prepared for a war of possibly more than three years. However, it was for Hitler to say when the war will begin, it is not for him or for his successor to say when it will end; it began when he wanted it, it will end when we are convinced that he has had enough."

Martha leaned against my shoulder while we took the steps one at a time. Something had broken apart in her down there while she listened. In silence, we walked down the hall into the bedroom she and Charlie shared. Winston Churchill faded behind the closed door.

"Martha, lie down for a while and I'll come get you later."

"No, I'll be fine. I'll just sit here." She patted the quilt beside her. "Come sit. I need you to stay here for now." She looked away from me, and let air escape from her lips, the same lips that had been so tight a few minutes ago. Her next words hung on a long breath. "If it's going over there, to that war, then…" she paused, "…I'm coming with you."

"What are you saying, Mart?"

Her hand grasped mine as though she was afraid to let go. Her shoulders rose and fell. She shook her head side to side like someone with a dogged purpose, ready to do battle.

"Martha? Say something? Anything?" She threw her arms over her head, lay back on the bed, and let her legs dangle over the side. The words poured out like a stream over rocks.

"I was the one to take care of my mother, not the other way around. I did everything I could. I took the doctor to her. I even found a priest. We weren't even Catholic!" Her hands flew up to her face. "But she died. She died in spite of all I could do, all God could do, all the doctor could do. You know all this. Why am I telling you again?"

"Maybe you need to say it again," I offered.

"There wasn't a person in my life I could lean on or trust. Mrs. McCarthy's home was a stopping off place. Not a family—just other kids, like me. Riffraff."

"Martha, no—"

She smacked her hand against the quilted mattress. "Where the hell am I supposed to be? I've been sent here, sent there, sent to an orphanage, sent to Canada." A rising wind had begun to rattle the shutters. Earl's voice echoed up the stairs, raised in protest to the news.

"Here, Martha. You're supposed to be here. We need you here."

She turned her head to face me and pointed. "No. People need you, not me. You make sure of that because you find places and go where you know you matter. Because that's what you need, Anna, you need to run to those places where you can look after wounded men and broken people. But you don't have to promise them that you'll always be there. Like you did when I came to live with you and Owen and Emily. You promised me. You promised. And then you left. Left me with Emily, my so-called aunt who, by the way, hated me."

Tears dripped from the corners of her eyes down onto the quilt

She sat up as I reached to her, and let herself fall against me while I absorbed her sadness.

◆

LATER THAT NIGHT I CAME INTO THE QUIET OF MY ROOM back at 53 King Street, threw my coat across the bed, and walked over to my desk, the one Dad had given me when I entered nursing school. I'd written many important letters here on this pine table, but this one was pivotal. I was about to write to the Matron-in-Chief of the Royal Canadian Army Medical Corps. The time was now. Time to leave.

With the haunting strains of Elgar's *Enigma Variations* drifting up from my father's study, I sat in my room and fashioned my good-bye.

MISS ELIZABETH SMELLIE, MATRON
ROYAL CANADIAN ARMY MILITARY CORPS

*Dear Miss Smellie;*

*Since my return to Canada in 1921, after serving with the Canadian Nursing Sisters throughout the Great War, I've been honored to continue in a supervisory role, to care for the men suffering from Shell Shock, at Rockwood Hospital Kingston Psychiatric unit.*

*I am writing to re-apply to the RCAMC as an experienced Nursing Sister with a request to be placed at a Canadian General Hospital in England.*

*My time during the Great War and my postwar work with men wounded both physically and mentally can provide valuable experiences on which to draw and with which to serve.*

*I will be 46 years old on my next birthday, which I realize is beyond the age limit at this time. My hope is, my knowledge and training will be of benefit, particu-*

*larly my extended experience in Canadian General Hospitals in both England and France.*

*Please find attached my record of service and my health records.*

*I understand from discussion with the Matron at Rockwood that I could be released from this hospital if my request for military service is accepted.*

*Yours truly,*
*Anna Johnson*
*Canadian Nursing Sister*

The music filled the hall downstairs as I walked toward my father's study. I felt like the eighteen-year-old I'd been when I told him I wanted to go to nursing school. Even my knock at his study door had that old tentative hesitation.

"Dad?" I cracked open the door.

"Annie. My goodness, is this not the most moving piece of music?" He sat in his large leather chair—the music surrounding him, his arm in the air as he'd always done, conducting as he listened. "Come, sit. Listen."

A moment of grief clutched at the back of my throat as he motioned to me to come sit by him. His hair, now white, fell across his forehead, as it always had whenever he gave himself to his music, or to the complexity of an elegant mathematics problem. He loved both equally.

He looked over at me, still conducting his music. A tall standing lamp shed a glow over what looked like hieroglyphics spread across papers hither and thither on top of his desk. Who knew what striking project he was involved in now? I sometimes wondered if he and Simon had more in common than just being fellow mathematicians. Simon a rocket scientist? Dad?

"Anna? This music." I waited. "This music is like you, my daughter. You are a countermelody to the world. You play your own music. You live your life elegantly and fearlessly."

What I'd come to tell him. He already knew.

That night I walked to the corner mailbox.

◆

FROM THEN ON, MY LIFE WAS A BLUR.

A telegram arrived with military speed. I was accepted, gratefully, so it read. I was to be part of a contingent of nurses heading for one of two Canadian General Hospitals in England.

Taplow Hospital in Kent was supplied by the Canadian Red Cross and needed experienced nurses. I hoped to go there.

◆

## May 1940

TIME MOVED ME CLOSER TO MY DEPARTURE, AND SOON the good-byes crept up on me.

I thought I'd be ready. I'd done this before. This time, for some inexplicable reason, I felt a finality to each farewell. I asked for no fanfare, no farewell gathering, and absolutely no tears. I chose to drive out to the farm early in the morning, three days before I was to take a train from Kingston to Halifax.

Martha met me at the bottom of the lane, flagged me down, and climbed into the car.

"I needed a few moments to say good-bye before everybody else grabs you. And to thank you for passing the torch."

The engine idled and spat while we sat in the morning light. Two horses in the neighboring field trotted to the fence and proceeded to chew on the grass by the lane. I'd geared myself up for these good-byes.

"Passing the torch?"

"I think you know, don't you, that with you gone, the job of the steadying influence on this family will be available." Her eyes brimmed, yet a faint smile twitched at the corners of her mouth. "I'm applying for the job, right here, right now. Me. I will be the core of this family. I will be who you believe I am."

"Here."

She reached across the seat, took my hand, and with no other words let a gold locket drop into my palm. "This is the one thing Ma left for me. I want you to carry it with you, for luck and protection."

"But shouldn't you give it to Sarah?"

"When you are back safely, and she is home too, you can give it to her. Now give me a hug and I'll disappear while you go say good-bye to all those people who are standing on the porch. I love you, Anna. Be safe and come back to us."

She jumped from the car, ran across the road, and disappeared into the woods. That was the last I saw of her before I left.

Dad drove me to the train station in Kingston three days later.

When I swung my bag and my pack out of the car, I knew I needed to keep moving. I saw him begin to step from the car.

"Dad. Remember, we said our good-byes back at the house. Just blow me a kiss, and keep the home fires burning." I walked away, letting the tears drip off my chin.

*Milree Latimer*

## June 2, 1940

THE DAY ARRIVED.

I was leaving Halifax to sail to Liverpool.

There was no great fanfare as we boarded *The Duchess of Bedford*. But I wanted to remember all of it: the troops tramping up the gangway, duffel bags slung across their backs; the overwhelming numbers of young soldiers moving in groups and lines across the pier; ships swallowing them, line after line.

My sister nurses from No. 5 Canadian General Hospital boarded with those of us who'd traveled from Toronto. For me, the oldest in a group of more than one hundred nurses, I felt the familiar excitement of the known and the not knowing what lay ahead. Martha was right—something in me came alive.

As I stood at the ship's rail and watched Pier 21 slip away, it occurred to me I might not return. It was a strange thought that had no reason attached to it, one I let drift like the wake of the convoy ships sailing at our side.

Halfway across the ocean, we received news that France had fallen to the Germans. Our convoy kept us safe and protected, even though the hazards of U-boats were constant. Fear rode with us like a lookout—all of us right down to the junior nurses were back-straight alert, along with the captain who never left the bridge.

But more than U-boats burdened my thoughts, while I, like the captain, stood my post at the rail.

Was Simon somewhere in France, now that the Germans had overrun the country? Had he been caught? How could I find him if he hadn't made it to England? Why did I think he might have?

However, I had a responsibility and a charge before me. I reached into the inside pocket of my all-weather coat, and placed my fingers around both Martha's locket and a picture of Simon.

Olivia had handed it to me as she said good-bye.

# Part Five

## The Escape

# Chapter Thirty-Four

*If any of us get lost, if any of us cannot come all the way remember there will come a time when all we have said and all we have hoped will be all right.*

—William Stafford, "A Message From the Wanderer"

### Early May 1940
### A town in northwest France ♦ Simon Lansky

Lily of the valley and primroses scented the French air. Flowers bloomed in spite of the daily horror that threatened me. Brutality encompassed the garden like an overgrown hedge.

I'd arrived safely, guided through woods and along rivers by a Belgian and a Frenchman, both hesitant to speak or ask about my situation. We'd traveled at night. When lights from trucks or tanks flashed through the trees, we'd drop to the ground. My face was scratched and bloody from rough dirt and sharp rocks.

They'd brought me through Belgium into France. We'd walked through woods and tramped over brush until my body felt like one of my old tattered bathrobes. I'd wondered when we stopped to rest for an hour if I would ever stand again, yet some primitive impulse, some need to be alive, charged my body to be upright and keep moving. The two guides were gone as soon as we arrived at the church. When dawn allowed light to seep through the clouds of early morning, Father Durand had led me into the church and down into a damp cellar under the altar, where I rested on a cot imprinted with the shapes of others like me.

Now I sat in a churchyard with only time to drink a cup of water and to breathe in the late afternoon air. My senses began to speak of freedom and hope. I drew in the beauty and the possibility that I might survive.

"As soon as it's dark, we must leave."

I ignored Father Durand's urgent tone. He was the priest of a small Catholic church in this town and he was to be the one to take me on to the coast. I had been led here near the border of Belgium and France, but I could not rest because German armies were already rolling over Belgium, the Netherlands, and France. When the priest beckoned to me to rise and go with him, I shook my head no. "A moment, please, a moment to finish my water." The stone steps, hard as they were, invited me to linger. Possibly a false sense of hope had slowed me down, that and the blisters forming on my feet.

"But no, monsieur, we must move on. The Germans have crossed the Meuse River into France, we must keep going."

"How far will we go tonight?"

"Monsieur, we need to travel as long as we can, we are both in danger. You must listen. You must pay attention. I'm going to give you a priest's cassock. We'll be two priests driving to the coast. There you'll be hidden in a church by the docks till a boat comes to take you out into the channel."

How bizarre it all seemed. I'd been transported into Belgium from Germany as a dead body, and now I was a priest. A brutal world surrounded my journey, a Catholic priest my guide. I stopped for a moment on the way back through the small church where I'd be changing into clerical clothing. I wondered at these people who endangered their lives for me, a Jewish teacher who only wanted to be with his daughters once again.

I'd discovered in conversation that Father Durand had begun helping Jewish men like me only a few weeks before, and I knew nothing of the two men who'd brought me to this small church in a French town. The Vogels in Germany and their French counterparts were a strange connection. German Quakers and a Catholic priest. No one told me why or how they had decided to help Jewish men flee the Germans. I chose not to question them. I chose to trust them and be thankful for their courage.

When Father Durand realized I'd stopped part of the way up the aisle of the church, he called back to me, his tone tight with urgency.

"Monsieur, please, we must hurry. We don't know exactly where the Germans are at this point." And there in the nave of a tiny church I removed my shirt and pants, wrapped them into a crushed ball, and stuffed them into a cloth bag. I'd need them again…maybe in England.

I took the borrowed black cassock, reached it over my head, and let it flow down around my body. In some peculiar way, the rough material and the heaviness around my ankles gave me a sense of comfort and protection. I inhaled the scent of candles and the smells of old wooden floors and benches.

"This will be our last quiet moment, Father. Let me thank you."

He stopped and looked to the ceiling, then his gaze dropped to my face.

"We must all do what we can."

We stood in our personal silence for only a moment until the rustle of his gown and his hand pressing my arm told me it was time to go. He walked toward the door, his hand still on my arm, "Monsieur, please. Remember if we are stopped by anyone, and unless someone speaks to you directly, I will be the only one talking."

"Father Durand. I speak fluent French. I learned as a young man while at university in France. Do not worry."

"Monsieur. You are Jewish. I understand, too, that you are a scientist. The Nazis will hunt you not just as a Jew, but someone valuable to their cause, I am sure. All we have is a few hours between us and possible arrest."

"I know everything you say is true, but the Germans have not yet invaded France. Am I not safe here with you right now?" I was hurrying to walk beside him, my earlier sense of ease gone. Fear and desperation began to work their way into my bowels.

"Did you not hear?" By now he was speeding up even more. "They have marched into France. They have crossed the Meuse River from Belgium into France. You are no longer on safe ground." His frustration with my apparent carelessness, and the danger for him, was palpable. He stopped at the door and stood in front of me, his palms together as though in prayer.

"Monsieur. Are you not terrified that you will be caught?"

I tightened the band cincture around my waist, looked at him, and spoke my truth.

"I am a German Jew, wearing the cloth of a Catholic priest. I have been transported out of my country in a coffin by people who chose to rescue me, to a place in France which, I now understand, has been invaded by my enemy, who at one time were my countrymen. Yes, I'm terrified.

And fearful I may never see my daughters again. The only person I can trust at this moment is you, a village priest whom I met yesterday. I am a mathematician, Father, but not a gambler. So yes, I am terrified, because everything I know about what is happening, everything that I've already experienced, says I'm doomed." I leaned into the door and pushed it open into the dark. "Now, are we leaving for the coast tonight. Or not?"

When we set out at two o'clock in the morning, Father Durand drove the bishop's 1937 black Citroen with his blessing. I hadn't known what to expect, but as we drove the dark streets out of town, I sensed an eerie quiet. When we reached the road going south, we became two priests making their way to the coast. Soon into our journey, we found ourselves inching in among bikes, carts, horse-drawn carriages, people struggling with any possessions they could carry. Everyone was looking to the south for a safe haven away from tanks and advancing German troops. Eventually, Father Durand and I turned west toward the coast where another church, another priest awaited.

Our silence filled the air in the car.

I saw as we drove toward the coast that there were individuals willing to risk their lives to help in whatever way they could. In the dark of night, I saw a farmer come out to the road on his tractor. He pulled a hay wagon and drove along the side of the road, picking up children and their mothers, beckoning to others to follow behind as he drove down his lane toward his barn. I could only assume he was giving some a night's rest. Soon we found ourselves alone on the road, the way ahead clear. Father Durand dared to switch on the headlights and pressed his foot onto the gas pedal.

"You've done this before. You seem to know the way."

"The Germans are moving west and south with their Panzers, monsieur. We will need to keep going as quickly as we can. We haven't much farther, but we need to move speedily."

In that moment I felt something surround my heart, a hopelessness that clutched like the darkness beyond the car. Down the road we could see shadowy silhouettes, uniforms of the French police at the side of the road. Three men stood in the headlights of the police van, hands shackled behind their backs.

Father Durand slowed the car and kept moving.

"Do not look out. Fold your hands as though in prayer."

As we swerved to pass the van, one of the gendarmes waved his flashlight toward our car and beckoned us to move on. Breathing resumed within the car, but no words passed between us.

"Father? Why are the French police stopping people at night here in the middle of nowhere?"

His hands clutched the steering wheel as he sat forward to peer beyond the headlights.

"I don't know, Professeur, but I am afraid we need to move more quickly. It's possible that the Germans are closer than we thought."

"But why are the French police…"

"I do not know. That's all. I do not know. I only know, there is no one we can trust."

His foot pressed on the gas pedal and we began to speed through the night.

I leaned my head against the window and closed my eyes. I thought of Olivia and Ilse, who believed I'd come home to them. Yet the reality was I was fleeing the best of the German forces, Panzers and infantry charging their way into France.

I watched the trees and the darkness slip past the car window. "Father Durand…you are a good man placing yourself in great danger for me."

He said nothing.

"Possibly," I said, with a sigh approaching a sob, "we're too late. You, all the others who've brought me this far, have tried. Maybe we're fighting a useless battle. I'm just one man. One Jewish man. I suggest you let me out of the car, and I will do what I need to do to survive or not."

Again, he said nothing…he drove. A town emerged from the dimness of the countryside.

A pale moon shone overhead as though someone had flashed a beacon. My shoulders drooped. My hand clasped the door handle ready to open it. I closed my eyes and imagined my girls waving to me. I looked over at Father Durand. Why wasn't he slowing down?

He had his hand on the wheel, the other waving and pointing—"Monsieur, monsieur! Look, look beyond." The moonlight reflected across water. A church sat among trees, and beyond was the channel.

"Where is this place, Father?"

"I can't say where, I can only tell you that…ah, there he is …" And like a ghost out of the night a man appeared, walking by the side of the road.

Father Durand slowed the car to a halt, shut the headlights down, and waited. The man came to my passenger window and beckoned. The moment either held promise or threat, but when I paused, my friend the priest tapped me on the back and gave me a gentle push.

"It is all right, Monsieur Professeur, he will take you to

a fishing boat that waits offshore."

"Father Durand," I turned to him and reached my hand to take his. "I am grateful. I don't…"

"Go. Go. I must leave here and so must you."

Darkness was taking on the gray light of dawn when I stepped from the car. How, I wondered, could I keep going in the light of day?

The man by the side of the road beckoned to a bag he'd set on the road. He said nothing, but pulled out rubber fisherman boots, ripped worn pants, a heavy sweater fraught with holes, and a flannel shirt.

"Change," he grunted.

"Here?"

His rolled his eyes to the sky, then pointed to me and to the bag. "Change. Here. Now."

He was a muscular, burly man with a thick beard, part of this line of men hating what was happening to their country and willing to do what it took to resist.

I looked around for a place where I might have privacy, but there was just the side of the road. The only sound was the gravel under the tires of Father Durand's car as he disappeared into the dim. I wondered that he'd left without the priest's robe I still wore.

"But the cassock?"

When the guide pulled on the cincture around my waist, I stepped away from him and began to disrobe. There'd be no time for modesty.

Within the hour, a gray fog had settled over the water. He'd been waiting for some kind of cover. We set off down the road until we reached a path through the grasses leading down to the beach. A scramble down a sagging seawall found us on a deserted foggy beach. Sand stretched along a shore where I expected we'd walk, me with no knowledge of where or why. My guide walked ahead of me, his head down. I followed. He stopped. Pointed out to the water.

There it was. A small fishing vessel sitting a few yards off the shore, rolling quietly in the wake of the waves. My passage.

He turned to me, lifted my arm, and pulled me toward the water. The tides were with us.

The boat seemed insignificant as it emerged from the fog, yet, however small it might be, it was my deliverance. We walked through the receding waters until my boots began to fill and water soon rose up to my waist. Just when I thought the journey might end here, I felt a tug at my arm. "The boat is over here," he whispered. I'd been walking out to sea.

Another hand appeared over the side of what now looked like a more dependable craft.

The guide stood in the water and finally spoke. "My friend will take you into the channel. An English fishing boat will meet you somewhere off the coast of Dover. God go with you, my friend."

"We will need God, Father Benoit," a fisherman on board said while I clambered in.

I turned as I settled onto one of the benches near the bow.

"That man who brought me here just now was a priest?"

"Ah, yes, monsieur, he is a Capuchin monk who pretends to be a fisherman. Already he has rescued many like you."

"And Father Durand?"

"Ah. He is a Jesuit."

The quiet sound of a motor cut through the thick fog and we began to move.

"We must not speak now, monsieur. The Germans have put patrol boats out in the channel. We will travel slowly. They will not expect us to be out in this fog. But we have done this before."

◆

WHENEVER THE REMOTE GROWL OF A DIESEL ENGINE sounded across the water, Rouall would silence our motor until the Germans disappeared into the mists. With a stop-and-start crawl, we made our way toward the English coast. One day, I thought, I'll realize what a miracle all this is, but for now, my desire to survive grasped at my chest. I wrapped myself in the thick gray wool of the blanket they'd given me and willed the boat across the water. A small light flashed twice, dimmed, and died.

There it was.

A fishing boat. An English fishing boat.

# Chapter Thirty-Five

*There is nothing more pathetic than caution
when headlong might save a life,
even, possibly, your own.*

—Mary Oliver, "Moments"

### June 3, 1940 ♦ Frontenac County ♦ Martha

The familiar smells of a morning kitchen surrounded me. Eggs frying. That was Olivia's wish. Toast, medium brown, that was Ilse's. Coffee warm on the woodstove, that was Charlie's. He liked to come in from working in the fields for a break and a chat partway through the early morning.

Rose, too, liked this time in the morning. She'd often cut through the backwoods to visit the neighbor, Ethel. "She's not been the same since George passed away," she'd say to me, as though redeeming herself for having the luxury of time—and for leaving the details of home and family to me. Earl, who'd finished his two fried eggs topped with bacon, pushed back from the table. "Ready, girls?" He reached for his brown wool sweater from the hook by the kitchen door.

"Time to go, don't want us to be late in the last month of school. It is the last month, isn't it, Ilse?" He grinned.

He'd volunteered a few months ago to drive the girls to school when Charlie and I, in company with Olivia and Ilse, decided it was time for them to leave the comfort and safety of my home-schooling and venture into the world of public school. Now he looked forward to the times alone with them in his pickup, as they chattered about their life and the newness of Canadian friends.

I missed those hours we'd spent together, the girls and me. We'd read stories, most in English. We'd practiced writing letters to Papa, which we saved and put away. I chose not to dampen their hopes they'd see him again.

I wondered if Olivia's desire to go to school might be another sign that for her, home was no longer Germany, and might never be again. Ilse's bed-wetting had stopped (and with it, Olivia's complaints about having to sleep with a bed-wetter). Our conversations about their papa had dwindled, but not stopped. We tried to keep some of the news about the war from them, which, now that they were going to a public school, was fruitless. The war was the topic of the community, even a small rural one like ours. Whenever I drove into Kingston to take them to synagogue, I saw more and more young men in uniform.

Ryan had joined the Royal Air Force and was over in England training to fly Spitfires. His letters were few and far between, but each one was filled with an excitement that worried me. How could he be excited about a war? My own daughter, who was nursing at Kingston General, still pushed to enlist as a military nurse. I knew I didn't have much longer to dissuade her, and forbidding her to join up was pointless. Charlie only chuckled when I'd say, "I'll just tell her she can't go."

"Well, Mart. She's your daughter, she has your blood in her veins. Something about 'dogged' runs through my mind. Did anyone ever try to tell *you* what to do?"

"I never was as bad as she is when it comes to stubbornness. That's your blood, Charlie Sloan." Yet in the midst of our wrangling, we secretly admired her determination to do something that mattered.

I missed Anna every day. I waited for a letter to arrive, and if one didn't come at least once a week, I'd imagine the worst. The headlines and the broadcasts from Earl's radio often sent my heart racing. There were times, no matter night or day, I'd grab Anna's woolen cardigan from the hook in the kitchen, wrap it around my shoulders, and walk up and down the lane. Back and forth, back and forth, until I convinced myself Anna was all right.

I'd call Owen once or twice a week. "Have you got a letter from Anna?" I'd ask, without giving him a moment to say hello.

"I haven't heard from her in the last few days, but I will surely let you know when I do. She's not in danger. You need to stop worrying."

Her own father did not seem concerned for her safety, but…

## FRANCE YIELDS TO NAZIS' DRIVE WITHIN 39 DAYS

### Ninth Country to Fall to Hitler in Two Years

### Shows Feeble Defense

### ABANDON MAGINOT

(Special from The New York Times
to The Globe and Mail)

War news had battered the airwaves and screamed from the headlines.

One day near the end of June, the postman drove down the lane to deliver a letter.

The morning was well underway when I sat at the kitchen table and ripped the seal of the flimsy airmail paper. I breathed in the smell of the paper, sat at the kitchen table, and smoothed my hand across the pale blue envelope with the red and blue stripes around the border. Earl had driven off with the girls, each of them telling him all they were going to do throughout the summer. I'd listened as they walked across the kitchen and out the door, Earl behind them, grinning, "Opa Earl, we'll help milk cows and drive the tractor. We'll help in the vegetable garden. Wait till Papa sees what we can do." I'd felt a chill, hearing their confident words. Now, though, I attended to Anna's letter.

Care cautioned me to unfold it gently. Each word was clear and distinct, written in Anna's neat script.

CANADIAN RED CROSS MEMORIAL HOSPITAL, TAPLOW, BUCKINGHAMSHIRE, ENGLAND MAY 1940

*Dear Martha:*

*I want to let you know that I'm well and happy to be back in uniform. I'm working once again with young men who have been battered and wounded, both physically and mentally. It seems that wars are still fought by brave, young men who are bloodied, damaged, bruised, and beaten, just as they were twenty-five years ago. But the weapons today are more dangerous, more horrific.*

*I can imagine you sitting at the kitchen table reading my rant, and saying to yourself, "Why does Anna* do this? Why does she put herself into places where she wants to scream out at the injustice of it all?"

And here we are, Martha, fighting the same enemy. When does it end? This intent to hate someone enough to kill him.

I'm not sure if my letter will pass the censor, but if it does: know that I write to you because you're the rock, Martha, and there's something I need you to do.

I don't know if you knew this, but when I left, I asked Olivia if she had a picture of her Papa.

This hospital is a Red Cross Memorial Hospital equipped by the Canadians. I know the area well since being here in the Great War. I specifically wanted to come here to look for someone we are both interested in finding. I'm in touch with another hospital where I worked in 1918.

There are some Jewish refugees nearby—I can't say more than that—but I intend to keep searching.

There's something I need you, Dad, and Charlie to do. All I'm about to say might be riding on false hope. But isn't hope all we have?

What I'm asking is incredibly difficult, but it might be possible. I need you to go to the immigration office and file some paperwork related to my search. I've included the instructions. There will be necessary papers. Travel passes, a passport. Can you find out what he'll need? Dad will have the information. He has known Simon for many years, he knows his status as a professor. As soon as I know if he is alive or dead, and then where he might be, I will send you a telegram. Remember, keep hoping.

This must be making your head spin, dear Martha.

*Take it in, consider. Talk to Dad, and of course Charlie. Now I must get to work. The war is not going well. I'm afraid we're in for an influx of wounded.*

*Bless you, dear Martha.*

*Anna*

Anna was right. She had made my head spin. Where would I even begin to investigate processing papers for Simon? And how would I do that for someone who possibly was dead, or still being hunted in Germany? The door to the back kitchen slammed. Charlie in for his early lunch.

"Mart?"

"In here, Charlie."

He stepped up into the kitchen and tossed his cap onto the hook by the door. Always a ringer. He never missed.

"I think you're still sitting where you were when I left this morning. Are you okay?"

Dear Charlie. All these years later since the Great War, he was still left with edges of anxiety if life seemed off-kilter. Me still at the kitchen table at eleven in the morning was unusual.

"I'm perfectly fine, Charlie. Come sit, and I'll make us a pot of tea. I need to talk to you."

## June 8, 1940

> **LANDING FROM 'INCREDIBLE ARMADA' HEROES REPORT CASUALTIES LIGHT IN FIVE-DAY MIRACLE OF FLANDERS**
>
> These Men Not Defeated But Wear Light of Victory in Their Eyes, Says Gregory Clark, After Interviewing Tommies "Back in Blighty"
>
> MAY 3 - 1940
>
> ARTILLERY SECTION, TWO GUNS LEFT GETS 25 TANKS ON MARCH TOWARD SEA

THE NEWSPAPER STORIES ARRIVED LIKE A CLARION CALL. Somewhere called Dunkirk was in the news. An extraordinary evacuation. Charlie and I glanced across the supper table as we listened to Olivia's litany of the day.

"One of the boys in my class called me a Hun today. Doesn't he know I'm not a Nazi?" "This is a hard time for you both, isn't it? I remember when I was a girl, and so many Irish were angry at one another. Some girls in my school in Dublin were cruel, just like that boy in your class."

"Did they call you names, Aunt Mart?"

"Ooh, yes."

"Like what?" Ilse chimed in.

"Oh, things like 'boggy orphan girl.'"

"But you were, weren't you? An orphan?"

"You know, I think we should talk about something pleasant." Charlie, always to the rescue.

"And what might that be, my son?" Earl joined in from the end of the table. "Okay. I have a joke," Earl tried again.

OUT OF PLACE

Rose, Charlie, and I groaned. Earl had introduced his knock-knock jokes to the girls. It appeared they'd never heard anything like them, and he delighted in their laughter.

"Here we go." Ilse and Olivia sat straight in their chairs, eyes pinned on Earl. "Knock, knock."

"Who's there?" Both in chorus.

"Atch."

"Atch who?"

"Bless you." Earl grinned and buttered his bread.

The girls laughed with delightful guffaws. Their braids jiggled. How lovely to see their eyes brighten for a few moments. For a while we put aside worry.

◆

THE NEXT DAY A TELEGRAM ARRIVED FOR OWEN.

I answered the phone when he called the house and sank to a chair as he read it to me.

# Chapter Thirty-Six

*I'm too much of a skeptic to deny
the possibility of anything.*

—Thomas Henry Huxley, *Life and Letters
of Thomas Henry Huxley*

### June 1940 ♦ Kent, England ♦ Anna

I STOOD IN THE ENTRANCE HALL OF ORPINGTON Hospital and absorbed the smells and sounds. In 1919 I'd walked out through these doors and thought, *Good-bye forever*. But, now, I guessed the Germans and I weren't finished. What a strange thought, the Germans and I having it out to the bitter end. Truthfully? I wanted to be back here. My heart beat out the rhythm of a military hospital. There would be moments of crisis followed by the miracle of survival. Possibilities for life lay within these walls, and I was soon to be back in the midst of it all.

But first. I picked up my military duffel bag, the same one I'd carried all through the Great War, and walked down the hall to Matron's office. I was making my way through the unfamiliar corridors of a grand new building just a year old. The old huts where hundreds of wounded had been cared for still stood outside on the grounds, as they had throughout the last war. For me the feel of No. 16 Canadian General Hospital, as it was then, lay out there in those huts. This was a different building, but still it was here to care for the damages of war. Possibly I shouldn't have felt this quiver of well-being running like a fresh stream down my spine, yet truth be told, I was glad to be back. Like a nun who'd returned to her abbey, I was home. My appointment with Matron, Miss Thompson, was immediate. I arrived at her door just as the wailing of sirens and the sounds of planes overhead brought Matron from her office, in company with two other nurses.

"We'll need to get to the shelter till the all-clear is sounded. Sometimes it's a drill, but we never know." She walked ahead and I came along behind her. My reintroduction to wartime had begun. After the all-clear sounded, Miss Thompson invited me to sit with her by a window that looked out on the lawns and the forsythia. A picture of peace. She poured tea as she talked.

"I'm not at all used to these raids, or the possibility of more serious ones. But I'm told by some of the boys who've been brought to us from Dunkirk that we'd better be prepared for some bad times. Herr Hitler is looking across the channel as we sit here." Tea poured, she dropped into a wooden, straight-back chair and sat sipping.

I wondered if she expected me to launch into my reasons for being here. I started. "You received my letter from the Red Cross Hospital in Taplow?"

"It's there on my desk, I've read it, and I'm assuming this is why you want to talk to me. I need to say something first, though."

"Miss Thompson, I…"

"Oh, for heaven's sake, call me Marion. You and I have seen enough battles and enough of war to be talking as colleagues. And that's where I want to start, as colleagues. What is this herculean task you've taken on, this finding a

Jewish man who you think may have been rescued and who you think may have been brought to England?"

"I worked here during the Great War, when it was all Quonset huts. I have memories of friends, of nurses I worked with—but, Marion, that's only one small reason. The head nurse at the Canadian Red Cross Hospital mentioned that Orpington has taken in soldiers who are experiencing shell shock. I've nursed those soldiers in my days here and in France, and probably you need to know, I suffered myself for a while."

For a moment she tilted her head and raised an eyebrow.

"You've a history of shell shock? And you want to return to nursing during this war, and…go looking for a Jewish refugee?"

"Oh, I'm…"

"No, let me finish. What do you need from me, Anna? Because I need nurses like you. This will be another nasty war, and if you survived the last one, and if you lost your way for a time—if it was shell shock and…you found your way back…I think we have a place for you and someone with your courage."

"Marion, there will be times when I'll need to leave—times when I'll need to go and—I don't know exactly how to explain it or how that might happen. I'll need to follow a lead when it comes up, whatever or whenever that could be. But I promise you, when I find him and send him home to Canada…and I will, I'll stay in this hospital, or wherever I'm needed for as long as this war lasts. And beyond."

"It could be a long war, Anna. You know that, don't you? We've lost the continent, the Germans are fierce and determined, and none of us know how long it might be before we get back there. I pray Britain is not in their sights, but I'm afraid it is. More men are being brought in from the evacuation, and they all have horror stories. What I'm saying is you could start here, today."

"And I will."

With those three words I stood up. "I need to go and change into my uniform."

"We'll have a spanking-new, crisp uniform for you in the morning, Sister. In the meantime, rest. You will need it."

A young nurse sped by me as I left Matron's office, her white veil flying behind her, like the wake from a ship.

◆

A FEW DAYS LATER I WAS BACK ON A WARD, AS THOUGH it was yesterday. One man, Eddie, lay on his bed. I spoke to him, but his face offered nothing, only a blank stare. He was an apparition in white—white sheets, legs bandaged to the knees, his head swallowed in a white helmet of bandages. He folded his hands like an obedient schoolboy when I walked into the sunroom where he lay. "Eddie, I'm Anna, or 'Miss' if you like that better. To your friend William over here …" I pointed with a waggling finger to a young man, a boy who lay on a stretcher cot with bandages over his eyes, his legs cut off at his knees. "To you, Will, I'm 'Lieutenant,' right, Will?" I grinned at him even though he only saw blackness. A weak smile started at the corners of Will's mouth. "Never, Lieutenant, never. You'll always be Anna Banana to me. And Eddie? He ain't gonna talk. He's gone away, ma'am. He's gone." Every day I felt a wonder that someone who was barely twenty years old, who'd never walk again, who'd already seen death hovering in the smoke from tanks and guns, someone like Will, could talk about someone else's pain with compassion and concern.

Last night, after being on duty for almost twelve hours, I'd sat on the floor of my room wrapped in the gray wool of my army blanket. And the monsters descended.

My days were swamped already with grief, anger, and disillusionment—theirs, those young men, and mine. We'd received word in the morning that ambulances would be carrying wounded from Bramshott Hospital to us—wounded souls and wounded minds. Our Matron had let it be known that I "worked miracles" with shell-shocked men. I wasn't any miracle worker. But I had been like them, those boys who arrived with blank eyes and wails that pierced my heart. I felt at first that I was in danger of disappearing inside my own disenchantment, just as I had years ago. The miracle we shared, these broken boys and I, was only that we listened to one another and we learned to talk our way through the labyrinth of horrors. One person at a time.

That's how I met Eddie, who'd come back in late May with the first wave of evacuees. Eddie, who lay on his bed, his arms folded behind his head, like a man taking a short rest. I sat with him some nights well into the darkness—I talked, I sang, as I'd learned to do with these boys. One night I began to unravel the story of Simon for Eddie's ears because I'd run out of stories to tell. I realized I found some solace in describing the farm, how Martha and I had rescued Olivia and Ilse, how we prayed and hoped we'd find this man, Simon.

"He's a friend of my father's, you see, Eddie—all that distance, all those years ago, he's almost family to us, to me." I talked as though I believed he could hear me.

And, one night, in the dimness of blackout-curtained windows, Eddie turned his head to me.

"I'm Jewish."

The next night, I went into the ward and walked to his bed. He was sitting up, his bandaged legs propped on pillows. A nurse had brought him a cup of tea which he'd taken with a tremulous hand. I stood at the end of his bed and he beckoned me to the chair where I'd sat other nights.

"Sister? We call you 'Sister,' don't we?"

What does a person do, when some nights hope rises? Begin to hope again, I guess.

I sat by him and waited for him to begin the conversation, on this night.

"I'm Jewish, and I know what's going on over there. Maybe I can help, maybe I can't, but I sure as hell can try. You need to tell me what you know."

This man, who'd lain on his back staring at the ceiling for days and nights, began to restore the grit that I'd lost. He did it with a story and a question I hadn't considered. Eddie told me about a camp where Jewish men from Germany who'd been rescued in 1939 were living, for now. It was called the Kitchener Camp. "If he's out there, we'll find him. You know these Brits. If he's landed on this soil, somebody knows where he is. They found all of us, didn't they, and brought us home?"

We talked, Eddie and I, each night. I'd come to him after my daytime duty and sit. Sometimes I listened, and sometimes I watched him tremble because he needed to tell his own story of horrors. Occasionally it was one about his own family. Those times I held his hand until the shaking stopped, and sometimes until he dropped off to sleep.

But one night he beckoned as soon as I walked into the ward.

"Sister, Sister… I've thought of something… come sit," he whispered, with a kid's attempt at quiet, and received a few shushes from other beds.

I hurried and dropped into my chair, my once-crisp white apron, now not so crisp, not so white, folded into my lap.

"Sit back, Eddie, sit back, you'll rip your bandages."

"No, Sister, listen. I know about some Jewish men who'd been sent over here to a camp near Sandwich. They've closed the camp, but some of them have gone to work on nearby farms."

"What are you saying? That I need to check out all the farms in southern England?" When I shrugged my shoulders, Eddie reached for my arm. I could feel an urgency in his grasp.

"No. You go back to the hospital in Taplow, and you go to something called Central British Fund, a group that's helped Jewish men leave Germany."

"Eddie, how do you know all this? How would anyone from this other group know about Simon?"

"Miss, you have to think like a survivor. I'm a survivor, been one all my life. I'll survive this war too, even if I have to go back over there sometime. People talk, especially here in the hospital, and because I'm Jewish, people like nurses and doctors will sometimes tell me what's happening out there." Eddie's voice was rising with excitement.

A muffled whisper traveled across the aisle from another bed: "Keep it down."

"Okay. You need to go to sleep. In the morning I'll contact the hospital at Taplow. Now, go to sleep."

The next morning, I called the hospital at Taplow. The Canadian Red Cross Memorial Hospital. A possibility glimmered.

# Chapter Thirty-Seven

*It will always be like this, each of us going on in our inexplicable ways building the universe.*
—Mary Oliver, "Song of the Builders"

### September 1940 ◆ Kent, England ◆ Anna

A LETTER FROM THE RED CROSS, A NOW-WRINKLED PHOTO, and a telegram had led me to the bottom of the lane leading to John Morley's farm. A squadron of Spitfires rumbled over my head, reminding me that air battles were being fought over the channel at this moment. I walked faster along the rutted dirt road. Word was that occasionally an air battle might move over land. I'd come this far to find Simon, and being caught in the midst of a dogfight was not part of my plan.

Anyone who had tried to discourage me from putting myself in harm's way had met with my stony stare. Even Miss Thompson shook her head now whenever I'd ask for a weekend or a day to go plunging after a new lead. Eddie, who was now able to walk, had been moved from the shell-shock ward to rehab. Every so often I'd look up from my desk at the nurse's station, and he'd be standing on his crutches, grinning down at me. Each time he asked the same questions. "Have you heard anything yet?" "Seen any Spitfires yet?" "Are you staying away from the bombs?" He was like an overexcited horse gnawing at the bit to get back out into the battle. "You're seeing more action than I am,

Sister." Some of the action was not what I wanted or needed. Bombings and aerial dogfights over the coast, sirens wailing, darkened operating theatres. War had awakened some of my old demons, but I was determined to conquer them. Searching out Simon gave me the purpose I'd needed for a long time. Eddie, who no longer lived inside his own hell, represented life's possibility to me. As long as young men fought wars, I'd be there. For me, hope reigned. I'd had a glimmer from one of the nurses at the Canadian Red Cross hospital in Taplow who'd thought she recognized Simon's picture. "He looks so like a man who was brought here after the camp for Jewish refugees closed. But he was a lot older."

I'd urged her on, not wanting to leave anything or anyone to chance. "Do you know what happened to that man? The one who was a lot older?"

"I'm not sure, but I think he was taken to the Isle of Man where some of the refugees went. That's if he made it—he was pretty sick."

CANADIAN MEMORIAL
HOSPITAL TAPLOW, KENT

*Dear Sister Anna:*

*Since you were last here, I've been thinking about the picture and your description of the man you're searching for. Another man arrived later in June. He was brought in by a local fisherman who was very hesitant to say where he'd found him. Only that he believed him to be a German Jew. How he knew that I can't tell you. When I asked him why he hadn't taken him to the authorities, he just said he thought maybe the Red Cross might be kinder.*

> *This man subsequently left us, and I'm sorry I don't know where he went. We gave him shelter and food for a few days, but he seemed anxious to move on. For all I know he could have been a German spy.*
>
> *As I remember he did have a resemblance to the man in your picture—this man's name, at least the one he had on his entry papers, was Thomas Bell. I remember you saying your man would probably be cultured. He did speak well.*
>
> *I don't want to send you off on a fool's chase, and I'm sorry I didn't contact you sooner, what with the bombings and the civilians adding to our military wounded, it's been a wild time. I expect you are experiencing the same thing at Orpington.*
>
> *My hope is in the midst of these barbarous times you find your man and send him home to his girls. You are a very courageous woman. I'm glad you are one of us. We need all the best nurses we can find.*
>
> *Maureen Alexander*
>
> *P.S. One other thing—the man I'm describing was a remarkable chess player. While he was here, he played chess with some of our patients. "Keep their spirits up," he said.*

I wished beyond reason that man might have been Simon. But by this time, I'd about given up hope. News of the occupation of France was alarming. Some around me were talking about the possibility that England might be next to be invaded. Nothing seemed to stop the German Army.

The RAF was an extraordinary force. Churchill himself had spoken about them in glowing terms. He believed the

Royal Air Force was all that prevented the Luftwaffe and the German Army from landing on British soil.

"Never in the field of human conflict was so much owed by so many to so few," he'd said, to remind us all not to despair.

I was so disheartened I was ready to give up. How might one man, one Jewish man, make it through the chaotic madhouse of what the world had become? How was that even possible?

I decided to write to Martha. One night, after I'd received the letter from Taplow, Miss Thompson sent me a message to come to her office right away. My knees were shaking as I walked in—I felt as though I'd been summoned.

And I had.

"You have a long-distance phone call from Kingston, Anna. I have the operator's number so you can return the call." A chair nearby caught me as I collapsed.

My hand shook so much, it was difficult to pick up the receiver from its cradle. I held the telephone, asked for the operator's number, and waited. In a miraculous few moments I heard Dad's voice at the other end.

"Anna. Anna. Oh my. Oh my."

"Dad, stop saying *oh my* and tell me what's wrong." I wondered if I could catch my breath long enough to hear his message.

"It's Simon." My chest went into spasm. Hope and despair collided. *This is how shattering feels.*

"Anna, are you there?"

"Yes, Dad, I'm here."

"He's contacted us. Well, me. We know where he is, Anna. We know where he is."

"Where?" I croaked.

"Here. I'll read it to you. He's working on a farm somewhere near Sandwich, Kent. Isn't that near you, Anna?"

The world and the room sped into a kaleidoscope of colors. Sounds from beyond the office mixed with voices and announcements, doors opening and closing, and somewhere a wail of anguish. I'd frozen into the moment. And, just as quickly, I came to.

"Dad, send me a telegram right away. Put down as much information as you can. Everything he's told you. As soon as you can—meaning now—go to Western Union. Send it here to the hospital. I'll…I'll go find him."

◆

AND SO IT WAS THAT I STOOD AT THE END OF A FARMER'S lane. I turned to the cab driver who'd driven me from the train in Sandwich and who still waited.

"You can go on, I think. We'll find our way back to the station, I'm sure."

"You sure, ma'am? I hate to leave you out here on your own. Do you have someone to go back with you?"

"Thank you, sir. I'll soon be meeting a friend and we'll go back to the station together."

An old stone farmhouse waited for me, one with a thatched roof hanging over its walls. Shutters hung with precision around sparkling windows. Smoke rose in curls from a tall chimney. Everything said home. I paused before I lifted my foot to the front stoop. What if this was all just another pointless ramble? What if Dad had been wrong? I lifted my hand to ring the bell.

Before I could grasp the ringer, the door swung open.

A tall, gaunt man stood at the threshold. Simon Lansky.

# Chapter Thirty-Eight

*And now you'll be telling stories*
*Of my coming back.*

—Mary Oliver, *A Thousand Mornings*

### October 1940 ◆ Frontenac County ◆ Martha

WE LAY ON THE BED, THE GIRLS AND I, EACH OF US IN our own world. Olivia's head was on my shoulder. I could feel her smile through the flannel of my nightgown. Ilse wanted to be different. She lay with her head on my stomach and giggled with the rise and fall of my breathing. Our nightly routine. "Tante Martha," Ilse said. "I have a story about Papa. Can I tell it to you? It's a story about him coming home."

I eased myself closer to Olivia and made room for Ilse to clamber up beside me, her head on the pillow, her arm across my chest, her hand barely touching her sister.

"You tell your story. Tell us how Papa is coming home." "Papa is very brave. I don't think he's afraid of anyone. Do you, Olivia?" Before Olivia could answer, Ilse kept her story moving. "And he has friends, lots of friends, so one day, all his friends decided they needed to help him."

As she warmed up to her idea and the possibilities her imagination wove, she pointed to her fingers—counting off, one by one, the friends: "Herr Vogel…"

"In English, Ilse, not German," Olivia muttered.

OUT OF PLACE

"You're interrupting my story. I need to tell it my way."

I tapped the top of Olivia's head with a soft reminder to let her younger sister have this moment. "Go on, Ilsy," I said. "Anyway, *Herr* Vogel was a friend, and Johanna his daughter. I know because they helped us. They'll pretend they're taking him on a trip like us, and they'll turn him into another person. What do you call that Olivia? What's that word?"

Without lifting her head, Olivia murmured into my shoulder, "Disguise."

"Yes. They'll disguise him, and no one, not one single German guard, will know him."

"Who will he be?" I asked. I'd been entranced with Ilse's stories before, yet I heard something else. Her story sounded to me like a prayer. "He'll pretend to be…" She paused for a moment. "He'll be a very old man. Like Opa was. Remember Olivia? How Opa had a beard and was all bent. No one would ever think someone like Opa could be Papa. Could they?"

"But how will this old man get out of Germany?" I wanted the story to keep going. I wanted to feed her imagination and her boundless hope. Ilse lifted her head and put her hand under her chin. "See, that's why I'm telling the story, because it helps to tell it even if it's not true. I haven't figured out how he's escaped. I just know he has."

The light of a child's belief can perforate the darkness of adult doubts. I'd learned this from Ilse and Olivia. I worried, though, that she sounded so convinced.

When Ilse began to falter and her voice weakened, a voice rose from the other side of the bed. Olivia sat up. "Remember how Papa used to like to quote Goethe to us?" Ilse nodded.

"Your papa quoted Goethe? Really?"

Olivia managed to frown at my doubt—only for a moment—and laughed. "It is true. He did. Sometimes we might smile a bit, but now I remember."

"Do you remember what he said?"

"I don't remember word for word, and it was in German. But I think it was *I love those who yearn for something impossible*. Papa is very smart, isn't he, Ilse? Remember how he'd teach us to play chess?" Before I could say a word, Ilse clapped her hands. "I remember. I remember how smart he was…is. Maybe he'll fly home to us on wings and we'll play chess when he's here."

"Ilse, I'm pretty sure your papa won't fly home." Now, I realized, we needed to talk. Story or not, it was time to prepare them for the possible worst. Anna had done her part. It was my turn to tell them the truth.

◆

IT WAS AFTER THIS CONVERSATION WITH THE GIRLS THAT we heard Simon could be on his way home. A telegram had come from Anna, couched in concern. After our initial elation, Charlie and I made sure the girls didn't see the telegram. Not yet. It seemed safer for Owen to keep it locked in his desk. When Anna found Simon, she'd taken him immediately to Orpington to the hospital. She'd written to us:

*He's a sick man. He's exhausted and drained. His escape has been inconceivable. Please don't say anything to the girls. Letter to follow.*

*Anna*

We'd honored what she'd asked of us. There were still too many "what ifs." Too many to allow our girls renewed hope, even though they generated their own buoyancy. "We talk to Papa every night," Olivia had told me. "Ilse believes we're protecting him when we tell stories about him and when we talk to him."

Olivia and Ilse had become two Canadian teenagers whose home was a farm in rural Ontario. They trekked off to their small-town high school each day. Olivia lived with passionate intent to be the best mathematician she could be. "Like Papa," she'd say. Ilse was the storyteller, the one who asked questions about her Papa, the one who believed what he'd said when they left Germany:

*We'll be together again, I promise.*

No matter what awful news blared from the radio, what headlines spoke of doom, Ilse said, "I know Papa is all right. I just know." She reminded me of myself, that young girl in Dublin, who believed the priest's blessing could save her ma. And it broke my heart, just as it had then, to listen to Ilse's innocent hope. When they asked about their papa, infrequent as it was now, the questions were couched in optimism. "How far is the English Channel from Germany?" This, Ilse had dropped on me one evening as we dried the supper dishes. "Have you seen a map? What do you think?" I'd stilled my hands in the soapy dishwater and waited. Ilse had gazed out the kitchen window at the twilight sky.

Like a colt that's discovered the open gate, she'd flapped the dishtowel in the air. "Of course. Silly me. Look on a map. Maybe I can even track Papa's escape. Do you think he's already out of Germany?" Two years since leaving him, they both believed. What was I to do with that question, with their certainty, when I knew how terrible the news was for so many? What did I know for sure? That Simon might be safe, but sick. Maybe already dead? What if he'd given up? What if it had all been too hard for him? I knew nothing of his horrific experiences as a Jewish man in Germany. All I knew was how the newspapers and the radio news spoke of horrendous crimes against Jewish people. Olivia and Ilse had told me about living in Berlin just before their father sent them away. They told stories of being chased, fearing for their lives. Their stories were fewer these days, but terror still lived somewhere in their bodies and now in mine. I'd become the holder of fears—my own, and sometimes Charlie's. Our Ryan was somewhere over the channel in a Spitfire—would he come home? Charlie, in his dark times, said no. It was hard to breathe on days when Charlie lost faith, or those evenings when Olivia sat on the porch steps and stared out at the night sky.

We all lived on a precipice of hope. "It's so wrong," I'd said to Charlie after we read the telegram. "So wrong that he's come so far, and now he may die."

Charlie had yelled at me that day, "Stop right there! No one has said he's dying!" The man who yelled was the Charlie who still awoke in the night not able to breathe.

All of us lived day by day with dread, fear dancing in and among us like a grinning poltergeist.

◆

## October 1940 ◆ Kingston, Ontario ◆ Martha

"You need to come away from the window, Ilse." Rose, Earl, Olivia, Ilse, and I sat in the front room of Owen's house, the room that looked out on King Street and the university campus. Streetlights, dimmed as a war measure act, gave small pools of light on the lawn and the paths across the way. Ilse had been darting from window to window, out to the front hall, back into the room. As soon as she dropped into a chair she'd jump again when a car drove by.

"Why don't I make us a cup of tea, maybe find a cookie in Owen's pantry?" Rose said.

"I think that would be lovely. Ilse, why don't you help Gran Rose?" I pointed to the kitchen and beckoned Ilse to follow her. When they were no longer in danger of hearing our voices, I turned to Earl. Olivia had disappeared into the overstuffed pillows of the chesterfield, one that held the memories of Owen's evening naps and university student soirees. She looked to me for reason to hope that all was well. Charlie and Owen had gone to the Kingston Station, where Simon was coming in on a late afternoon train from Quebec.

"Earl, do you think something has happened?" "Martha, I think it's something as simple as the train is late." Earl and his practical nature subdued my doubts for a moment. Olivia reached across the chesterfield to take my hand. "It'll be all right, Martha. It'll be all right."

She'd taken to calling me Martha since her seventeenth birthday and in a way, it was comforting. These days, I missed the calm that Anna's presence could bring to me. *You've left me with a huge task, Anna*, I'd say into the pillow at night after I'd wished the girls goodnight and kissed Charlie on his sleeping eyes. *Yes, you are there in the midst of bombings, and who knows? You could get yourself killed. Then what do I do?*

Anna was faithful and wrote letters to all of us, sometimes two a week. In some of those letters, particularly to me, she'd write about Simon's struggle back to health.

The letters told of how she'd once again found her feet in the midst of a war, and how clear she'd become about staying in England. I'd decided I'd find other ways to keep her in my life. I just didn't know how right now. Tonight was not the time to worry about that. My thoughts drifted, with the background of voices, Earl and Olivia, the rattle of dishes in the kitchen. Every car that passed by was like a breath gone astray.

Car headlights shone on the trees across the road and turned into the driveway beside the house. A leap from the couch and I realized Olivia was at the window, then heading to the front door, shrieking and cheering as she ran. Ilse erupted from the kitchen, letting the swing door fling itself back and forth on its hinges. Rose, dusting her hands on her apron, was in pursuit. Charlie and Owen were barely out of the car, moving to open the rear door wide with a flourish. A very tall, very thin man disentangled himself and emerged from the back seat, his head high, his face alight. I stayed on the porch and hung onto Earl's arm to keep myself steady.

I stood witness to a man who'd defied history to keep a promise and find his way home.

# Epilogue

*A few words together and don't try
to make them elaborate
This isn't a contest, but the doorway
into thanks.*

—Mary Oliver, "Praying"

### 1968 ♦ Dublin ♦ Anna

Why did Martha suggest we meet at Christ Church Cathedral here in Dublin at Evensong? Why not a pub?

Were we mad, the two of us, sitting here in this mystical place, one that Martha believed was like a home to her? The choir's white gowns glowed in the candlelight. Their voices lifted to the clerestory high above.

Why now? Why here?

We shared age and arthritis. But neither of us had lost the taste and spirit for the unknown adventure. Martha had chosen this cathedral for a sought-after reunion.

The last time we'd been together was when I'd flown back to Canada from my home in Kent for Dad's memorial. My father had lived until his 85th year, still waiting there in his study for his daughter, Anna, to make up her mind to come home. A regret that haunted me. I'd waited too long.

Bless Simon for becoming the son my father had wanted. They'd become his family—he, Olivia, and Ilse. They'd shared a house. Owen and Simon shared teaching positions at the university until Owen could no longer make his way over there to his office. They shared grandchildren over the years. Owen sent letters and pictures to me, pride and gratitude written into every line. Always at the end of his letters, he wrote how he missed me, but knew I'd found my home "there on the southern coast of England."

Martha and I sat together at the back of the cathedral nave, shoulder to shoulder, the music lifting us away and beyond all the years.

*Martha Sloan. Whatever is this about?*

She turned to me. "Anna…thank you."

"Is that why we're here, in a church in Dublin? To say thank you?" I reached to take her hand.

She waved me off. "No, Anna. We're here because I need to tell you my story before I go home. And I needed to tell you here, where it started."

"But I know your story, Mart."

"Remember how I told you about running to this church to find a priest for Ma?"

"Yes. I remember. You found a priest to go back home with you, to give your mom last rites."

"I found a priest, but this is not a Catholic church, Anna, and when the priest told me that, I was devastated. All Ma wanted was to be blessed by a priest, and I couldn't even do that for her. And when I ran back home, she was already gone." Her eyes were brimming with unshed tears. "So, I told her the priest was there, and he'd brought her blessings. I lied to my dead ma, Anna. I lied." All I could do at that moment was reach for her.

"Martha, you have given your ma so much. You've been brave all through your life. And you've created a home for all the people in your life—and most importantly for yourself. You have nothing to regret."

Martha smiled. "I never could fool you. You are the one person in the world who could make all this right for me."

"Martha. What's going on?"

She turned away from me for a moment, and in that distinctively Martha way, straightened her shoulders. When she faced me, I realized something was very wrong.

"I have cancer, Anna, and it's not going to get better."

"Oh, Mart." As I lifted my arms to gather her in, she raised both hands.

"No, please listen to what I have to say. I need to get this out before I go to pieces with you, my safe person. I need you to help me, Anna. When I go home, I'll need to tell the kids I have cancer. But I just needed to come here first, and ask…will you come home, when the time comes, and make sure they're all right?"

I held her hand in mine and nodded.

"Remember the wharf in Quebec? You greeted me like a good friend would greet another. You were everything I needed when I was saying goodbye to my life in Ireland. I knew I'd always be safe with you. You were the one who taught me about good-byes and what they can teach us. I don't think I ever said thank you, though. You've taught me about bravery, that feeling scared is how we are sometimes. Not so bad, not so bad." Her voice wavered only for an instant, until I heard that deep resonance. "You've taught me about the magic of living, Anna, and the sweetness of good-byes."

◆

I KEPT MY PROMISE TO MARTHA. WE ARE THE KEEPERS of promises, all of us. I was there when she died. We were all there. In place.

We said good-bye and sent her on her way, on to her next adventure. That Irish girl, running down Henrietta Street.

# Acknowledgments

My gratitude:

To Jaclyn Desforges, author, poet, coach, and invaluable and gifted editor who encouraged me to go deeper into myself and into my story. Working with Jaclyn is like having my own private master class in writing a novel.

To Barb Morris, who has a wise and keen eye for the well-written phrase and a love of words. She is a gifted copy editor and writer, a constant friend, and a remarkable cheering section.

To Genie McBurnett, who encouraged the storyteller in me, who listened over many cups of tea, and who has supported my passion for story with unflagging enthusiasm and love.

To Laura Jeffrey, my artistic, musical friend who brought her talents and intuitive expertise to her reading of my early outlines, ever urging me on to write this story.

To Luminare Press, where Patricia Marshall and her team of talented editors and artists turned my story into a book that I treasure. Thank you! Jamie, Denise, Kim, and Melissa.

To Jane Kirkpatrick, an author whose stories have inspired my love for historical fiction, for our generous conversations where I learn. Each time we talk I remember why I want to write.

To Sandy McCormack at Pacific Northwest Writers Association, for her wisdom, her laughter, and her ever-present, enlivening "Yes, you can!"

To Paul Saltzman, who, in the midst of a busy documentary filmmaker's life, took time to listen and comment upon ideas about the Jewish people in early- and mid-1930s Germany.

To Diane Dober, who came to one of my book club talks for *Those We Left Behind*, and in one serendipitous conversation became a font of information about Jewish people escaping the Nazis. Sometimes the threads of stories find connections if we pay attention to those around us.

And to Annie Peace, who gave me gladness of heart and ever-present encouragement, and who listened to whole paragraphs over many phone calls and Skype meetings.

To Pam Blanchard, who listened to the story as it unfolded and kept asking for more.

To Phil Tompkins, my nephew, who drove me around the city of Kingston and the countryside of northern Frontenac County while I told him the story and he found Martha's and Anna's homes, all the while entertaining me with his stories and his wit. Most fun I've had while researching.

To Dr. Cynthia Toman, Associate Professor (retired), Faculty of Health Sciences, School of Nursing, University of Ottawa, for her generous gift of time, emails, and knowledge about Canadian Nursing Sisters in the Great War and the Second World War.

I'm fortunate to live in a community here in Central Oregon that values and sustains books and reading. My local booksellers, Brandon at Herringbone Books in Redmond, Oregon, and Tom Beans at Dudley's Bookshop and Cafe in Bend, Oregon, are ambassadors for the independent bookstore and a local community of authors. My gratitude also to Andrew, manager of Barnes & Noble in Bend. All, ever encouraging.

To writer friends Kate Ayers, Kristin Bak, and Kake Huck, who know from the inside out the joys and perils of the writing life.

To the Library and Archives of Canada for soldiers' and nurses' stories, letters, and diaries.

To the British Home Children Advocacy and Research Association in Canada, which prompted my first glimmering of an idea for this story.

To ever-present friends, unfailing in their belief that I have a story to tell. Thank you, Liz. Thank you, Heather D. Thank you, Carol H. Thank you, Catherine C. Thank you, Celine. Thank you, Julie.

To my niece Heather, who continued to spur me on with love and care.

To my niece Kath, a first reader whose excitement about my later-in-life passion for writing matches mine.

To Claire Bass, my step-granddaughter, who expresses delight in my need to write. She, a budding writer herself, also read my story. That's family dedication for you.

To my mother, long gone now, who, all those years ago, passed on to me stories about her days as a private duty nurse during the 1920s, for those tales she told and those I imagined.

To my families…east and west. My gratitude to you all, for taking me into your lives— Janice, Steve, Alex, and Jack. Tom, Bob, Jen, and Carter. John, Jenna, Claire, and Olivia.

And to that lovely man, Jerry, who's never been surprised that I'm a storyteller. Just like him.

# Author's Notes

I begin with truth-telling words: *This is a work of my imagination.*

Yet.

"Out of Place" blossomed because of my curiosity about orphaned children who were sent from Ireland to Canada in the early twentieth century, one of whom was my late husband's father. As I searched out his journey, I discovered he'd sailed on the SS *Dominion* in 1907. I contacted the British Home Child Advocacy—and it was then my imagination began to unfold.

I took a family story and created the image of a fifteen-year-old Irish orphan girl, and the character, Martha McGrath, came alive. After discovering she couldn't be a Home Child because she'd traveled from Dublin to Kingston to be taken in by family (Home Children were more often placed on farms with strangers), I seized fiction's freedom. Martha sailed on a ship from Liverpool to Louise Basin, Quebec, in company with other Home Children. Thus her orphan story became wrapped in a time, a place, and, ultimately, a family. Historical research can take a writer into unexpected places, creating characters who appear on the page as though they've been waiting to be seen. Anna's story and the friendship she and Martha nurtured is fiction; the worlds in which they lived were real in time and place.

My gratitude to Professor Cynthia Toman, Associate Professor (retired) in the School of Nursing at the University of Ottawa, for her generosity of time and response to my questions about Canadian Nursing Sisters in the Great

War and the Second War. Anna Johnson, Canadian Nursing Sister, emerged from my imagination, but Professor Toman provided encouragement and knowledge of how Anna's life as a Nursing Sister during the Great War might have been.*

Settings are the places where stories and the characters live. I was fortunate to search out those places in Kingston and northern Frontenac County where Martha's story played out. They became more than descriptions on a page on the day my nephew Philip, a creator of film stories himself, drove me around the city of Kingston to find where Martha lived with the Johnsons, and north to the countryside where her farm might have been. We found an old limestone house that very well could have been Professor Owen, Emily, and Anna's home. We discovered farms and farmland in the countryside of North Frontenac that gave grounding to the Sloan family and the influences they had on Martha. That ride around the city and the countryside was a boon to my imagination and to the veracity of the story.

Serendipity plays a role in research. I am grateful for a chance meeting at a book club, where I met Diane Dober who helped me be the truth-teller of Professor Simon Lansky's fictional escape journey. Immersed in the stories of a place and time, I read, I read more, I listened to my characters, and I imagined them into life in the midst of their eras. I could not have created this story without the letters, the memoirists, the storytellers, and the historians. If there are mistakes or deviations, they are truly mine.

Selected further reading can be found on my website, www.milreelatimer.com.

*Cynthia Toman, 2016. *Sister Soldiers of the Great War: The Nurses of the Canadian Army Medical Corps.* Vancouver: UBC Press.

Made in the USA
Middletown, DE
21 March 2021